SECRET DIARY

of a

RECTOR'S DAUGHTER

The story of a young girl in a Somerset village during the Great War

Maisie Stone

Pen Press

© Maisie Stone 2014

All rights reserved

No part of this publication may be reproduced, stored in a retrieval system, or transmitted in any form or by any means, without the prior permission in writing of the publisher, nor be otherwise circulated in any form of binding or cover other than that in which it is published and without a similar condition including this condition being imposed on the subsequent purchaser.

First published in Great Britain by Pen Press

All paper used in the printing of this book has been made from wood grown in managed, sustainable forests.

ISBN: 978-1-78003-773-8

Printed and bound in the UK
Pen Press is an imprint of
Author Essentials
4 The Courtyard
South Street
Falmer
East Sussex
BN1 9PQ

A catalogue record of this book is available from the British Library

Cover design by Jacqueline Abromeit

SECRET DIARY

of a

RECTOR'S DAUGHTER

*Best wishes
Maisie Stone.*

Chapter 1
April 1914

"At last!" Charlotte Carr runs down the Rectory steps and slips through the hedge to the graveyard, clutching her old straw hat against the blustery April wind. Her fair hair is held back in a ribbon, her faded skirt and button-up boots are clean but shabby, as befits an impoverished rector's daughter.

Charlotte (also known as Lottie) has waited for this moment all the morning. Now her father is occupied with a visitor she can at last make her move. "That's the trouble with father," Lottie thinks indignantly, "he's very nosey when it comes to God and religion. He would demand to know what the problem is, why I'm saying some special prayers." And Lottie wants to keep this particular problem to herself, for once.

"Morning, Potter!" she calls to the gardener busily weeding around the tombstones. The old man touches his cap. "Morning, Miss Charlotte, fresh wind." Lottie stops by his wheelbarrow, watching the old gardener working with his hoe. "Quite a few daffodils left, they're still looking pretty."

Potter straightens up and nods. "We'll need to put them seedlings in soon, Miss Charlotte, for a bit o' colour in the summer – hope you don't mind me sayin', like."

Lottie smiles, noticing the lines on Potter's weather-beaten face. "I'll help you with that, Potter, you need a bit of help." She holds onto her hat in the wind. "We'll do it together soon, those beds around the lawn, I think, don't you?" The old man nods and bends down to his weeding again. "Them seedlings is comin' along a real treat in the greenhouse."

Lottie hurries along the path and pushes open the massive studded entrance door of the ancient church. The musty atmosphere envelops her as she slides into a pew and buries her head in her hands, half kneeling. Then she opens her blue eyes again, looking around the lofty vaulted nave, now thankfully deserted.

"No, it's not wrong to ask, I know it's not. He will help me, I know He will."

She closes her eyes and bows her head again. "Hallo, God, it's me again. I've been so worried," she whispers earnestly, "it's my bust, you see. It's just growing too much and I'm finding it embarrassing – all the young gentlemen look at me now. I'm having to wear loose blouses to cover up. So, please God, can you help me? Is there anything you can do? I'm quite desperate. Thank you very much."

She wriggles back on the pew, then slides forward, hands together again.

"I'm sorry to ask you this, dear Lord. I know it's a rather selfish request, but I've got no-one to turn to, now that dear mother is" – her voice falters – "is no longer here. Thank you, God. I'm doing my best to look after father and help him in the parish, now Bella is gone. Oh and please help me cope with my extra duties, as I feel rather inadequate just now."

Lottie leaves the pew and bows to the altar, then hurries out of the church. She heaves a sigh of relief as she turns into the tree-lined Church Lane towards the village. "Might work," she thinks to herself, "it was worth a try. If not, I might have to go into Taunton and buy myself a decent brassiere."

She reaches the village and the blacksmith looks up from his anvil as she passes his forge. "Morning, Miss Charlotte, nice day."

"Good morning, Peter, yes, indeed."

"Miss Bella settled all right in Lunnon town?" he asks.

"Yes, very well, thank you, she's fine."

Lottie carries on walking along the village street, nodding and smiling to various people on the way. She passes the village school and sees the children at play during their mid-morning break. The girls are skipping and playing chasing games, the boys kicking a football or bowling hoops, all chattering and laughing as they run about. She waves to the teacher, Miss Fairmile, just about to ring the bell for lessons once more.

She recognizes the dapper figure of Major Post with his neat moustache by the bakers and he lifts his trilby hat to her, then hugs her warmly. "Good morning, Lottie, how are you today?"

"Very well, thank you, Major, and you?" Lottie is very fond of the Major, a friend of her father's and also one of his church-wardens.

"Absolutely tickety-boo, spring has sprung, I do believe!" he replies, smiling broadly. "Heard the cuckoo this morning, so it has! And how is Bella doing, have you heard?"

"We had a postcard last week, yes, she's settled very well in her new post, thank you."

"Oh good. I know she'll do well, she's so bright."

"And what's the news of Ronnie, how is he getting on at Cambridge?" Lottie asks. The major's eyes light up and he nods and smiles. "He's finished his finals and worked very hard, so we're hoping for a good result. Should be home next month – so, tally-ho!"

The major begins to take his leave, then turns back. "Oh, by the way Doris says if you need any help with the Sick and Poor visits she'll be only too pleased to help. She'll be in touch with you."

Lottie beams, her blue eyes warming at the news. "Why, that's very kind of her. I could do with the support, I must admit, now Bella has gone and mother is… um… no longer with us."

The traditional Sick and Poor visits fill Lottie with dread, now her sister has gone away. Trailing round the cottages and hovels with pots of jam, old clothing, bibles and prayer books. Only Bella could make visiting vulnerable parishioners seem like fun. They had been in fits of laughter at times, in between houses, but now on her own it suddenly seems a dreadful chore looming on the horizon. They had of course performed this duty with their mother before she died, mother always so smiling and patient. Lottie still remembers obediently following her in and out of the houses, giggling with Bella, carrying her basket of 'goodies'.

The major lifts his trilby again. "Well, I must be away, delighted to see you, m'dear. Give my regards to your father. I'll see him on Sunday, of course."

As Lottie continues on her way through the village she is assailed by various village folk, much to her dismay.

"Excuse, ma'am, I got some jumble, where should I be taking it?"

Lottie hesitates. "Um, leave it outside the Village Hall, thank you." Hope that's right, she thinks. I know father doesn't like it left at the Rectory.

A buxom villager leaning on her garden gate, two toddlers clutching at her skirts, calls out as Lottie passes: "My Iris wants to go in fer the May Queen, miss, who picks 'em, can you say?" She gives a nod to an equally buxom young girl standing by the cottage door, picking her teeth.

Lottie looks doubtfully at the girl, who doesn't exactly look an innocent young maiden, but answers: "M'm, I think you should see the school-master, Mr Duff. He would be able to tell you all the details. Good-day!"

I don't think Old Duffer would approve of that young lady somehow, Lottie thinks. And anyway I think they're voted in by other pupils, have to be under 18.

A thin-faced worn-looking woman approaches and says timidly: "Beg pardon, miss, you are the vicar's daughter? Sorry to bother you an' that, but can the vicar 'elp us, me 'usband's sick and no money coming in... Six little'uns to feed, awful coughs they've got. We're in a tied cottage, y'see, on the Squire's estate. Terrible damp, it is. I've told Squire Madely but he won't do nothing about it..."

Lottie had heard talk of Squire Madely and his reputation as a bad landlord so was anxious to help. "What name? And the address? I'll tell the Reverend, but I can't promise." Hope I can remember all this, she thinks.

So many problems! Lottie's head is spinning, but then she reaches the end of the little street as the church clock strikes eleven o'clock and suddenly breaks into a run, seeing the horse-drawn post-cart approach the red pillar-box ahead.

"Hallo! Can you wait? I've got one here!" She produces a letter from her pocket and hands it over. "Thank you, postman."

The postman nods and touches his cap. "Thank you, ma'am." He empties the box, climbs back into his cart, flicks the reins and proceeds down the lane, edged by leafy hedges and banks of primroses. Lottie gives a rueful sigh and watches the cart clip-clop on its way. "Another one on the way to you, Bella. How on earth am I going to manage without you?"

She makes her way home through the village at a brisk pace, head down, hoping not to be accosted by any more villagers. Lottie winces and fingers her clothing. Her bust is feeling most uncomfortable now. She can hardly breathe. She had bound them up with crepe bandage to flatten them this morning. 'What a pest this is!' she thinks, 'now I know how the Chinese ladies felt having their feet bound!'

She wonders what awaits her back at The Rectory. Her father is a dear soul, a good parish priest and a loving father, but his organisational abilities leave a lot to be desired.

When dear mother died, Bella had coped with him admirably, whipping him into shape in a firm but kindly way. But since she had left two weeks ago, father had now slipped back into his old ways, sitting happily in his untidy study smoking his pipe, surrounded by piles of books and papers, writing a new prayer or a letter to the Church Times, blissfully unaware that he should be at a meeting or conducting a christening.

Some people in the parish thought the Rector a little eccentric, as he was apt to stroll through the village mumbling to himself when he had a lot on his mind. But he wasn't at all! Lottie knew he was doing God's work, thinking lofty spiritual thoughts about the Epistles of Paul the Apostle, his special study. And then sometimes he would forget to brush his hair, particularly now mother was not here to keep an eye on him. So all in all it was a big job, Looking After Father. And it didn't help that Lottie was almost as disorganised as her father!

I must try and improve things, Lottie thinks worriedly as she enters the house. I'll have to introduce a new system for the 'hatches, matches and despatches' as they call the births, marriages and deaths. Father has been known to scribble a date and time for a christening or wedding on the back of an envelope, after meeting someone in the street. That is just not good enough, Lottie thinks. He should be entering it into his big appointments diary. I must tackle him about it. Perhaps a separate book for each would be a good idea, then I could transfer them into his big diary.

But, too late, as Lottie approaches the study, she can hear raised voices and then a florid-faced man and a weeping woman holding a baby are being ushered out by the flustered-looking rector, apologising profusely. Oh no, Lottie thinks, what now?

When he has seen the couple out, the rector hurries back to the study, shaking his head, a worried frown creasing his brow.

"What happened, Father?"

"Most unfortunate, there were two George Smiths, one was buried last week aged 88, George Edward Smith, and the other one was that couple's first-born son, George Edwin Smith, whom I christened last Sunday. Unfortunately on the notices posted in the church porch the names were mixed up. I shall have to reprimand Mr Daly.

"…oh no," cries Lottie, suppressing a smile, "no wonder the couple were upset!"

Lottie takes her father's arm. "First of all, I'll fetch a nice cup of tea and then perhaps it might be an idea if we reorganise the 'hatches, matches and despatches', what do you think?"

She fairly skips down the corridor to the kitchen to ask for some tea. She is just so relieved that for once it's not her fault, but the verger's.

THE RECTORY
15th April 1914

Dearest Bella,

Thanks for the p.c. Glad to hear you are settling down well with Aunt Hilda in London. I am missing you so much already. Have you started your new job at the Language School yet? And are there any decent fellows there, or are you still saving yourself for Ronnie Post?

Please write at once and tell me your news, a proper letter this time! I do so miss our long chats over breakfast and dinner. Father is hopeless at 'chatting' as you know and also, poor dear, far too busy with his parishioners to talk to little me. He also seems rather distracted these days. I'm sure he's worrying about his eldest daughter living in wicked London town! But if I mention you, he says "I'm sure she's keeping busy, Charlotte", in rather a cross voice and gives me the parish newsletter to type from his dreadful handwriting.

S-o, we are jogging along here at The Rectory in much the same old way as before. Mrs May and Emily send their best wishes to you. Emily is walking out with a new young man now. He's called Fred and he waits around outside the back door for her to come off duty. He's a reed-cutter or something on the Levels. She puts her hair up in a special way when she sees him and puts rouge on. I shall have to think about putting my hair up once I turn 18 in August. You will come back for my birthday, won't you, Bella? You're so clever with hair. I need you to style it for me.

I still miss mother terribly. I know it's been two years now but I still think of her every day and keep her photograph by my bed.

Mrs May is very 'put out' that you've gone away. You were the lively one, she says. "It seems very quiet without Miss Arabella now", is all I hear from her. "No piano playing, no shrieks of laughter."

I've started doing the weekly Sick and Poor Visits with Mrs Post now, much to my relief. I was dreading doing it on my own. She has been very supportive since mother died, hasn't she? We still go on a Thursday and trail round all the cottages, it's so dreary, as you know. Mrs Post takes it all very seriously and is very dutiful and kind to everyone, especially Bennie the deaf-mute in Oak Cottages. She gave him some fudge she had made last week, as a special treat. Not like when you and I did it, Bella, eh? We did get the giggles at times, remember? It was always such fun with you. How about the time we gave one poor harassed mother two pots of Mrs May's best strawberry jam and some clean linen and one of the little darlings (there were 8 from memory) tipped all the jam over the linen – what a mess! What a hoot!

Tethercombe is looking very pretty now that Spring is here. All the daffs. are out and primroses on the banks and the bluebells will soon be appearing in the woods. The cottage gardens in Sheep Street are a riot of yellow and pink blossom and the plane trees in Church Lane are gradually coming into their new leaf, like dainty sprigged muslin. We desperately need to brighten up our garden before the Fete in July. I really must try and help Potter more, as poor father never gets time for gardening. I will try to put in some seedlings next week and feed the roses with Bessie's poo. How we all miss dear mother's green thumb! The garden hasn't looked the same since she died.

Father had his first visitors to the church yesterday and Mr Gander chose some really joyous hymns for Easter Day. St. Stephens looked absolutely beautiful decorated with all the Easter lilies and spring flowers. The sun was streaming through the stained glass windows like a kaleidoscope.

There was quite a good congregation, all the regulars including both the Trevithick boys.

Well, dearest Bella, must close now and am hoping and praying you are happily settled with Aunt Hilda. Please give her my fondest love. Haven't seen the old stick for years. Please write SOON with ALL your news! I want to hear about all your new beaux, every detail!

Best love from your devoted sister,
Lottie
P.S. Hope you're not missing the Poor Visits too much – you're the lucky one, you've wriggled out of it!

SECRET DIARY

of Charlotte Mary Carr

20th April 1914

My breasts are still growing! I can't believe it. I am mortified. Only three years ago when mother was still alive they were small and pointy. But now there's suddenly been a spurt of growth and all my chemises are becoming tight for me. I must be at least 36 inches round the bust now. I have started wearing loose blouses and shawls when I go out, as I feel very self-conscious about them. Went to church yesterday and prayed they wouldn't grow any more. Hope it works. But maybe I should get a proper brassiere soon. I wish, how I wish dear mother were here to advise me. And I do miss Bella so. Have been flattening them a bit by binding them up, as I feel all the young men are looking at me now. But it's not working, it's too uncomfortable and keeps slipping. Wish I had small, pert breasts like Bella and not these horrible pendulous things. I feel so conspicuous.

21st April 1914

Went into Taunton on the bus secretly today without telling father. Was fitted for a proper supportive brassiere from the corsetry department of Bentalls Department Store. When the assistant told me the size I had to ask her to repeat it, as I couldn't believe it. I am now a 38" large size. I felt quite hot and flustered after this news as I tried on different brassieres in the cubicle. So, anyway, like it or not, I am now the proud possessor of three pairs of Excelsior brand brassieres, very stout and serviceable cotton, not exactly the dainty silk lace-trimmed garments Bella no doubt buys in London. But at least I feel more comfortable now. I wonder if Bella will be jealous of my fuller bust?

Will have to look after my new undergarments as they must last for a long time, as money is tight in our household and I'm not yet earning any money. It was difficult to explain to father why I needed so much extra spending money. I didn't feel I could be frank with him. So I just said it was for personal items. He probably thought that meant sanitary pads! No doubt thought I'd bought a year's supply when he saw the receipt!

25th April 1914

The second anniversary of dear mother's death. I put a small posy of flowers on her grave, the woodland flowers she loved so much, primroses, anemones, violets and a sheaf of bluebells. Shed yet more tears. I gazed at the polished granite tombstone with its stark inscription:

> MARIE ELIZABETH CARR, beloved wife of
> *Horace Carr, Vicar of Tethercombe and*
> *Loving Mother to Arabella and Charlotte.*
> *Born 12th February 1866*
> *Slipped away 25th April 1912.*
> *Now at peace*

'Slipped away'. How I hate these euphemisms, so Victorian. Father had chosen the words. She didn't 'slip away', she died after a painful illness that lasted three months. She looked so thin and gaunt at the end, but was so brave and uncomplaining. And so I hope you are now at peace, dear mother, for you deserve to be.

At the time of her death everyone was still reeling with shock from the 'Titanic' disaster which had happened two weeks earlier, and I remember wanting to scream at them: 'I don't care about the Titanic, my mother has died, not a stranger, but my mother! The 'Titanic' disaster, though appalling, had to me been pushed into the background by my dear mother's death.

I still miss her so. Why, oh why did she have to die so young, only 46! She was the kindest, sweetest person in the world and so brave about her disability. Father says it was God's will, but I can't accept this and have only just resumed my daily prayers, for I felt God had deserted me. I see other girls out with their mothers, girls I was at school with, and feel quite jealous and bitter, though I know this isn't a Christian feeling.

I knelt at the grave and had a little chat with mother as usual, telling her my problems. I knew I could be frank with her. "It's my bust you see, mother," I began. "It's grown so much and I'm embarrassed about it. I've been praying it will stop growing and I've bought myself a proper brassiere now, so that might help. I am trying to be brave here without you, mother dear, but it's so hard at times, especially now Bella has gone to London."

Can't write any more, too upset.

Sunday 26th April 1914

Went to church as usual. Am slowly getting used to going on my own now and sitting in the front pew. It seemed very odd at first when Bella went away and I felt very self-conscious. Also, sitting in the front pew you can't see who is behind you, without peering rudely over your shoulder. And of course there is father, right in front of me in the pulpit, so I have to be on my best behaviour. Watching him give his sermon (dutifully typed by me) I held my breath, hoping there weren't too many errors!

Tom Trevithick was there as usual, but not his brother, Luke. Luke only seems to come at Christmas and Easter these days. Tom nodded and smiled at me as the congregation filed out. He seems a nice fellow, quiet and reserved, I believe in his 30s. Older than his brother anyway, but still unmarried. I know he has a dairy farm at the top of Turners Hill. Luke is very tall and dark-haired, with dark, penetrating eyes and scares me rather. Bella always said they were our sworn enemies, because of something which happened years ago, but I have only vague memories of the incident as I was too young. I tend to avoid him if I see him in the village as he looks you up and down in an amused way, whereas Tom is more open and approachable, slow and easy-going with a stocky build and a fine moustache.

Tom was lingering by the lych-gate when I left the church porch and as I approached him he smiled and said "Good morning, Miss Carr". So I stopped and had a little chat with him about father's sermon. I didn't like to tell him I knew it backwards!

Well, we ended up taking a little walk together! We went down Church Lane, across the village green, past The Manor House where Major Post and his wife live and round Church Lane back to The Rectory again. It was quite pleasant chatting to him about local matters and we admired the gardens we were passing, so pretty now spring is here. I found I could talk quite easily to him. He seems a good sort, one of those comforting, rock-like people.

When I got home and apologised to father for being late back for lunch, I was surprised. He wasn't cross at all and seemed quite happy about it. Wonders will never cease! Perhaps he wants to marry me off! At least it must mean he approves of Tom.

* * *

Lottie is in St. Stephens, polishing the lectern and humming the hymn 'All Things Bright and Beautiful' to herself. M'm, how she loves the rich smell of beeswax polish! And how satisfying it is to see the ancient timbers nurtured and shining once again. Two of the lady helpers are off sick, so Lottie had at once volunteered when Mrs Witherspoon, the doctor's wife, asked for some help yesterday. Lottie has also arranged the altar flowers. A few tulips from the Rectory garden have been added to Mrs Witherspoon's hot-house lilies and irises, so they make a fine display.

M'm, she can smell the fresh fragrance wafting across to her now as she gives the lectern a final polish.

'There! That's better!' Lottie is just about to pick up her cleaning cloths and leave the church, when the big entrance door is pushed open rather forcefully. The formidable figure of Mrs Violet Doubleday is standing there, etched in the doorway against the sunlight. She is waving a booklet and as she advances down the aisle, Lottie can at once see she is not amused. Mrs Doubleday is a long-time resident of the village and an influential figure, a church benefactor and vocal on several local committees. Lottie's heart sinks.

She remembers the old lady from childhood when she once reprimanded Bella and herself for daring to giggle during their father's sermon one Easter Sunday when their mother was absent. They called her 'Mrs Poo-poo' after that, or Mrs DoublePee, which only led to more giggles. Father had been preaching the parable of the Prodigal Son at the time, while looking daggers at his errant daughters in the front pew.

"Ah, Miss Carr, just the person I wanted to see. I called at The Rectory just now, but the vicar seems to be out, so your housekeeper said you might be here."

She comes to a halt in front of Lottie and once again flaps

the booklet in Lottie's startled face. She is panting somewhat from the exertion of hurrying down the aisle and her wide heavy-bosomed figure, clad in full-length black bombazine and a grey felt hat decorated with cherries is now almost blocking out the morning light streaming through the stained-glass windows. Lottie steps back in alarm as she ventures to ask in a timid voice. "Can I help you, Mrs Doubleday?"

Mrs Doubleday clicks her tongue in annoyance. "It's not help I want, young lady. It's an explanation and an apology. Where is my name, that's what I want to know, where is it? And also I speak on behalf of several other valued members of the congregation, Colonel Carruthers and the Spencers to name but two. Where is the recognition in this magazine?" She flaps the booklet once again and Lottie can now see it is the Parish Newsletter, duly typed by herself and distributed only last week. Lottie fixes her eyes on the bobbing cherries and tries to think calm thoughts.

Mrs Doubleday is obviously trembling with rage about something, but Lottie is still in the dark. "I'm sorry, Mrs Doubleday, but what is the problem? Shall we sit down?" Lottie indicates a nearby pew.

But this only seems to anger Mrs Doubleday even more. "I shall sit down when I want to, young lady." She comes even closer to Lottie. "I understand that you now type out the Parish Newsletter for your father, is that right? Your sister, Arabella, has gone away, am I correct?" Lottie nods, wondering what's coming.

Mrs Doubleday shakes her head. "We had no problems when Arabella undertook this important task, but now, I'm afraid this just isn't good enough. You'll have to wake up your ideas, Miss Carr. Do you realise," she splutters, "you have entirely missed out the complete list of church benefactors?"

She nods, breathing heavily. "Missed us out. That's what you have done. A lot of people are very angry."

Lottie gives an audible gasp, shocked to the core by this news. She holds her breath, dreading what is coming next.

Mrs Doubleday leans against the newly polished lectern, sweating profusely and panting in her voluminous gown, Lottie is annoyed to see.

"We are quite happy to donate. My family has been donating to the church for over 40 years, did you know that, young lady? Quite happy to donate, as I say, but," a frosty smile passes across her thin lips briefly, "we do expect a little recognition. That's all we ask. A little recognition."

Phew! Mrs Doubleday gives a deep sigh and then seems to collapse into a nearby pew, panting heavily and fanning herself with the booklet.

Lottie is horrified and knows her father will be really angry and upset when he finds out. A list of benefactors giving continuing financial support to the church faithfully appears in the Parish Newsletter every month and many of the donors would feel hurt and unappreciated if this didn't eventuate. She thinks wildly back to last week when she typed the Newsletter out for father. Glory be! It must have been the day she had gone to mother's grave. She had felt rather distracted and upset afterwards and can only think she had turned over two pages at once, when copying details from a previous Newsletter.

"May I see the Newsletter, Mrs Doubleday?" she asks sweetly, recovering her composure and the old lady hands it to her. Lottie scans the pages quickly and realises that is what has happened. Obviously she should have checked it more thoroughly herself. But privately she blames father for not doing so. It was the first time she had typed it for him, after all. However, what's done is done. Best to be really apologetic and contrite, she thinks. She composes her face into a serious dutiful expression.

"I do apologise, Mrs Doubleday. I don't know how this terrible mistake happened. I can only say I'm a novice at producing the Parish magazine and I have a lot to learn."

She ventures a small smile. "I do hope you will forgive me and I can assure you, it will never happen again."

Mrs Doubleday gets to her feet and leans on the pew, sniffing and tightening her lips. "Well, I sincerely hope that it does not, young lady. I will be speaking to the vicar about this, oh yes, but I'm glad to have your assurance that the mistake will not be repeated."

"I'm very sorry about it," repeats Lottie as she follows the irate lady up the aisle. "And please pass my apologies on to the other members of the congregation whose names were unintentionally omitted." They reach the entrance door and Lottie runs forward to open it for her. "Needless to say, we do appreciate your continuing financial support and an apology will appear in next month's magazine." I'm sure this is what Bella would have said, Lottie thinks desperately.

Mrs Doubleday grunts and sighs. "I should think so too and now I'll bid you good-day, Miss Carr."

And the stout figure of Violet DoublePee sweeps pompously up the path, the daffodils waving and nodding on either side, like bowing courtiers.

Phew! Lottie leans against the church porch, her heart beating wildly. Not a good start to the day! Hope I handled that all right, she thinks. I must be more careful next time! I must check it all more thoroughly. Although I don't particularly like her, Mrs DoublePee is a very important figure in the community and it's not a good idea to cross her.

She thinks back to the incident in her childhood and giggles. She remembers father reporting to mother at lunch that she and Bella had misbehaved in church. However, quick-witted Bella had then piped up: 'But I thought the parable of the Prodigal Son is all about forgiveness, father,' and was promptly sent to her room for being impudent.

As Lottie closes the church door and slips though the hedge to The Rectory, she sees the family pony and trap returning up the drive-way. Her heart fills with dread. Now to face her father.

Chapter 2
MAY 1914

SECRET DIARY
of Charlotte Mary Carr

10th May 1914

Tom has asked me to the Empire Day dance! I am so excited! Have had rather an eventful day all round (for me), as Tom turned up unexpectedly this morning and said did I want to come to the market at Dunster with him? So I set aside my charity envelopes, hastily donned my hat and jacket, left a note for father and off we trotted.

It was very busy at the market, although as usual I had hardly any money to buy anything, except a few new handkerchiefs and a couple of penny-dreadfuls from a pedlar selling second-hand novellas. There were plenty of ragamuffins about, so one had to watch one's bag and purse.

There was a one-man-band there which was amusing, an old gaffer strapped up with a big drum and cymbals, also bells and pipes, very diverting. Then we bumped into Major and Mrs Post by the flower stall. They are so sociable and kind! I went with Mrs Post to Hanburys, the big drapers nearby as she needed to buy some damask table napkins. How I love the smell in this shop! It was so interesting looking at all the materials and bolts of cloth, also seeing the cashier up in her little eyrie giving the change which she then shoots back along the wires, with a ding-a-ling! Mrs Post then suggested we had tea together at the Little Gem Tea Rooms opposite. So we had a pleasant little get-together and the Major insisted on paying the bill, then Tom took me home. And on the way back he asked me to go with him to the dance! Of course I said "Yes".

I have been to the Empire Day Dance before, of course, but never with a regular young man as it were. So it's much more fun going with someone and I know Amy is going with Bertie so we can perhaps all go together.

Going back to Tethercombe, Tom dropped me off in Church Lane and as I approached The Rectory I could hear the haunting sound of the muffled tenor bell tolling solemnly from the tower. I knew father was there conducting a funeral service for one of the villagers. It sent a chill down my spine. I can never hear this bell now without remembering the terrible day of mother's funeral. Maybe I felt worse because it had just been the anniversary. Anyway, I had to flee to the sanctuary of my room to get a grip on myself. But it wasn't a good time. For Emily was sweeping the front porch and, as I ran up the stairs sobbing, Mrs Post was shepherding a gaggle of Women's Club ladies into the back dining room for a meeting, and they all looked up at me. But in my grief all I saw was a blur of faces and didn't care what they thought of me. Honestly! There is no privacy in this house! There are times when The Rectory is like Piccadilly Circus!

How I wish dear Bella were here to console me! I do miss her so! In the weeks after mother's death we were a great comfort to each other, one being strong when the other was weak and vice versa.

But now I have to be strong on my own. Bella has gone to live in London and that's that. She was given a wonderful opportunity of a good job and she took it.

Of course I've got father here with me, but he's so busy with the parish and a bit unapproachable at times. I love him dearly and once asked him if he missed mother very much and he admitted he did. They had been married for 25 years after all and were very close. That was quite an admission coming from him, as he's not very good on emotional matters. But then he added rather piously: "But the dear Lord is my constant companion, so I'm never alone." That put me in my place!

I glanced at the photo by my bed. Mother's familiar calm face smiled back at me. Memories flooded back – her soothing hands and voice when I was ill with some childish complaint; her laughter as we shared an old family joke; and her sharp brain suggesting the perfect word as I laboriously struggled over an essay for homework, for she was well read.

A tap on the door interrupted my thoughts and Mrs May was

standing there with tea and sympathy. She is a dear. "Thought this might help, Miss Charlotte."

After a while I pulled myself together and started thinking about the matter in hand, i.e. what on earth am I going to wear to the dance?! That's a real worry! I've got a couple of formal evening dresses but they're not suitable. I would love something new, but daren't ask father for any more money this month. I looked through my wardrobe and dragged out all my clothes. What a dreary collection!

But I did find my pink floral blouse with the frills down the front which hides my bust quite well and is not too faded. Alas, no suitable skirt. I seem to have put on weight on my top half and lost it round my hips, so nothing fits properly. My next idea was to make myself a skirt. Or then again, maybe Bella has some old cast-offs I could wear. Some of the things she has tossed out are better than the ones I'm wearing now. I can't borrow from Amy, as she's a much bigger build than me.

Then I remembered there is a remnant material table in the haberdashers in the village. So tomorrow I'm going down there with the last of my meagre spending allowance to see if they have anything suitable.

11th May 1914

I have just had the most embarrassing morning of my entire life!

As I was getting ready to go down to the village, a small ragged boy arrived at the back door with a note for me from Grandmother Carr. My heart sank. She gets very forgetful now and often sends these little notes asking for help. Sometimes they are long, rambling incoherent letters. Other times they are short and to the point. This was one of the latter. It read:

> *"Charlotte. Please fetch me Izal toilet paper and medicine for dyspepsia urgently. Grandma."*

My heart sank even further to my buttoned-up boots. Just when I was eagerly anticipating a rare morning to myself to browse through the materials, now I had to run errands for Grandma! I felt annoyed, but if I hurried I could still do it and be back for lunch. I bundled up my hair hastily with a scrap of ribbon, jammed my hat on top and cycled down the drive-way.

As I rode down Church Lane I realised Grandma had not sent any money with the note. So now I would have to buy her things first with my precious money, take them to her cottage (a good mile away) and then go back to the village for my own purchases, when she had reimbursed me. Aargh!! I was rapidly becoming more and more frustrated. I was normally very patient with the old lady, now in her 80s and steadily becoming senile and increasingly deaf. I loved her dearly, but now and then, I thought, it would be nice to have just a few hours to myself.

I went into the village store and bought Grandma's things, bundling them awkwardly in my arms, intending to put them in my bicycle basket. As I left the shop hurriedly, still in rather a bad mood, I somehow managed to trip over an iron boot-scraper by the doorway and fell flat on my face!

The toilet rolls flew off in all directions and the medicine bottle shattered on the paving stones, spraying thick creamy liquid everywhere, including all over my skirt. "Oh!!" I cried out in alarm and a tall, well-dressed figure passing by turned round and stared at me as I lay there, sprawling alongside a horse trough. It was Luke Trevithick.

I was never more embarrassed in my life. I felt such a complete fool, lying there in an undignified heap, my clothes awry and my hair fast escaping from its ribbon, my hat in the gutter. And the last person I wanted to encounter in such a situation was Luke. Our paths hadn't crossed for years and I was still rather wary of him, after the incident at the party.

He came at once to my aid, bending down and offering his hand to pull me up. But I could see from his expression, that amused, arrogant expression, as I struggled to my feet, nursing my scratched nose and bruised elbows, he was doing his best to stop himself from laughing. He doffed his boater politely. "It's Miss Carr, isn't it? Are you all right?" he asked as I bent down to pick up the toilet paper.

I nodded, fuming inside and refusing to meet his eyes.

"I'm Tom's brother, Luke. Let me help you. Hope you haven't cut yourself," he added, retrieving the last of the errant toilet rolls from the village street. He returned them, but it had been raining and they were now sodden and ruined.

The shopkeeper came out and started anxiously fluttering about and other people passing by were now staring. A nasty little boy bowling a hoop actually stood and laughed. I felt so conspicuous. I kicked the broken glass into the gutter with my boots in a most unladylike manner. And then to my horror tears started to spring into my eyes, as I realised I would now have to buy some more things and was rapidly running out of money.

Luke's dark eyes scanned my face and seeing I was upset he put his arm lightly around my shoulder. "Don't get upset now," he soothed, "it's nothing to worry about."

"I've got to get some more things for my grandma," I sobbed, the shock of the fall setting in, "and now I haven't got enough money…"

There I was sniffling and bawling like a child, shoulders heaving and somehow it was all made worse by Luke's sympathetic gestures. And to my further embarrassment I suddenly realised I was exposing a deep décolletage! The buttons on my blouse had come adrift in the fall and, horrors! my pin-tuck chemise was now fully revealed. I buttoned my jacket across my bust firmly, tried to smooth my hair and clutched my hat. A deep blush was now suffusing my face and neck, as I struggled to retain just a modicum of dignity. I blew my nose, raised my chin and finally met Luke's dancing brown eyes.

Was it sympathy and understanding I saw there, or mocking humour and amusement? I wasn't sure. I pulled myself together and tried to see the funny side of it. I gave a weak smile and a nervous giggle. "I must look such a mess… I'll go back home and get some more money, clean myself up…"

"No, no," Luke said, reaching into his pocket and thrusting a handful of silver coins at me. "Here, have this – is it enough? Pay me back anytime, no hurry. Give it to Tom sometime."

I gave him an embarrassed look. "That's very kind of you, thanks." I shook my head. "I feel so foolish!"

Luke merely laughed and shrugged. "Accidents happen. It can't be helped." He began to walk away and then turned back again, grinning. "By the way, I hear you're going to the village dance on the 24th." I nodded. "I might see you there. I think you owe me one dance at least – is that agreed?" He put out his hand and I shook it, smiling reluctantly. "Agreed."

As I went back into the shop again, trembling all over, I mused over what had happened, cringing with embarrassment at the memory. What must he think of me? Luke Trevithick, now grown into a handsome young man whose flirtatious reputation in the village was legendary. And now, I didn't know what to think of him. I was somewhat bemused, liking him and mistrusting him in equal measure.

13th May

Have to record this incident which happened today. I was in the back garden picking some flowers for the sitting room, when Mrs May called me from the kitchen door. I could see she had someone there with her and when I drew close could see it was the gypsy pedlar who comes round the houses now and then, selling a few things.

The gypsy gave her wheedling smile at me as I approached and held up a bunch of ribbons. "Pretty ribbons for a pretty girl!" she sang out. "6 for a 1d. All different colours, see?"

Placing my trug of flowers on the ground, I looked through them and picked a few out and gave her a 1d. from my pocket. She smiled showing broken teeth in her sallow face, framed by greasy lanky jet black hair. She was wearing a voluminous skirt and old boots, also a bright turquoise patterned blouse and grimy scarf tied round her neck. Mrs May stood by, clutching the pegs and a basket she had bought and smiling as she looked at my pretty ribbons. Then Emily appeared in the doorway, flushed and excited. "I'm ready to have my palm read," she said smiling. "Here's the 3d. for you," handing over the silver coin.

I was intrigued. I'd never seen a gypsy read anyone's palm before. The gypsy eased her bulky frame down on the back step and Emily sat beside her holding out her hand.

The pedlar held her hand and began to trace the lines on the palm. "Ah yes, you have a long life in front of you - a long and happy life."

I was a bit sceptical. I could hear Bella saying now – 'hardly surprising, she's only 17', but I was also more than a little curious.

"Yes," the gypsy continued, her black eyes narrowing, "and now I can see on this line here a few dark clouds are looming..."

"Oo-er!" Emily's face fell, "what does that mean?"

"Can't say, dearie, but now," the gypsy pulled Emily's hand closer, "I see the love line and it looks – yes, it looks happy, but he will go away, then he will return to you."

"Oh!" Emily cried, her face completely blank, "where will he go I wonder? But he comes back...?" I knew she was going out with Fred and that this news was important to her.

"Anything else?" Emily said impatiently, "can you tell anything else, will I get married and have babies, will I?" The gypsy shook her head. "No more, dearie, that's all."

She got up with surprising alacrity and was about to push her old pram with its load of ribbons, plants, pegs and baskets off down the path, when I called her back, suddenly thinking I would like to have my palm read. "God bless you, dearie," she said, all ingratiating smiles. "Cross my palm with silver first, mind."

I ran to my room to fetch some more change and sat on the step. I was glad father was out, as I don't think he would have approved of his daughter sitting on the back step conniving with gypsy-pedlars.

She took my hand and began to trace the lines on my palm. "Oh yes, my dear, I predict a long life and a healthy one. You've got a lucky face, miss, I can see that."

"And what about the love line," said Mrs May, teasing me and winking.

"Ah, the love line, yes I see – I see a tall, dark stranger come into

your life and he will be romantic and true..."

I withdrew my hand, suddenly cross. What nonsense this was! Tom wasn't tall and dark and he certainly wasn't romantic. I stood up. "Thank you kindly, I have to go now."

And I ran indoors, utterly confused and embarrassed. It was only when I reached my room that I realised the description of the man could easily fit Tom's brother, Luke. What silly rubbish it was! I could never get too involved with an arrogant man like him.

THE RECTORY
14th May 1914

Dearest Bella,

Thanks so much for your welcome letter received last week. My stars, what a dizzy lifestyle you're leading!

Your new job sounds ideal for you. You are so fluent in French – I am glad to hear you actually have contact with the students as well as doing translation work in the office.

Your social life in London seems very busy. Am so pleased to hear that Aunt Hilda has made you so welcome. She is a brick. No doubt as a spinster her life is usually rather quiet, although you say she is quite intellectual? You must be looking forward to the concert at the Wigmore Hall with her.

How wonderful to see Marie Lloyd on the stage in person! I would love to go to the Music Hall one day. And you have joined a tennis club! I can just see you hitting the ball gracefully over the net in your new white tennis dress, on the lawns of that lovely house. You are a lucky devil, Bella! You get all the fun. Meanwhile I'm stuck here in Tethercombe looking after father. (Labour of love, of course!)

Now, your new beaux! That Peter Plunkett sounds a real bore, I should definitely drop him. And Cyril seems a bit weedy to me, although his sister sounds quite fun. What a strange name, Evadne.

But Rupert Everingham – now he seems to figure prominently in your letter, Bella. Is he handsome? You don't say, but he sounds a perfect poppet to me. But then you add, quite casually, he has a CHAUFFEUR, so he must be well-heeled! I should cultivate him if I were you!

Thanks for the WPSU ribbon, though in truth I can't see myself wearing it down here. I think I would get arrested on the spot by Constable Perkins. Interesting how they chose the Suffragette colours of Green, White and Violet. I didn't realise they stood for Give Women the Vote. I must confess I was a trifle shocked by your interest in the Suffragette movement, Bella. I do have to be honest, as you are my sister. I have conveniently "lost" that page of your letter, as I'm sure father would be very disapproving to say the least. I know "Votes for Women" is a worthy cause and you do say you're in the "Suffragist" non-militant wing, but please promise me you will be careful, Bella. Don't get yourself arrested for pity's sake! And don't go on hunger strike. You don't want to end up in Holloway, being forcibly fed, it sounds quite horrible. Father would have a fit.

We had a frightful to-do here last week. I am so scatty! I made a ghastly error in the Parish Newsletter and missed out Mrs DoublePee and a lot of other benefactors! Father had to issue a grovelling apology in the magazine and he even sent Mrs PP some flowers from that posh new florist in Taunton to keep her sweet. Needless to say I wasn't very popular with father for a few days, but as I'm the only one who can type around here, I've still got the job!

Such a hoot! To redeem myself I have been helping Potter in the garden and have now planted hundreds of seedlings (mainly marigolds and marguerite daisies) all round the lawn. I also fed the roses in front of the terrace. So hopefully by July the garden will be looking quite colourful for the Fete. I have also started on some sketches, mainly flower studies and local scenes, to sell at the Fete. Dr Witherspoon has said he knows someone in Porlock who would help me frame them cheaply.

The only minor domestic drama we had last week was that there was a mouse in the kitchen and Emily swooned at the sight of it. Father made a rare joke and said it was a church-mouse come to join its own! I think he had been doing the accounts and was reminding us we are all poverty-stricken.

(Mind you, on his stipend, I'm not surprised.) As Pussy Carr was nowhere to be seen, Mrs May meanwhile calmly set a trap with cheese and caught it behind the dresser within 10 minutes! She is very practical and fortunately not the fainting kind. Other news, Davey the stable-lad missed his lift home in the Carter Paterson van and had to stay the night. He insisted on bunking down in the hay-loft, but we gave him a blanket and fed him, dear lad.

I have been going out with Tom (Trevithick) for about 3 weeks now, mainly just walks after church. He is a very pleasant companion, despite what you may think.

But now I am all of a dither, Bella, the Empire Day dance in the Village Hall is coming up and I don't know what to wear. May I borrow something of yours? I have a pretty blouse I could wear, (my rose pink floral), but need a long skirt. I cannot ask father for any more spending money this month, so am looking for material to make a skirt. My friend Amy is also going to the dance with her young man and she has said she will help me do my hair. I am quite excited about it. So think of me on May 24th. Will close now. Look after yourself and BE CAREFUL!

Your loving sister,
Lottie

* * *

"And now we've run out of silver polish, this is the last straw!"

The Rectory is in chaos! An important visitor is arriving tomorrow, no less a personage than the Bishop of Bath and Wells. Mrs May and Emily seem to be getting in such a flap preparing his room, and cooking and cleaning that Lottie has offered to dash down to the village on a mercy errand to fetch urgent supplies.

She emerges from the shop into the village street, now gaily decorated for tomorrow's Empire Day celebrations with Union Jack flags and coloured bunting. She looks up and down the colourful displays and smiles to herself. "I really must come and see it all tomorrow."

Lottie loves Empire Day, 24th May, and remembers what fun she and Bella had in their childhood on this day. The Morris Dancers clapping their sticks and jingling their bells; Magic Lantern shows, egg and spoon races, visiting troubadours and coloured minstrels playing banjos. The children will be relishing a day off school. There is always a wonderfully jolly festive feeling all over the village. Lottie sighs: 'Almost want to be a child again.'

She makes her way to the pillar-box to post another letter to Bella. She misses her sister so much and feels the need to keep in regular touch with her. As she pops it in the box, she sees a pony and trap approaching down Turners Lane at a spanking pace. And as it gets near she sees it's Luke Trevithick. He has a young lady with him who is holding onto her hat firmly as he sweeps her along. Lottie doesn't recognise her, but she looks very young and pretty with dark hair. She acknowledges Luke with a smile and a nod and he waves back grinning and then calls out: 'Mind your step!'

Lottie blushes and gives a secret smile, suddenly recalling their embarrassing encounter recently. But then she remembers the Dance tomorrow evening and wonders whether Luke will be there to claim a dance with her. She still has mixed emotions about him.

She lifts her chin. 'I don't give a jot if he's there or not,' she thinks defiantly, kicking some stones on the road as she begins to walk home. But then she muses: 'But I suppose if he is I'd better accept out of politeness – after all he did help me the other day and he is Tom's brother. One can't bear grudges for ever.'

When Lottie arrives back at the Rectory her father greets her in the hall rather testily and Lottie's heart sinks. "Oh, there you are, Lottie. I wanted to speak to you and I didn't know where you were." He sounds quite peeved. He's frowning and looking anxious, his eyes darting about nervously behind his spectacles. "I went to the village…" Lottie murmurs apologetically. And I was already running an errand for Mrs May, she thinks indignantly, but bites her tongue and follows her father into the study. When father gets into a flap like this, it's best to placate him, not argue with him. "What is it, Father? What's happened?"

The Revd Carr looks flustered and agitated and lights up his pipe, drawing on it heavily. He gives a deep sigh. "First of all Colonel Carruthers turned up complaining again, something about torn hymn books, oh and his family pew not being polished properly and the choir-boys talking during the sermon. So I had to pacify him as he's a benefactor, especially after that Newsletter business. He's such an old fusspot. Now I discover this…"

And he points an accusing finger at the large leather-bound open book on his rather untidy desk. "It's my diary, Lottie, you haven't been bringing it up to date. Bella always did that for me, so that I know exactly what I'm doing each day." He sighs and begins to wring his hands and pace about in his flowing cassock, not a good sign.

He's obviously getting over-anxious about the Bishop's impending arrival, Lottie thinks. "Oh, I'm sorry, father. I don't think you told me about that. (I know you didn't, she thinks) I'll do it in future…"

"…and so now we've got a clash, I've got the Bishop arriving tomorrow morning and there's also a Parish Council meeting. I can't have that, I really can't, it's all too much." The Revd peers out of the window short-sightedly and shakes his head. "I did so want everything to go smoothly when the Bishop is here…"

Lottie goes over to him and pats his shoulder. "I'm sure it will, father, I'm sure it will. I will help you all I can. Now, what shall we do about the Parish Council meeting, cancel it or could Major Post deputise for you, perhaps like he does sometimes?"

The Revd Horace Carr's face lightens somewhat. "Yes, he could, couldn't he? I hadn't thought of that. He's such a splendid reliable fellow, the Major. So good in a crisis."

Lottie nods, relieved to see her father calming down at last. "Would you like me to go over to the Manor House and ask the Major, Father? I could go on my bicycle now, it's no trouble."

The Rector's face creases into an angelic smile. "Could you, Lottie dear? That would be splendid. You are a good girl. That would be a real weight off my mind."

"And would you prefer the meeting to be held at The Manor House perhaps instead of here? Would it be better, do you think? Keep it out of the way of the Bishop, perhaps?"

The Rector nods. "Good idea." He reaches across and gives Lottie a kiss on the cheek. "My dear girl, you're learning fast, I do believe, learning fast."

Lottie grins as she goes into the hall. "Why, thank you father!" A rare compliment indeed, whatever next?! And she hurries to the kitchen to give poor harassed Mrs May her much-needed silver polish. Then, it's off to the shed to find her trusty steed.

Chapter 3

JUNE

THE RECTORY
2nd June 1914

Dearest Bella,

Thanks so much for the special picture post-card from Yorkshire. I shall put it in my album, it is so pretty with its padded satin flowers and embroidery. I've got quite a collection now. What lovely countryside it looks there in the Dales and your weekend house party sounded great fun in that big mansion. You are obviously having the time of your life with Rupert and his set of friends. Nice to have some time off from the office.

Hope you're not forgetting your local friends, though, as I saw Ronnie Post the other day. He is such a lovely fellow. He dropped his mother off here in his new Morris Oxford. Very smart motor car. He looked so dashing in his blazer, with his fair hair flopping over his forehead. He still holds a candle for you, Bella! He has now graduated from Cambridge (Law Degree with 1st Cl.Honours) and has just started working for a firm of solicitors in Dunster. He kept asking when you were coming home and I said maybe the Fete weekend in July and also for my birthday in early August. Do hope you will be there, as WE NEED YOU to help out at the Fete. You are such a born organiser, Bella.

Well, now for my news about the Empire Day Dance! I had the most lovely time possible! In the end I wore my pink frilly blouse and that skirt of yours (so thanks for the loan), the dark blue cotton with a little flared pleating at the front. And I wore a matching pink ribbon in my hair. Amy did my hair for me quite nicely up on top and she let me have a dab of her 'Californian Poppy' scent behind my ears, which was quite over-powering! I put it on once we had left the house, as

I didn't think father or the Bishop (more later) would approve!

Tom was very attentive and we danced a little, though in truth he's actually a bit flat-footed and not much of a dancer. We got on well together as a foursome with Amy and Bertie, even though the two men are both very taciturn. But Amy and I chattered enough for all of us! Tom's brother, Luke had said he was going to attend, but he didn't turn up. Apparently Tom said it was his birthday that day and he'd gone into Dunster drinking with his pals. He also said: "That's typical of Luke, he's very unreliable," which seemed a bit of a grumpy and disloyal thing to say about your own brother to me.

But it was such a festive atmosphere there with all the red, white and blue bunting across the Hall, the Union Jack displayed proudly on the wall next to the pictures of the King and Queen and the lively country music from the village band. I really enjoyed it, watching the dancing and listening to the music. I particularly loved the fiddle music.

Father put in an appearance mainly to say the Blessing before the food, but he didn't stay long, as we had the Bishop of Bath and Wells (no less!) staying overnight. Apparently father knew him at Oxford. The Bishop seemed a very pleasant man, if a trifle pompous, but he seemed very interested in my sketches (can't think why) which happened to be out in the hall awaiting collection by the framer.

After the dance I went back with Tom to see his mother's tapestries which were wonderfully worked. Their lovely stone Georgian farmhouse 'Three Chimneys' is at the top of Turners Hill and would afford a wonderful view of the surrounding countryside in daylight, I should think, but it was beginning to get dark when we got back.

Tom has invited me to lunch for a date next month and also Father has asked to meet Tom, so I shall have to arrange a little tea party perhaps. They have a cook/housekeeper who comes in daily to look after them, but the place did seem a bit shabby and seems to lack a woman's touch.

I think I have exhausted all the news now. I am gradually getting a few things organised for the Fete. Lady Pemberton has agreed to open it for us as usual, which is good. Ronnie has said he will dress up as a clown to amuse the children and will look after the skittles game, so that's a start.

I think I can persuade Grandma to knit a couple of matinee jackets. I'll have to remind her how to cast on (remember?) The Misses Tiptree have very kindly offered to make some of their weird soft toys. And lots of ladies are making cakes, of course. Promise me you will be here for it, Bella. I shall be MOST DISAPPOINTED if you don't come. And father will be VERY CROSS! By the way I have got father's diary more organised for him now – I stick a big notice on the wall above his desk "WEDDING TODAY 3 p.m." or "FUNERAL TODAY 11.30 a.m.", so he can't miss it! He quite likes it! I did feel it was necessary as he is getting so forgetful.

Will close now. Please write a proper letter SOON!

Best love,

Lottie

SECRET DIARY

of Charlotte Mary Carr

4th June 1914

Have been day-dreaming about the Dance for over a week now, in between my daily tasks, savouring every moment. It was so lovely, I did enjoy it, but couldn't quite understand why it was I enjoyed it so much more this time than other years when I've been with Bella. But when I analyse it, it must be because I had Tom beside me and I therefore felt more confident.

Other years I've always been a bit shy and self-conscious and also (have to admit it) in Bella's shadow rather. Bella is always so flirtatious and self-confident and (let's be frank) a bit of a Bossy Boots! I know she means well, but she always tries to organise everyone all the time. So I'm actually finding it quite liberating to be able to organise myself for once!! Or at least, I am trying! Tom has a very steadying and calming presence, even though he is very quiet. I feel safe with him and am becoming quite fond of him. He didn't give me many compliments at the dance. I don't think he's one for fancy speeches. He just gazed at me and said: "Very fine and dandy." That is his favourite phrase! Very fine and dandy. (Fortunately my scratches and bruises had healed up nicely). And he just gave me a kiss on the cheek at the end of the evening and squeezed my hand. He really respects a girl. I don't think I'm quite ready for proper kisses yet. I think perhaps I was a trifle disappointed that Luke didn't come to the dance. He did say he would. But I'm still a bit dubious about him, especially after the embarrassing incident in the village two weeks ago. He's rather brash and arrogant, everyone says so, and also it now seems he can be rather unreliable at times, so perhaps all in all we were better off without his company.

Anyway, I was pleased with my outfit in the end and Amy did my hair nicely. I was quite daring and put on a little lip colour.

Amy is a true friend – we both had such fun together, giggling away over nothing at all, just like we did at school and secretarial college. She has just secured herself an excellent post as companion to an elderly lady over at Porlock and will have to live-in, so I shan't see much of her which is a shame. She was my only local friend from school, as most of the other girls are from Taunton way.

I really must try and find myself a paid position soon, but seem so involved with father and the parish that it doesn't seem feasible at the moment.

15th June 1914

Saw Luke T. to-day when shopping in village. He raised a hand to me and called: "Good morning", then climbed on his horse and galloped away up Turners Hill! Rather rude behaviour, I thought. But perhaps he was embarrassed about not coming to the Dance. He has a terrible flirtatious reputation locally, goes out with lots of different girls, I'm told. Of course, Bella went out with him a few times the year after mother had died. When I'd asked her about him she'd just said: "Oh, Luke – yes, he's quite good company, he's improved a bit," that's all.

She confided to me with a giggle that once he'd been an usher at a friend's wedding and for a prank he and another chum had written 'HE-LP' on the soles of the bridegroom's shoes! So when he knelt at the altar some in the congregation started tittering (although most people were shocked), much to the bewilderment of the vicar (not father) conducting the service (and the bridegroom). Hilariously funny yes, but rather immature behaviour, I would say. The marriage ceremony is a very serious occasion. I couldn't see Tom doing that. Dear Tom, I'm becoming quite attached to him. He's quiet, yes, but has a solid sort of dependable presence which is rather comforting I find. It's nice having someone to look after me now when we go out. And he's certainly a regular church-goer, much more so than Luke.

I do miss Bella so! It will be so good to see her when she comes for the Fete. We can have a long chat like we used to do when she was at home... She can tell me about all her beaux in London and her job. She is leading such a busy life up there, but knowing her I'm sure she loves it.

I do hope she doesn't drop dear Ronnie Post in favour of some smart-set Londoner. I love dear Ronnie, he is such fun and yet so nice. He and Bella have been good friends for years now, since grammar school days and then of course he went off to Cambridge and Bella went first to Taunton and then to London, so who knows who will eventually be my brother-in-law?! The big mystery! And, more important, who will be my love, my special love? I often wonder when I see the silvery moon shining down, if under that same moon is living and breathing a man who I will eventually fall in love with and marry. Where is he?! Who will it be?!! Will it be TOM?!!

19th June

Found something today which made me realise father does still have loving feelings for mother. He had asked me to bring down his Bible Study notes from his bedside drawer and while searching through the drawer I happened to see a Christmas card and gift tag there in mother's hand-writing 'To dear Horace with love from Marie, Christmas 1911' – the last present she probably gave him before she died... Dear father, it touched me that he had kept it all these years. He was very supportive to her during their marriage. Her foot disability meant she had to wear a surgical boot, but she was so brave about it. She always made light of any problems, particularly bearing in mind she was in the public eye so much, being a rector's wife.

30th June 1914

I don't often read the newspaper, but have done so today, as father seemed very vexed by something which has happened in Europe recently. I had seen him talking very gravely to Revd Sims, our curate, earlier in the day. When I asked him what it was about, he said that someone called Archduke Franz Ferdinand has apparently just been assassinated at a place called Sarajevo (wherever that is) and everyone seems to think it's going to cause trouble in Europe – it might even cause a war.

Can't imagine our little quiet Somerset backwater here could be affected by something that has happened so far away, but father has said we must all pray for peace. He is going to mention it in his prayers in church on Sunday.

* * *

"I don't want to alarm our parishioners," Lottie's father's earnest voice drones on, "but I do want them to realise there is a problem in Europe which could be serious. Some of them don't even read a newspaper, you know. In fact," he blinks hard, "some of them can't even read!"

"Of course," Lottie murmurs as she sits poised at the typewriter in the study the following Saturday, "I do understand." It's a warm, oppressive afternoon. The study reeks of tobacco fumes as the vicar has been in there smoking his pipe for some time. Lottie pushes up the window further to get more fresh air. A blow fly is buzzing against the window pane. She gazes longingly out of the window to the sunlit garden. Lottie would love to be out getting some exercise riding Bessie or visiting Amy, but realises that father comes first and she has to do her duty.

In the light of the sudden turn of events in Europe, the vicar is writing some special prayers for the Sunday service. She looks at her father with deep affection as he pores studiously over the Bible and also selects hymns which have a particular significance for the occasion. Dear father, she thinks, he is so dutiful and conscientious when it comes to looking after his flock. Lottie sometimes wonders whether the congregation realise the trouble he goes to every week when writing sermons or special prayers. She hopes they appreciate his diligence and wisdom, as he searches for the perfect phrase or quotation from the Bible. The vicar's eyes light up and he jabs the prayer book excitedly. "Yes, here we are, Lottie, we'll start off: 'Give peace in our time, O Lord, because there is none other that…'"

There is a brisk knock on the door and Mrs May enters with a tray of tea-things. She beams at Lottie and her father as she sets them down on a side table. "Beg pardon, sir, sorry to interrupt, but Mrs Carr Senior has arrived unexpected like. I've put her in the front parlour. She's asking for you, sir."

"Oh dear!" Horace Carr immediately looks flustered and worried behind his horn-rimmed spectacles. He hates being interrupted when writing his sermon.

Lottie rises from the desk and pats her father's shoulder. "I'll go to her, Father, don't worry – you carry on with your writing…"

Horace Carr gives a relieved smile. "Oh, thank you, Lottie, could you? Mother is a dear soul, but she does tend to ramble on at times. I wonder what she wants? She doesn't usually come at this time, does she?"

Lottie goes into the parlour to see the small figure of Grandmother Carr bending over by the fireplace, tipping the contents of a capacious carpet bag out onto a low table. "Hallo, Grandma, this is a nice surprise! What have you got there?"

"What's that? Speak up!" She holds up her ear trumpet. "Oh, hallo, young Lottie." She gives her a wet kiss. "Look, I've brought you some baby things for the Fete. Haven't I done well?"

She smiles through ill-fitting dentures and holds up a little matinee jacket for Lottie to see. It is striped in different coloured wool and very bright to say the least. As Lottie takes it from her she can already spot a few dropped stitches and decidedly uneven tension, but she has to smile. "Why, it's – um – it's lovely, Grandma, very colourful!" Lottie tries to hide her giggles. She can't imagine who would buy it at the Fete, apart from a few Romanies. "That's very kind of you, grandma. Oh, and another one, well, I never!" Grandma produces yet another little jacket, this time knitted in brown and navy-blue stripes. "Well, I found all this spare wool, you see in my knitting bag and I thought I might as well use it."

"Very good idea, Grandma. Very thrifty! Now you sit down here and I'll fetch you a cup of tea."

"And I've made some bibs, as well, from old towelling, look!" Grandma proudly holds up a clutch of several little baby bibs, somewhat basically cobbled together with blanket stitch and some ribbon. "My stars, you have been busy. Thank you very much my love."

Lottie leaves the room to fetch a cup of tea for the old lady. She has done so well to produce all these things, she is over 80 now, she thinks. As she hurries back to the front parlour with the tea, to her surprise she almost bumps into Mrs. May showing Grandmother Carr out through the hall!

"Can't stay for tea after all, Lottie, sorry dear. I've got my friend Lucy waiting in her trap out here for me, forgot to mention. Love to Horace.' And she hurries out down the steps, clutching her bag over one arm, still chatting away.

Lottie starts, a little confused, then kisses and thanks her again, waving goodbye as the old lady is helped into the trap by Potter who was digging nearby.

She shakes her head, laughing to herself. 'My dear grandma! She's getting a bit forgetful now!' And as she gathers all the baby-things together from the table, Lottie looks hard at the tiny garments. Oh no, grandma has sewn on buttons but there are no button-holes! She clutches her head in mock despair. 'Now I'll have to sew on some ribbons or press-studs or something!

Heigh-ho! These things are sent to try us!' And Lottie returns to the study to continue typing for father.

Chapter 4

JULY

SECRET DIARY

4th July 1914

Went back to lunch with Tom at Three Chimneys after church today. It really is a topping spot up there, with a panoramic view all the way round from Porlock to Dunster and Dunkery Beacon in the distance on Exmoor, the Bristol Channel glinting far away on the horizon. Had a very enjoyable lunch, gammon and fresh vegetables cooked by Mrs Bryant their housekeeper, followed by apple pie and fresh cream from their dairy.

I had been secretly hoping that Luke would not be at home, as he still makes me rather uneasy. But he was. He was very late arriving and Tom became quite annoyed with him. As brothers they don't seem very compatible. Their black Labrador, Benny, came in with him and sat at Luke's feet by the table, until Tom ordered him out quite roughly. "No dogs in here, you know that!"

Luke seemed different this time, not quite so charming somehow. He kept teasing me and interrupting when Tom and I were speaking. I think he'd been in 'The Bull'. I felt distinctly embarrassed at times. Particularly as yesterday I had accidentally overheard Emily gossiping to Mrs May. She said that some of the easy village girls go up to the farm to visit some of the local young men after dark, just wearing their long dresses with nothing on underneath! And Luke's name was mentioned! I was so shocked! I blushed to my very roots and ran into the garden to recover my composure. I have tried to put it from my mind, but every time he looks at me now, I find myself thinking about it. Wicked impure thoughts!! Good job father isn't a mind reader!!

Then as Tom was pouring the coffee, Luke challenged me – asked me if I felt that people who didn't go to church could be just as good and virtuous as regular church-goers. It was an old argument between him and Tom, apparently and they wanted me, as the daughter of the Vicar, to settle it for them. I mumbled words to the effect that there are probably good and bad amongst them both. Of course Luke was triumphant and felt he had scored a point over Tom. There seems to be a bitter rivalry between them which I found difficult to deal with. But perhaps this is how it is with brothers. It certainly isn't like that with Bella and I and never was, even when we were growing up. Our parents insisted on good manners and a calm environment at the table to aid digestion and any differences had to be settled in private.

THE RECTORY
9th July 1914

Dearest Bella,

Thanks for your note about the stuffed toys. Quite understand you haven't got time to make any yourself. Grandma has already delivered some things she has made, a few matinee jackets and other baby things which is kind of her, even if they are a bit weird!

The schoolchildren have made lots of colourful posters advertising the Fete and Sale of Work. They are posted all over the village and Dudley Sims is organising bunting around the Rectory gates, very gay. Potter is working all hours doing the garden and is up a ladder trimming the big hedge as I write. His son, Sam has come to give him a hand once or twice. The flowers I planted have bloomed (much to my amazement) and the garden is now looking quite colourful. The roses are in their full glory under the terrace – they are beautiful this year. Potter has done a wonderful job.

Won't stop for more now. See you on the 14th hopefully. I've forgotten what you look like! We shall never stop talking!!

In haste, much love from Lottie

P.S. Very kind of A. Hilda to send a jar of sweets as a prize. Please thank her from us all here. So sorry she can't come down.

SECRET DIARY

12th July 1914

Tom came to tea to-day and met father formally for the first time. I could tell he was very nervous when he walked in the front parlour holding his cap and began to sit down on the tea-trolley! Fortunately it was empty at the time! When Mrs May did bring the tea-things in, we had some of her lovely shortbread, also dainty little fairy cakes and a big caraway seed cake, as well as cucumber and cress sandwiches, so she did us proud.

I'm afraid father is not very skilled at putting people at their ease – that was mother's forte. He mumbles away and fidgets with his spectacles and his cuffs. So it was left to me to lead the conversation and try to steer everyone in the right direction.

Tom recovered his composure after a cup of tea and told father all about the workings of his dairy farm. In fact once he got started it was hard to stop him! He was very respectful to father and called him 'sir' all the time.

They discovered a mutual love of cricket and began to discuss in tones of awe the batting skills of Jack Hobbs and the bowling expertise of Colin Blythe, both England Test players.

But then the conversation turned inevitably to the Fete which is this coming Saturday 15th July. Tom at once offered to donate some apples for the Apple Bobbing Contest which pleased father enormously. And between them they negotiated a fair price for the strawberries Tom is bringing for the strawberry teas, also fresh cream from his dairy. He also said he would bring a pony and give pony rides for the children, great idea. Some of Tom's farm labourers are coming on Friday to bring the metal chairs and trestle tables up from the Village Hall for the Tea Tent, so that's a big help, also help erect the big marquee. So the little tea party ended quite amicably, with father as usual having to dash off to some meeting at The Manor House.

Tom looked quite relieved once father had gone and gave me a spontaneous hug as he said goodbye. Father said later at dinner that he thought Tom was a very pleasant young man and seems very capable, which I suppose is high praise from father. It also pleases him that Tom is a regular worshipper and of sober disposition, from a well-respected local family, who were also regular church-goers. He seemed impressed by the fact that both Luke and Tom had attended the Taunton Academy for their education, the best school in the area. So, I think that means he approves of him – thank goodness for that! At least they've now met.

17th July 1914

Phew! Have been so busily occupied lately, I'm exhausted! The Fete went well, I thought – we were lucky with the weather. Bella was an absolute brick as usual and her help was indispensable. The summer house looked so pretty, where the strawberry teas were dispensed – the Misses Tiptree had decorated it with masses of roses from their garden. Took a photograph of it with my box Brownie. It was such a sweet moment when the lamb went to sleep in its little pen, before anyone could guess its weight. Nobody liked to disturb it, until dear Tom stepped in and blithely picked it up, muttering "silly women!" Grandma's knitted baby jackets were (amazingly) sold, but we had priced them very low. Such a pity Lady P. was indisposed and so couldn't declare the Fete open. But Major Post gamely did the honours – only trouble was he was then presented with the bouquet of flowers meant for Lady P., when father had already suggested they should be sent to her at The Grange with good wishes for a speedy recovery.

Hence we had to get some more flowers – luckily Mrs Witherspoon gave us some from her rose-garden. She is so willing. Potter wasn't too happy with the state of the lawn after the Fete, but although he keeps grumbling, I'm sure it will eventually recover.

THE RECTORY
18th July 1914

Dearest Bella,

Just a few lines to say a big Thank You for all your help at the Fete.

It went very well I thought and all the folk seemed to enjoy themselves. This has been such a marvellous summer. The strawberry teas were very popular. You were a real brick to take over the tea tent at such short notice when Mrs. Pike went into a swoon because of the heat. Good job someone had some smelling salts handy!

I thought Ronnie was so good as the clown, doing cartwheels all over the lawn and chasing the children with his big flapping feet! And he ran the Skittles game so well. He's a real card and yet so amiable too, isn't he? The cake stall scored a hit and the Apple-Bobbing went well too. How children love getting wet! Two of the gypsy children were caught stealing rock cakes and had to be spoken to severely by Old Duffer. But he was in genial mood and didn't report them to Constable Perkins, who was patrolling the lane outside, keeping an eye out for any Romanies and vagabonds lurking about. And Tom's pony rides were very popular, too. The infamous Tiptree soft toys sold quite well, despite being a bit 'floppy'.

Father reckons we've raised over £100 for the church tower Restoration Fund, that's not the final figure, it may be more. And most of my little pictures were sold – there's hope for me yet as an artist! In fact, curiously, I've since received a letter from the R.S.P.C.A. enquiring whether I would consider doing some sketches of animals, to be made into post-cards to promote their work. Don't quite know how the gentleman got my name, but I am thinking about it, sounds quite promising.

Bella, my pet – it was so lovely to have you back again and have a real heart-to-heart with you. I do like the sound of Rupert E. but must admit I am biased in favour of Ronnie P. as I know him and his family. I will bear in mind what you say about Tom, but I am very fond of him and he makes me feel secure, so am happy with the friendship at the moment. Let's hope the rumours of a war in Europe don't materialise. It's a frightening thought. I am praying every night for peace.

Seeing you again has made me realise how much I miss you. Mrs May said how nice it was to hear you playing your Chopin waltzes once more! I'm afraid I don't play the piano much these days.

I loved your hair in that chignon – very swish! It must be such jolly fun to work in London, but father seems to need me here at the moment. I do like to give him some support. Am glad to hear you are scaling down your interest in the Suffragettes, after Aunt Hilda's warning. Do hope you will keep it that way, as it would break dear father's heart if you got yourself in any kind of trouble. I hear the police treat them very roughly when they arrest them, so do be careful. I believe Mrs Pankhurst was arrested this week outside Buckingham Palace, trying to present a petition to the King. Let that be a warning to you, Bella dearest!

Glad to hear you are now doing some voluntary work for the poor and crippled children with Aunt Hilda. The Sunshine Club sounds a wonderful idea. I will ask around locally to see if there is a suitable house available for rent here for them. Father wants me to help raise funds for the Christian Mission in Bechuanaland in Southern Africa, to support the Missionary Society. He knows the Chairman, apparently. I said I would think about it, but frankly I would rather support local causes – what do you think?

Re. the Trevithick family and Luke – when you went out with him must have been one of your mad moments after mother died, as I thought you said he was your sworn enemy, after what happened at the party. He has got a bit of a reputation as a philanderer now locally, I'm afraid. All the village girls ogle him with their bold eyes. Have heard shocking gossip about him, but can't put in a letter. Will tell you sometime.

Mind you, he is handsome. I saw him the other day with a girl from school who can only be described as 'fast' and you know I'm not usually nasty about people. She looked a real minx, wearing thick make-up, etc. They were coming out of

'The Bull' together and she was laughing in a very raucous way. I'm afraid I looked the other way so that I didn't have to acknowledge Luke. Perhaps it's just a wild phase he's going through. I remember you said to me once that most men have to sow a few wild oats before they marry. Maybe that's what he's doing. He was very kind to me when I had my little accident I think I told you. He's also v. good with disabled children. I have seen another more compassionate side to him – will tell you some day.

Well, I must be toddling, sister dearest, and will look forward to seeing you in a few weeks' time for my birthday. Come down for the weekend to make it a longer time.

With best love and kisses, your affectionate sister,

Lottie

P.S. To my surprise I have been asked by the Girls Friendly Society to be their local patron – am frightfully flattered! Don't think the duties are too onerous!

SECRET DIARY

20th July 1914

Tom has proposed to me! I am so happy! It was very romantic. We were walking home yesterday evening at twilight under the overhanging plane trees along Church Lane, when he suddenly asked that Very Important Question out of the blue. I was just pointing out an owl in a tree, when he stopped in the lane and clutched at my hand. Then he said, quite abruptly: "Would you do me the honour of becoming my wife, Lottie?"

I was so shocked that I said "Yes" immediately, then thought afterwards I should have said I'd think it over. My mind seemed to go into a spin. Once I was in bed I became quite nervous. What had I done? I had accepted the first man who came along! But I am convinced he is the right one for me and I'm sure mother would have liked him. That is my yardstick. Father seems to approve of him, too.

But I don't know what Bella's reaction will be. She said such a funny thing when she was here for the Fete after she'd met Tom. I said to her I liked Tom very much and she said: "Yes, Lottie, I can see you like him, but do you love him? Does your heart flutter and your knees go weak when you see him?' I just stared at her, thinking she was being fanciful and worldly-wise..."

Then she said quite seriously: "When you meet a man you can love and respect who also excites you and makes your heart flutter, then that's the one you should marry."

That's nonsense, I thought. I don't give a jot what Bella thinks. Tom makes me feel happy and secure and I'm very fond of him. What more can a girl ask? Bella's new London friends are putting strange ideas in her head, if you ask me.

Anyway, Tom has suggested that we have an engagement period of two years as I am only young, so that we are sure of our feelings. He is going to ask father for my hand in marriage this weekend. Can't believe I'm engaged!

* * *

"I have to go into Taunton on Friday to see the dentist," Tom announces a week later, "so perhaps we could choose the ring, Lottie, while we're there. What do you think?"

Lottie is somewhat bemused. He could have put it a little more romantically, she thinks indignantly as she steps down from the trap, after an afternoon cup of tea at Three Chimneys. Am I going to be fitted in between fillings, she wonders?!

Lottie is in a daze after becoming engaged, her mind a whirl of conflicting emotions. The security of loving and being loved by someone as kind and trustworthy as Tom is marred by slightly guilty feelings about her duty to father once she is married.

But now her spirits suddenly lift when she remembers father has said she can have a new dress for the engagement party. So it begins to enter Lottie's young head that maybe while Tom is at the dentist, she could be looking at dress-shops. Poor Lottie is so starved of new clothes that it is an absolute treat for her to be able to buy a new dress. Not to mention choosing her engagement ring with dear Tom.

"Very well, that's fine," she answers, "providing father doesn't need me on Friday. What time is your appointment?"

"11.30, so I'll pick you up at about 10.00 if that's all right with you, and then we can have a cup of tea perhaps once we get to Taunton..."

"...and I can look for a dress while you're in the dentist," Lottie smiles. What a pity Bella isn't here, she thinks, her mind buzzing. We could have such a good day together choosing a dress and looking round the shops. Going shopping on your own isn't much fun at all.

"Oh, you're buying a new dress?" Tom seems surprised.

"Why yes, for the party! Father said I can choose one. He's very kind. It's not every day a girl gets engaged, you know!" Lottie smiles. Tom is a funny fellow, she thinks. I suppose he's not used to women. He doesn't understand they like to have new clothes now and again.

Lottie leans across and gives Tom a hug. "You're a funny one, Tom! You do amuse me! See you on Friday! Bye!" And she runs off up the Rectory drive-way laughing merrily.

Tom gives an uncertain laugh and a wave of his hand and climbs back into the trap, a puzzled look on his face.

* * *

Lottie is having a lovely, self-indulgent time in Taunton, a real treat for her. She is inspecting all the dress-shops and has tried on five or more dresses already. Then out of the blue in one of the shops she hears her name called and there is her friend, Amy, standing before her, smiling and clutching several bags. She has a rare day off from her job and, although she can only spare half an hour before she meets her mother for lunch, the two girls soon discover Miss David's, an exclusive new boutique just off the High Street. Within minutes they have picked out the most divine pale blue muslin dress just arrived from Paris. It is fashionably flared, with a lacy over-skirt.

'It's an absolute dream!' cries Lottie as she pirouettes in the cubicle, looking at herself from every angle in the mirrors. 'I love it!' She looks at the price ticket and gasps. 'Oh dear, I hope father won't jib at that amount…'

She feels guilty when she thinks of her impoverished father on his small stipend. But then remembers that mother had left some money to be spent on her daughters.

"It *is* your engagement party," Amy reminds her, "you've *got* to have it. The colour suits you so well."

Lottie hesitates, then nods. "I agree." She takes it reverently to the shop assistant, hovering nearby. "I'll take this dress, please."

"Thank you for your custom, madam. It fits madam perfectly, but if madam requires any alterations, we have our seamstress here who can do the job."

Amy looks at her fob watch. "Help, after one, I must go, please excuse me deserting you, Lottie, but I have to meet my mother…"

"Oh no!" cries Lottie, "I didn't realise it's after one o'clock. I was supposed to be meeting Tom at 12.30." The two girls giggle.

"Will he be very cross, do you think?" asks Amy, a twinkle in her eye.

"Oh no," Lottie replies, "he's very placid. I've never seen him lose his temper."

Amy gives Lottie a kiss on the cheek. "Must go. See you soon. Bye, Lottie."

"Bye, Amy, thanks for helping me choose – what luck we met up! Hope to see you at the party. Bye!"

Clutching her exclusive dress bag containing her precious purchase encased in pink tissue paper, Lottie hurries along the sunlit street to the Little Gem Tea Rooms where she arranged to meet Tom.

She feels elated with her extravagant purchase and stimulated by Amy's company – and she's on her way to meet up with her brand-new fiancé! Lottie is blissfully happy!

As she waits at a street corner to let the busy horse-drawn and motorized traffic pass by, her eyes are drawn to a paper boy's poster as he shouts out the latest news.

'WAR RUMOURS GROW' it reads in big capitals and

Lottie's heart gives a disbelieving jolt. 'No,' she thinks, 'not now, I'm so happy, I've just got engaged, there can't be a war, surely not.'

Everyone passing by is stopping to buy a paper and standing reading the news with grave faces, some people are shaking their heads and talking solemnly to other passers-by.

Perhaps we won't be affected too much by it here, Lottie thinks as she turns into the little side street where the tea-room is. Glancing at her watch she sees it's twenty past one. She opens the door of the café and sees Tom sitting at a corner table. He doesn't look too happy. In fact, he's got a face resembling thunder-clouds and rises to his feet as soon as Lottie appears. Lottie can't help noticing he has been reading a newspaper with its grim headlines while waiting. He almost growls at her and taps his pocket watch.

"Where have you been? I've been worried about you. Look at the time, you're really late!"

Lottie continues to smile broadly and waves her dress shop bag. "I'm sorry I'm so late, Tom. I happened to meet Amy by chance and she helped me choose a dress – a lovely dress. You will like it, I know."

Tom seems to flinch as Lottie flings her arms around his neck and plants a kiss on his cheek. Then she sinks down at the table, tired by the morning's shopping. "I'm sorry to have kept you waiting, dearest," she says meekly.

Tom grunts ungraciously. "I expect you would like a drink or something?" he asks her tetchily, as the waitress approaches.

Lottie is rather taken aback. Placid Tom has been replaced by grumpy Tom. She is not used to being spoken to in this rather abrupt fashion, particularly in public.

"I'd like a sandwich and a cup of tea, please," she replies quietly, determined to maintain her dignity and keep the peace.

Tom isn't comfortable in the town, Lottie decides. She had realised this earlier when they had arrived in his new motor. The Model T-Ford did look magnificent, she had to say. It had just been cleaned by the stable-lads and the black bodywork was gleaming, the red leather upholstery shiny and polished and the brass lamps twinkling on the front. Tom had stopped outside the dentist, not realising he was blocking an alley-way. And when a delivery driver politely asked him to move away, Tom had been quite rude and curt, although he did eventually move the car. He had also shouted at two ragged boys who were admiring his car. I suppose he was nervous they would damage it when he left.

"A pot of tea and some cheese sandwiches for two," Tom snaps at the girl.

"And then afterwards perhaps we can begin to look for the ring," Lottie continues hopefully.

Tom shakes his head and takes out his pocket-watch. "We haven't got time now, Lottie, I'm sorry. I need to get back to the farm. And my tooth is bothering me rather…"

Lottie claps her hand to her mouth. "…oh, Tom, I quite forgot, do forgive me. How did you get on at the dentist? What did he do?"

"He's put a temporary filling in it – I have to come back for a proper filling next week. So it's still aching."

Lottie clasps Tom's hand. "I'm so sorry, Tom. We'll come back and choose the ring another time. I quite understand if you don't feel well. We'll go straight home when we've had something to eat."

As the waitress brings the refreshments Tom picks up the newspaper on the table and waves it at Lottie, his forehead wrinkled with concern. 'And this news doesn't help, either…"

Lottie nods sagely. In all the unaccustomed excitement of seeing Amy and buying her lovely dress she has completely lost her head. She feels instantly contrite. She can now appreciate how worried and strained Tom must feel with the threat of war looming. Pull yourself together, Lottie and be serious, she reprimands herself. Stop thinking of frivolous things like dresses.

She puts her hand over Tom's on the table and squeezes it. "Don't worry, dearest, it may not come to war. But we should all pray for peace, that's what Father always says, pray for peace. So let's do that right now…"

Chapter 5
August

THE RECTORY
5th August 1914

Dearest Bella,

Just a few lines in haste following the dreadful news. We had all heard the rumours, of course, but nobody thought it would actually happen, somehow.

One feels shielded in this quiet little village, although I am sure that it not the case in the capital. It must be truly upsetting to be in the thick of it, although knowing you I'm sure you find it exciting!

Here, as you can imagine, everyone is very shocked by the news. People are gathering together with grave faces by the village shop passing newspapers around. No-one knows quite what is going to happen. There is an atmosphere of shocked disbelief pervading.

When I heard about it yesterday from Dudley Sims (who had just travelled from London and heard it there) I rushed to tell father in his study. He was very concerned naturally and immediately said he would have to change his sermon.

I did say at first to father that I would willingly cancel the engagement party, but in view of the fact that the men will be going off to war within a week or two, father advised me to carry on with it. So, we have now brought it forward and it will be held this coming Saturday 9th August. So do hope you can still come and we will make it a combined engagement and birthday celebration, as my birthday is only the next week.

Sorry it's such short notice but do hope you can come down on Saturday morning and stay a couple of nights perhaps. In view of the circumstances we are not making it a big celebration. Just family and a few friends, perhaps 12 of us at the most. We have invited the Posts and the Witherspoons and Ronnie has said he will be there, even though he is I know champing at the bit to join his father's old regiment (the Royal Somerset Rifles, I believe). He is the eternal optimist – he will cheer everyone up!

Must fly now, as father is writing a special sermon.

With much love,

Your affectionate sister,

Lottie

P.S. Please may I borrow your silver evening sandals?

SECRET DIARY

5th August 1914

My heart stood still when I heard the terrible news about the outbreak of war! I am horrified at the idea but am trying to push it to the back of my mind. I cannot believe that dear Tom may be taken away from me! Am hoping fervently that by some miracle he will not have to go and slipped into church this morning to pray that God will grant my wishes. It seems so fateful to me that just when I have made such a momentous decision to get married, this beastly war should be declared! Fate is very cruel at times.

However, I am trying to be brave and am going ahead with the engagement party on Saturday, although it's so difficult to be happy and gay when there's such a mood of doom and gloom everywhere. All very unsettling.

Anyway, Mrs Post is very stoical and kind and has said her cook will make a special cake and ice it, and the Witherspoons have said they will provide the champagne which is v. good of them. (Also very tactful, as I doubt father would have bought any, as he disapproves of intoxicating liquor in the house, apart from sherry at Christmas time). I have spoken to Mrs May about the supper arrangements, so one has to try and carry on as normal.

Fortunately Tom and I have already chosen the ring last week in Taunton. It is a lovely ruby and diamond cluster on a heavy gold band. And father very kindly said I could have a new dress for the occasion! So (with Amy's help) I chose the most divine dress from a smart dress shop in Taunton and now have that in readiness hanging in my wardrobe. It is so pretty! Can't wait to wear it! Pale blue muslin with a ruched bodice (which hides my bust quite well) and is flared with a delicate lacy over-skirt. Très élégante! Made in Paris and frightfully expensive, but father was very good about it. And I am hoping that Bella will style my hair for me, if she can catch the early morning train from London.

But this news of the war has cast a cloud over my happiness and I can't work up too much enthusiasm for anything. Tom seems very edgy and tetchy about it all. Obviously I think he is already worrying who will look after the farm if he and Luke have to go to war.

To cheer myself up have treated myself to a pair of silk stockings, cobweb sheer, to wear at the party. (Bit of a change from the thick darned lisle ones I used to wear to school!) Please forgive me, dear Lord, for this self-indulgence, I prayed as I went on the bus to Dunster. I had spotted an exclusive little shop there selling handbags and gloves, etc. An expensive treat from my dwindling allowance, but no doubt the last I will have, now war is with us.

Am also hoping to borrow Bella's silver evening sandals too, as luckily we are the same size.

THE RECTORY
12th August 1914

Dear Amy,

I must thank you so much for your letter and the birthday gift and pretty card. It was very sweet of you to remember me. The 'Soir de Paris' is just divine – a beautiful scent and in a very elegant dark blue glass bottle which looks very fetching on my dressing table.

    I was so sorry you and Bertie were not able to come to my engagement party, but I quite understand your brother's 21st party had to take precedence, being brought forward by the war.

It went very well, just a small gathering of friends and family. No-one feels much like celebrating at the moment, do they, in the light of current events. But we felt we should go ahead with it, as all the men may be off to war soon. It seems hard to believe. We have had a spate of hastily arranged weddings here in the village in the last few days, so father is being kept busy. The bells have never stopped ringing! You must feel the same as I do, you can't bear the thought of your dear Bertie going to fight in France. Has he enlisted yet? And your brother, too? There is a patriotic fervour sweeping the country, isn't there, and all the men seem to be caught up in it. The recruitment posters are proving very effective.

But anyway, Bella was able to come down from London, thank goodness, and she did my hair beautifully, back off my face a little and tied at the back with a blue ribbon which matched my divine new dress. Thank you for helping me to choose it. Everyone has admired it. My ring is lovely, a ruby and diamond cluster on a gold band. I shall have to show it to you when next we meet. Major and Mrs Post came along and Dr and Mrs Witherspoon too – they are all old friends of father and I have known them all my life. And my dear Grandma was there. She is very deaf now but I think she still enjoys these occasions.

Ronnie Post brought his new Amberola phonograph along which was fun. We were able to play some lovely tunes, all the current favourites on the cylinders, "Drink to Me Only", "It's a Long, long Trail Awinding", etc. so that was a pleasant diversion. Ronnie is a real card, you must meet him! Bella also played the piano and Doris Post sang "Ah, Sweet Mystery of Life!" She has a fine contralto voice and sings in the choir.

We even had a little dancing and some champagne – made me a tiny bit tiddly, but it was lovely to dance with my dear fiancé. Bella and Ronnie danced the tango very stylishly, which was fun to watch. They made a handsome couple, Bella with her titian hair and Ronnie with his shock of blonde hair. We are going to a photographer's studio soon for him to take some formal photographs of Tom and I and the family, so I will show you them in due course. We did invite Luke, Tom's brother, but as usual he was late arriving. Luke has already enlisted and is off to join his regiment next week. Tom is worried about his farm, but he wants to serve his country and is going to the Recruiting Office very soon.

Well, I must close now and hope you are enjoying your new post with Mrs Ponsonby. She sounds a very important lady with all her committees. Glad to hear you have been made so welcome at the church there. I will write to you now and then if this is all right with your employer? It's such a shame we can't see each other so often now. Perhaps I can ride across the moors occasionally and see you on your day off.

Give my regards to Bertie and wish him well. As always my love to you,

Your friend,

Lottie

SECRET DIARY

14th August 1914

At last I can set down some private thoughts about my engagement party last Saturday. It went very well, although everyone seemed somewhat subdued when they first arrived, with the awful news of the war on their minds. Ronnie was a real brick as usual and cracked a few weak jokes to break the tension a little. Everyone gathered round and admired my beautiful ring, while they sipped sherry, although it was oppressively hot and I for one would have preferred iced water!

But I felt so happy to be engaged to dear Tom – he's a rock to me. And his gift of a fine pearl necklace was a complete surprise to me and looked perfect with my outfit. My new dress was exquisite – I felt quite glamorous in it! Bella did my hair so nicely too, that I felt quite confident and poised, for once in my life. Tom declared that I looked 'fine and dandy' – his favourite expression, and it was like hugging a big friendly bear when I danced with him, very solid and comforting. He is not very demonstrative when it comes to kissing and fancy words and never gives me flowers, but he does like hugging me! Luke was really late arriving and when he did he barged in through the French windows, which were open due to the heat.

Father looked quite shocked and bewildered, as he was just about to say Grace. Everyone was just raising their glasses for a toast to Tom and I, prior to cutting the cake. Bella came forward at once with a glass of champagne to make him welcome, but Tom's face spoke volumes!

I think Luke had been with his pals in Dunster drowning their sorrows (or was it celebrating, I don't know) as he had apparently just enlisted and is off to join his regiment next week as a commissioned officer, a Second Lieutenant. The events of the war have happened so quickly, my mind is in a whirl. It's hard to realise that all our menfolk will soon be taken away from us.

But I have to record a special moment. As I danced with Luke later in the evening a strange feeling went through me – I thought I was going to swoon. And Luke whispered in my ear, "Your dress matches your eyes, Lottie." It wasn't so much what he said, but the way he said it. Very low and intimate. I didn't know quite what to say. So I just stared at him, as he swept me forcefully round the room with his broad shoulders and muscular body. My heart started to race and I became quite breathless My thighs began to shake. I expect it was the unaccustomed champagne.

It was a very odd, overwhelming sensation I'd never felt before, as if I was irresistibly drawn to him by a magnet.

Anyway, Luke took me outside onto the terrace into the fresh air to recover, before anyone could make a fuss. It was lovely to feel the cool air on my flushed cheeks. Luke gave me a glass of water, then just sat there staring at me saying: "You have blossomed into a beautiful flower, Lottie," which made me blush even more. It was a warm, balmy night. I could smell the heady scent of the roses wafting up as we sat there. It all felt quite surreal…

THE RECTORY
18th August 1914

Dearest Bella,

Thought I must write a few lines and trust you had a good return journey last week. Sorry you had to rush away so soon after the party, but we quite understand how busy you are up in London, now you are a working girl!

So glad you could come down. Thanks so much for all your help, and for the loan of the sandals. And for the gift of stationery for my birthday! It is top quality vellum and I shall really enjoy writing letters on this.

Luke has now gone to join his regiment (The West Country Fusiliers). We had a farewell drink with him at Three Chimneys to wish him well on Saturday. A few of the farm labourers were also just about to go off as well, so hurrah to our brave boys! Amy's brother, Richard, is hoping to join the Royal Flying Corps as an air mechanic and he is going soon to start training in Wiltshire.

I went into Taunton yesterday with Dudley Sims the curate. He had heard there will be shortages of everything soon, so advised us to stock up on essential supplies, petrol, coal and coke, candles, oil, wicks, sugar, tea, bulk flour, etc. Once we eventually reached the shops we had to queue for everything, but obtained most things. We drove there in the pony and trap and as we reached Taunton we passed the railway station and there happened to be a troop train just about to leave.

Well, my word, what a crowd of people seeing them off! We had a job to get through. They were all waving flags, cheering a column of soldiers and singing 'Rule Britannia' and the National Anthem. There was a band playing there and I could even hear people in the crowd singing that Phyllis Dare song 'Oh, we don't want to lose you, but we think you ought to go'. Very moving. And relatives and friends were all hugging their loved ones, husbands, fathers, brothers and sons, crying and sobbing and waving flags. It was a very stirring sight.

A real sense of patriotism is sweeping Britain – I'm sure it's the same in London. There are wild rumours that the Germans have already invaded Scotland from Norway, but father says that is a false claim, so I hope he is right. It is a bit worrying.

Here boys as young as 15 or 16 are enlisting, having lied about their age. They all want to serve King and Country and put down the menace of the Hun. But it does seem very young to be a soldier, I feel.

The Posts told me to-day that Ronnie has now left to join his regiment at Taunton, so I imagine he will soon be on his way to France. God speed dear Ronnie!

You must be so worried, but he is a born soldier like his father and so anxious to be off. But take comfort, Bella. They say it will only last a few months. It should be all over by Christmas. Major Post said he's sure it will only be a short scrap, and being a military man he should know.

I will close now and hope you can pen a few lines when you get time. I know how busy you are.

With love from

Your affectionate sister,

Lottie

SECRET DIARY

22nd August 1914

Have had an unexpected letter from Aunt Hilda about Bella. I was surprised to receive the letter, but even more surprised by its contents. For Aunt Hilda has informed me confidentially that Bella has now left the Language School and been appointed by the War Office to do secret war work using her language skills. It is all very cloak-and-dagger and Bella cannot speak to anyone about it (although obviously she has confided in Aunt Hilda), as she has signed the Official Secrets Act!

Aunt Hilda didn't want father to know this news, as she felt he is a born worrier and would start to imagine Bella was now a spy or doing dangerous work or something. And this is not the case apparently (thank goodness).

She has warned me that Bella may use her Suffragette interests and also her charity work as a cover for when she has to work extra long hours for the War Office. I had heard that the Suffragette Movement is now scaling down its demands and demonstrations in the light of the war situation. Mrs Pankhurst has said that she will now work with the Government to ensure women are employed and treated fairly in occupations formerly held by men.

I have written back to her at once of course, thanking her for letting me know and saying that I will still continue to write to Bella c/o Auntie's Chelsea address, so that Bella does not 'smell a rat', as it were.

Aunt Hilda said she thought I was a sensible 'gal' and that she felt someone in the family needed to know where Bella was working. Auntie also gave me her private telephone number so that in case of emergency she could pass on a message to Bella.

I know father is intending to have the telephone connected at The Rectory soon and meanwhile we can always use the public telephone at the Post Office, or the Posts and Witherspoons have said we can use theirs.

I have extended an invitation to Aunt Hilda to come and stay with us here, if the situation in London becomes too fraught, but she is such an independent old stick I can't see her taking it up. I'm sure father won't mind my inviting his sister without his permission. He is very fond of her, even though they don't see too much of one another.

Well, my stars, what a surprise! Might have known Bella would be snapped up by the War Office, she is so bright. All those extra lessons with Madame Clemenceau have finally paid off! And this does explain why she hasn't written much lately and also why she left so hurriedly from the party. But I mustn't breathe a word to father, or he would be worried sick.

* * *

"Coo-ee, Lottie!" Lottie is in the garden tending the roses under the terrace when she has an unexpected visitor. The exceptionally warm dry spell of weather is continuing and Lottie is doing a spot of watering to help Potter. She looks up and to her surprise sees her college chum, Polly Tremayne, cycling through the Rectory gates and then call her name, as she pushes it up the steep driveway.

Lottie at once puts down her watering can and runs to greet her friend. It's ages since she has seen Polly and the two girls hug each other warmly. When they left the Taunton Ladies College last year they had all issued heartfelt intentions of keeping in touch, but since then the months have slipped away somehow without any contact.

"Polly! This is a lovely surprise! How are you?"

"I'm fine, Lottie, how about you? I hear you're engaged now – congratulations!"

Lottie's blue eyes sparkle. "Why, thank you, I'm well. Now, will you have a drink? Let me get you some lemonade. Sit down here under the arbour and I'll fetch some. We certainly need it to-day."

Lottie runs indoors and asks Mrs May to bring out a pitcher of cooling lemonade and a plate of biscuits, then she rejoins her friend.

Polly is sitting under the trellis of the rose arbour, surrounded by red, pink and yellow trailing roses. She's taken off her hat and is stretching her legs. She makes a lovely picture with her smiling demeanour in her light summer dress.

"Phew! It's so hot today."

But Lottie is curious. "So, how is it you're round this way?" She knows Polly lives near Taunton.

"I was visiting my aunt over at Dunster with my mother and when I realized how close I was to you I thought I would pop in to see you, so I borrowed my aunt's bicycle. I've got an idea for an outing – would you be game?"

Lottie nods. She would love an outing. People seem to think once you are engaged you are always with your fiancé, but Tom is busy working at the farm most of the time and so she doesn't see that much of him. Life can be pretty dull just doing a few parish duties for her father, particularly now Bella and her friend, Amy are no longer around.

"Polly, what's your plan, I'm all agog!" Lottie grins at her chum, noticing she is wearing her dark silky hair in a different style now, off her face, with an alice band.

"Well," Polly begins, "you remember Clara Pocock I'm sure." Lottie nods. "I happened to see her the other day in Taunton and you'll never guess, she is driving now!"

Lottie gasps. "Brave girl! I'm not game enough yet, are you?"

"No fear, but her brother taught her apparently and then of course he's gone off to war now – yes, awful, isn't it? – and he said that Clara can drive his car while he's away!"

"Oh, lucky girl! So, come on, is she taking us somewhere?" Lottie says somewhat impatiently.

Polly gives a tinkling laugh. "Hang on, old bean, let me tell you. Clara has got to deliver something to her uncle in Allacombe, apparently, near Minehead and then she thought why don't a few of us chums take a picnic and make a day of it – go to the beach at Minehead! Cheer ourselves up." She is suddenly serious for a moment. "The news of the war is so depressing for everyone, don't you think?"

Lottie clasps Polly's hand. "You're right, Polly. We all feel a bit low at the moment. We need to keep our spirits up. What a good idea. And when are you thinking of going?"

Polly shifts in her garden chair as Mrs May approaches with a tray of refreshments. 'It's rather short notice, but it's tomorrow – can you manage that?'

Lottie looks a bit doubtful. Tomorrow is Friday and she usually types father's sermon then. However, maybe she can persuade him she could do it just as well on Saturday instead. "I'll just go and ask father. Hope I can. Won't be a moment. Help yourself to a glass of lemonade. Thank you, Mrs May."

Lottie soon comes back with a smile on her face, hurrying across the lawn, her blonde hair bobbing as she moves. "Yes, that's fine, Polly. I'd love to come."

Polly hugs her friend. "Oh, I'm *so* glad. It will be fun, particularly if this fine weather keeps up. Oh, do let me see your ring and you must tell me all about your fiancé…"

* * *

It is a still, windless day on the beach. Every sound is carrying clearly in the warm air, children chattering as they make sandcastles, the sea-gulls crying as they swoop overhead.

The girls, Lottie, Polly, Clara and Victoria had stopped on the cliffs above Minehead, the sky a cloudless blue, the sea sparkling below them and Clara had duly delivered her parcel to her uncle in nearby Allacombe. Then feeling peckish they had opened up the picnic baskets and devoured the tasty titbits provided by their various house-keepers. Game pie, chicken sandwiches, hard-boiled eggs, crusty bread, all washed down with home-made lemonade in stone bottles wrapped in a blanket to keep cool, followed by fruit cake and some lovely fresh fruit, strawberries and cherries. What a feast!

Lottie is really enjoying the company of her friends. She'd forgotten how well they all get on together. They are swapping stories and news of other ex-pupils they all knew, having a giggle about the teachers, comparing notes about job prospects and of course talking non-stop about men, clothes and the war. Lottie is the only one amongst them to be engaged and they seem to be in awe of her, as if she had acquired a new status. They all admire her beautiful ring and she shows them a photo of Tom and herself wearing her new blue muslin dress from Paris at her engagement party. Lottie tells them about Bella's new position in London and also about Amy's post as a companion at Porlock, and Clara and Victoria tell their news of their office jobs, too, in Taunton.

Now, they have stowed the picnic baskets away in the car boot and are down on the beach, the wide sweep of the sandy bay stretching before them. The sea is flat and calm at low tide, little lapping waves breaking gently on the sand. Out to sea one or two small craft are reflected in the water. A few children are happily splashing in the sea, jumping over the little waves.

"Let's take our shoes off, girls!" cries Clara, laughing and with one accord they do so and walk along the wet sand, feeling the rippled ridges cool and firm beneath their bare feet. Clara is very daring, wearing trousers and smoking, but most of the other girls are in cotton skirts and short-sleeved blouses. Lottie is wearing a simple blue and white cotton dress with a dropped waistline and carrying her flat sandals.

"Anyone game to go bathing in the sea?" asks Victoria. But the girls all shake their heads. No-one wants to embark on the tricky procedure of donning a swimming costume in public, draping a towel over vital body parts and trying to emerge with dignity somehow still intact. It's a step too far!

Instead they potter about on the beach, exploring the rock pools, paddling, picking up sea-shells and gathering sea-weed. Suddenly Clara points up in the sky. "Hey, look girls! A plane!" They all crane their necks to see the small aircraft which is doing swoops over the beach and the sea, quite an unusual sight. It comes low enough for them to see the pilot wearing goggles and they all wave at him.

"Let's hope it's friendly!" Victoria says and they all soberly remember that across the English Channel in France and Belgium the planes are not so friendly.

After a while when the shadows begin to lengthen, the girls reluctantly decide they should return home and begin the long trek back along the sands and up the cliff path to the car.

Once home and as she stands waving goodbye to the girls, Lottie suddenly realises she feels stimulated and refreshed. She needed this day, this unexpected day to herself, to put things into perspective. It's great to know she has the support of her old friends. And now after this brief respite she feels happier and stronger to carry out her duties or whatever the weeks ahead will hold for her, now the country is at war.

Chapter 6
SEPTEMBER

3rd September 1914
SECRET DIARY

Bicycled round to see Tom to-day at Three Chimneys. He had said he was going to the Recruiting Office last week to enquire about enlisting, have the medical, etc. But I heard nothing from him and began to worry. And then I heard the Army had closed the Office temporarily now that the first wave of reservists had gone to France, but was re-opening this week. As I went through the village I couldn't help but notice the lack of young men. The butcher's son has gone, also the postman and the cobbler's son, Peter the blacksmith, all replaced by older men. The population has been reduced to women, children and old folk. It suddenly brought it home to me and sent a chill through my heart.

But it was hard to imagine Europe so troubled on a day like this. Beautiful autumn sunshine shone forth as I cycled over the old packhorse bridge by Turners Hill. Early blackberries are already appearing in the hedgerows, sky was cloudless, the birds were singing their little hearts out. As I passed the fields full of newly-reaped sheaves of corn, the scent of new-mown hay was in the air, there were notices of forthcoming Ploughing Matches posted on farm-gates. The annual cycle of the seasons was still making its presence felt, despite the war. Tom's lovely fat cows were contentedly munching their lush pasture in the meadow, as I approached the farm. Out of the blue I thought of Luke and wondered where he was. Pray to God he's faring well.

Once I arrived at Three Chimneys there was no sign of Tom in the yard, just milkmaids gossiping in the dairy as they churned the butter. I went into the farmhouse and found Mrs Bryant in the back kitchen busily engaged making crab apple jelly. When I enquired after Tom she nodded towards the next room and I found him in the armchair by the range. He was drinking a glass of whisky, Benny stretched out at his feet on the flagstone floor – this at 11.15 in the morning! I was really shocked. Shocked to see him sitting idle during the day, but also to see him drinking spirits at this time! He has never done this, to my knowledge.

He was just sitting there, listlessly flicking through the 'Dairyman's Journal' and didn't get up. I asked him what was wrong and he was quite testy with me. "Can't a man have a drink in his own home now, without an inquest?" he said. I was taken aback. He doesn't usually speak to me like that. I went over to him and put my hand on his shoulder.

"What's wrong, Tom?" I repeated and then as I said it, I knew it had to be what the Recruiting Office had said. "What happened at the Recruiting Office? Are you going to enlist?"

He just sat there, his shoulders slumped, and wouldn't meet my eyes. "Bit of a shock, Lottie. Can't go," he said and I could see the tears welling up.

"Can't go even if I wanted to – I had a medical and they say I've got a heart murmur, or some such, I'm unfit to serve my country!"

And then he banged his fist down on the armchair and started to weep. I put my arm round him and tried to comfort him. Benny even looked up at his master with his soulful dark eyes and put his paw on Tom's knee, sensing something was wrong. I was surprised at the news about his heart condition, as he always seems fairly fit and does a fair bit of manual work round the farm.

"I had rheumatic fever when I was a child," he said, "they say it was probably caused by that. Now they say I can't do no heavy lifting."

I tried to cheer him up and think positively. "It's probably for the best, Tom. You wouldn't want to leave the farm to someone else to run, would you? And the Government is encouraging farmers to support the home front, keep the farms going. It's for the best, you'll see. Now, let's have a nice cup of tea, shall we?"

I could see Mrs Bryant hovering anxiously in the background, but I waved her away and made the tea myself. I bustled about and found some cake in a tin to give him with the tea.

And then as I saw him sitting there in the armchair with his head bowed, I suddenly realised. God had answered my prayers. Tom wasn't going to war. But all at once I felt oddly flat – and wondered why.

4th September 1914

Am rather worried about Tom. He has become very quiet and withdrawn since his rejection by the Army Recruiting Office. I hadn't realised how much enlisting meant to him. He greets me when we meet, then sits quite silent and morose, only replying in a monosyllabic fashion when I speak to him. He has also become very lethargic around the farm, only doing strictly what is necessary. I feel desperately sorry for him, but it's beginning to make me feel depressed as well.

I suddenly realised to my surprise I am missing Luke – he might be a bit wild and flirtatious, but at least he's got an optimistic attitude towards life. I even miss his teasing – never thought I'd say that! I had spoken confidentially to Dr Witherspoon about Tom's condition and he said it sounded indicative of a serious depression. Tom had obviously been very distressed that he couldn't serve his country, particularly as Luke was out there doing just that. And I knew there was fierce rivalry between the two brothers.

Also I suddenly remembered Tom had told me the other day of an incident that happened in Taunton, when a stout, well-dressed lady handed him a white feather, saying 'You know where you should be!' This obviously had not helped the situation, for he had been embarrassed and upset by such a nasty rebuke accusing him of cowardice in public. I was really angered by this. If I had been there I would have confronted the lady and told her a few home truths.

We don't get much news from the battle front. Tom has only received one letter from Luke since his departure and that had been censored, so we still didn't know where he is stationed. He just said conditions were bad and they had had a lot of casualties in his battalion. He had added a P.S. "Wish I had some of your stew, Lottie (I once made the boys an Irish stew), the food here is terrible and please send socks, the trenches are cold and wet."

When I read that I took up my knitting needles that evening with added enthusiasm, even though it isn't my favourite occupation. And I included Luke in my nightly prayers, along with Ronnie, Bertie and Emily's Fred. May God protect our brave boys and bring them safely back home!

THE RECTORY
5th September 1914

Dearest Bella,

Thank you for your letter, quite understand how busy you are at the Language School these days. Your charity work with the Sunshine Club sounds really worthwhile and also your meetings with the Suffragette Movement. Yes, I too had heard they are now tempering their demands, in order to help women find useful jobs. No doubt we will find many more women working locally here, on the farms and in various occupations. I have noticed there are now women working on the buses and railways as ticket collectors and cleaners to replace men gone to war.

And Tom has already taken on a couple of women. He is still rather suspicious of them, but they seem to be doing a sterling job hoeing, working in the orchard and milking the cows. I agree with you, they can do as well as the men, if not better! Let's fly the flag for women!

By the way, I doubt whether I can find a house now for the Sunshine Club. There was a large mansion standing empty on the Taunton Road for some months, but it seems to have been requisitioned by the Government for a convalescent home now, so that's out. But the children are welcome to come on a day visit, have a picnic, visit a farm, etc. We can always give them cocoa and buns!

We have all been busy here too, now that the country is at war. I gave my first talk at a Girls Friendly Society gathering last week. I was very nervous, but they were only young girls of 12 and 13, not exactly a critical audience! I gave them a little demonstration of tapestry work and also the rudiments of sketching to start new interests for some of them. Miss Rowntree, who is on the G.F.S. Committee, has said it's very important to keep morale up during war-time and father agreed. We handed out sketch pads and pencils, also there were coloured embroidery cottons and rough hessian materials available for sale for a few pence. Also I spoke a little about life in The Rectory, as well as a brief lecture on hygiene that I was advised to give by Sister Fletcher from the Cottage Hospital. (She did ask me to do V.A.D. work at the hospital, but I have declined, as I feel I am fully committed already.) So anyway, I have made a start with the G.F.S. and shan't be so nervous next time.

And now I have started a Knitting Group in the Village Hall on a Monday – yes, me, the world's worst knitter, don't laugh! But following Queen Mary's plea for women to send the troops socks and balaclavas for the winter, I thought I should set an example and start a group in the village. In truth I have never knitted a pair of socks in my life, so will have to read a manual or ask Mrs Post how you turn the heel as I have absolutely no idea! It looks very tricky to me. There is also a big demand for bandages, so we will be doing some bandage rolling as well, hopefully a simpler exercise. Thankfully, I believe the Women's Club is also organizing knitting groups and so the dear boys over there will soon be engulfed in socks and balaclavas, mainly coming in parcels arriving from a certain village in Somerset.

Poor father is in a bit of a state. He's got the Harvest Festival and Harvest Supper coming up soon of course and now he's lost his mainstay, Dudley Sims (gone to be Chaplain at an army base near Exeter) which is a big blow to him. And on top of all this he has had many unexpected pleas from wives of Reservists, mainly for money. They seem to think he is part of the Government and can conjure up this Separation allowance they are entitled to out of thin air.

One poor woman turned up at the back door in tears begging for money or food, saying she had two sick children and no food or money in the house, now her husband had gone to war. Mrs May thought it was a gypsy pedlar at first. Regretfully father had to harden his heart and turn her away. He did try to assure her that the money will eventually be paid and could only advise her there is a Soup Kitchen in Taunton, if she can find a way of getting to Taunton, that is! Father sounded quite strict when he spoke to the woman and muttered, "We're not a charity here," when she had gone. But I could see the episode had troubled him. His eyes looked suspiciously moist behind his spectacles. He's quite soft-hearted basically, but obviously he can't start giving hand-outs to anybody who comes to the door. He did say later he may speak to the Bishop about it, who could hopefully make overtures to the Government and perhaps speed things up. There is simply no money in the kitty for father to help these people in the village. There is the Poor Fund, of course, but that is kept for the utterly destitute and homeless.

Maybe your Suffragettes could think of organizing some group to represent the interests of these poor women as they are really rather desperate, poor souls. They need their government allowances, need to receive them regularly. In fact, I am thinking of organizing a local Soup Kitchen myself, if I thought there was enough demand.

Am trying to "look after" father a bit more now, as he seems a bit flustered by the new demands on him, poor dear. However, Major Post as church-warden has said he will take on some of the donkey work that Rev. Sims did around the parish. He is such a brick, very decent of him. Hurrah for the Major!

Well, I must stop here, before I get too carried away on my high horse! Do look after yourself, dear Bella and I would love to hear your news when you have time.

As ever, your loving sister

Lottie

* * *

"Ouch! Bother!" Lottie has pricked her finger when doing her hassock tapestry, as she sits on the terrace one warm afternoon, It's a curious design of church steeples and bells, mainly in grey with a red background, with 'God is Love' in white at the bottom. Now there is blood seeping all over 'God'. 'Of course, it would have to go over the white bit, not the red', thinks Lottie irritably, dabbing at the blood-spot with her hankie. 'Now I'll have to cover that up with some extra horrid little cross-stitches. Now I know why they're called 'cross-stitches'!' And she jabs viciously at the canvas, suddenly tiring of her occupation. She's feeling in rather a bad mood today, missing Bella more than usual. Her monthly curse arrived early today, making her feel lethargic and head-achey. Lottie has gone back to using soft cotton rags which can be washed and used again, to save money. She had started using sanitary pads, but then decided they were just too expensive. These are needy times. She has to watch the pennies.

Then suddenly she can hear a childish voice chattering in the lane and looking up she sees young Dan Fogarty, son of the local thatcher, passing by in the lane with his mother. She waves to them as they go by and the young boy waves back enthusiastically, a big grin encompassing his flat round face.

Despite her mentally handicapped son and two other children, Mrs Fogarty does a lot of voluntary work for the church, sorting jumble and cleaning the pews. She is a real treasure, one of those people the vicar relies upon to keep the church running smoothly day-to-day. Lottie is full of admiration for her and seeing Dan she is reminded of an incident a few months back.

She'd met Luke by chance one late afternoon, as she was wheeling her bicycle which had developed a puncture. She was quite relieved to see him, as her back was aching from picking strawberries in Tom's strawberry beds, so was grateful for Luke's offer to wheel it for her through the village.

Luke told her quite casually in conversation he had just climbed Dunkery Beacon with some chums that day, the highest point on Exmoor at 1700 ft. "Great view," he had exclaimed, "as far as Wales to the north across the Bristol Channel and Dartmoor to the south." Lottie was impressed. She had never done that, although she and Bella had enjoyed walking on the moor with their mother when they were younger.

They were soon chatting away, but then realised they were being followed by Dan who is about 15 in years but a mental age of 5. He is a harmless enough boy, but still makes her feel a bit creepy. To Lottie's surprise Luke ruffled the boy's hair and chatted with him, then asked if he wanted a ride on the bicycle. The boy was a slight build, so wouldn't damage the tyre.

Dan shouted, "Yes, please, mister!" and Luke helped him onto the seat and wheeled him along for a few yards, Dan laughing and calling out to a few women chatting over the garden fence nearby. "Look at me, look at me!" But after a while Dan grew tired of this game and wanted to get off and go and tell his mother of his big adventure. Lottie was amazed Luke had bothered with Dan. Tom's brother compassionate and caring? Well, what a surprise! He had changed since childhood.

But she didn't know Luke. For as they neared the Rectory gates down Church Lane he suddenly sat astride the bicycle and pulled a face, imitating Dan perfectly and shouting, "Look at me, look at me!"

Father had always taught the girls not to mock the afflicted, but Lottie collapsed with laughter, for it was so unexpected. Then Luke chased her through the gates with a grotesque limping gait and contorted face, making her shriek with laughter as she ran with her bicycle up the driveway.

Lottie thinks of this episode as she watches Dan and his mother continue down the lane, giggling to herself even now at the thought. And she soberly reflects that Tom never makes her laugh like that, he's always down in the dumps these days. But the brothers are two very different personalities and Lottie realises she must be patient with Tom who is rather depressed at the moment. She will just have to hope he comes out of this bad patch and cheers up soon.

Coming out of her reverie, Lottie waves to Dan and his mother and then to her dismay spies the formidable figure of Mrs DoublePee approaching down Church Lane, clad in her usual black bombazine, despite the warm weather. She appears to pass by the Rectory gates first of all, then notices Lottie sitting on the terrace and turns to come up the steep drive-way. Oh no, not Mrs Poo-Poo!

Lottie had tried to slide down in her chair, hoping not to be noticed, but now alas, it is too late. Mrs Doubleday is huffing and puffing her way along the drive-way steadily towards Lottie. What has poor Lottie done now? She awaits the confrontation nervously. She had often noticed Mrs Doubleday casting a glance in her direction in church or at social events and felt it was a critical gaze, since their meeting in the church back in April.

Lottie rises from her basket chair and goes down the steps to the lower terrace, forcing a polite smile to her lips.

"G-good afternoon, Mrs Doubleday, can I help you?"

"Ah, Miss Carr!" Mrs D is obviously out of breath after negotiating the steep driveway. "I did hope I would see you…"

Lottie's heart sinks yet again. "Oh yes…?"

The old lady comes to a halt in front of Lottie and removes one of her gloves and fans herself with it. "Good afternoon, Miss Carr. Warm day, is it not?"

Lottie indicates a garden seat nearby. "Would you like to sit down?"

Mrs Doubleday shakes her head. "Thank you, but I won't stop. I'm on my way to visit someone."

Lottie wonders what's coming. Is it more reprimands? She racks her brains thinking what sins she might have committed that could have come to the attention of Mrs Doubleday.

"I just wanted to say, young lady, that I think you're on the right track now. Yes!" She grunts and nods, her grey curls bobbing. "You made a few faux pas earlier but you are now doing quite well in the parish, we are all agreed."

Lottie is astounded – and amused. "Why, thank you, Mrs Doubleday, that's very kind of you to say so."

"…credit where credit is due, I say. Things seem to be going quite smoothly in the parish now I do believe, despite these difficult times and I'm glad to see you are helping in the war effort. You are setting a good example. Everyone is pulling together – there is a good community spirit, do you agree? I think your father must be quite pleased with you."

Lottie tries to hide her amusement at the patronizing tone

of the old lady's comments, but she knows they are well-intended and it is praise indeed, coming from such a normally harsh critic. Indeed, there is even a shadow of a smile crossing the old lady's face as she speaks. Lottie is frankly amazed.

"Well, it is s-so kind of you to let me know," Lottie blurts out, not quite knowing how to respond. She shrugs. "I'm only doing what I can. I will tell father that you have called. And if you need any help at any time, please let me know." Lottie knows Mrs Doubleday is a widow and sometimes in delicate health.

"Thank you, my dear. Well, I must be away, I have to meet my niece. Ah, there she is now." A young woman with a small toddler is making her way along Church Lane and Mrs Doubleday waves to her. She turns back to Lottie, a smile on her lips. "I wonder, would you like to meet her? She's visiting from London with her little son."

"Why, yes, I'll walk down with you," Lottie says, 'to save them coming up the steep driveway.'

As they approach the young woman, smartly dressed and wearing a pretty hat trimmed with flowers, the little toddler begins clapping his chubby hands. He is a sturdy little chap with solemn brown eyes, dressed in a sailor suit and pulling a little toy behind him. "This is my niece, Alexandra, and her son, Henry Stuart Valentine. Born on St. Valentine's Day, bless him. This is Miss Carr."

"How do you do, Henry?" Lottie says, smiling and bending down to shake his hand.

"We call him Stuart," puts in Mrs Doubleday.

The little boy's face crinkles into a beaming smile and he mumbles, "Hallo.'"

'How old is he?' Lottie asks. "Nineteen months and full of mischief," smiles Alexandra. "We're going to feed the ducks, aren't we, Stuart?" The child nods gravely.

Mrs Doubleday beams as she gazes at the child, a sight Lottie has never witnessed before. "He's walking so well now, Alexandra. Last time I saw him he was a little unsteady." She is obviously so proud of her great-nephew, despite being deprived of children herself. "Alexandra's husband is a flying officer in the Royal Flying Corps," explains Mrs Doubleday.

"Brave man, where is he based?" Lottie asks.

"At Hendon at the moment," Alexandra smiles broadly, "he adores flying, he's training young recruits before he goes on Ops., mainly reconnaissance work." She shakes her head. "Most of them have only a few hours' flying time before they go off."

"I wish them well, I shall pray for them all," says Lottie. "I hope you enjoy your visit down here. How long are you staying?"

"Just a few days, Aunt Violet is looking after us very well. It's so nice to come into the country, after London."

The older woman turns to her niece. "Miss Carr is doing such a splendid job in the village with the war effort." Lottie shrugs modestly. "There is a very good community spirit here now we are at war."

Mrs Doubleday takes Stuart's hand and turns to Lottie. "Well, my dear, we must be off now…"

"Very nice to have met you," Lottie nods to Alexandra and waves her fingers at Stuart who waves back solemnly. "And thank you for your kind comments, Mrs Doubleday, nice of you to call."

And the strictly no-nonsense matron makes her dignified way along Church Lane with her niece, little Stuart running ahead pulling his little duck on wheels, anxious to feed the real ducks on the village pond.

And as Lottie returns to her chair and her tapestry she is somewhat bemused, but in a better mood. It's good to know that 'Aunt Violet' is definitely human after all. And nice to know someone finds her behaviour satisfactory. For she never receives much praise from Tom these days, that much is very clear.

Chapter 7
OCTOBER

THE RECTORY
10th October 1914

Dear Amy,

It was lovely to see you briefly in Dunster last week, but I realise you had to dash away to meet Mrs Ponsonby. I have to say she looks a bit formidable! And yet you say she is quite lonely, being a childless widow. I'm glad you're enjoying the post.

Life in Tethercombe has never been so busy! We have had the Harvest Festival and the Harvest Supper to organise and it all went very well, a lovely gathering in the Village Hall. I usually love this celebration in the Church year, but I felt this year no-one's heart was in it properly, with the news of the war so prominent. There are more pressing matters.

I am now running a Soup Kitchen three times a week from the Village Hall and it's proving very popular. We are feeding upwards of 20–30 people a day. Now the price of food has risen so sharply people are finding it hard to feed their families properly and so father agreed with me that there was a demand for it. Lots of farms and more affluent families are donating vegetables and a few chickens, etc. and the Red Cross has supplied large cooking pots and urns, etc.

Matilda Rowntree and I run it between us. Do you know her? She worked for The Red Cross in Exeter for a number of years. She's in her thirties and very practical. She's quite a character – doesn't stand any nonsense from our customers at the Soup Kitchen. I met her through the G.F.S., as she's on the Committee. She takes a rather sceptical view of some soldiers' wives who claim they have no money to feed their children. She reckons they spend it all on drink. And perhaps she's right in some cases!

The baker's shop is giving us any bread and buns which haven't sold. Also, the miller is providing us with free flour which is a big help, just a couple of sacks now and then. So despite everything, this war is fostering a real community spirit! Anyway, we just keep it simple and dole out soup and bread, also tea and buns, and the mugs of Bovril and Oxo are very popular too. The food is basically free, though donations of one half-penny are invited but rarely received. The only problem I encountered on the first day was I didn't have a big enough spoon to stir the soup with and had to resort to the end of a garden rake! Happy days! Fortunately the recipients are so hungry and grateful I'm sure they won't notice if there are bits of grass floating about in the soup. Or they might think they are herbs!

We have also got our first refugees in the village. Major and Mrs Post are housing a Belgian family for a limited time who had to flee from chaotic conditions in their village near Ghent, following the German invasion, so the war has indeed come to Somerset. Indeed, Mrs Post has now formed a Belgian Refugee Committee and is fund-raising for it by holding luncheon parties/Sales of Work, etc., as she believes it is a growing problem.

Oh yes, on the domestic front, Emily (our parlour-maid) has surprised us all by handing in her notice. She's gone to work in a munitions factory in Birmingham! They all sing while they work and apparently they can make really good money there. But of course it is dangerous work and can turn skin and hair yellow, hence they are often called 'canaries'. Bit of a risk, eh? Still, we have to keep our boys out there supplied with armaments. Must tell you, Amy, Emily said such a spiffing thing in a letter to Mrs May. When they are packing the munitions in the boxes some girls pop in a letter to a soldier, giving their names and addresses and sometimes a photo, hoping the boys will look them up when they are home on leave! How romantic is that?! Poor chaps, they need a bit of hope and light relief out there. And perhaps the girls do, too, working in those terrible factories.

What is the news of Bertie and Richard? Good, I hope. I pray to God every night that this awful war will soon end and our boys can come home again safely. These are troubled times we are living in, my friend.

Father didn't want to replace Emily, said we had to make do without a parlour-maid now we are at war. But Mrs May put on her 'tight lips' look, so we now have Elsie, a scullery maid, who does the rough work, black-leading the grates and the range, bringing in the coal and lighting the fires, etc. She is a tough little thing, comes from Bristol, but she is very cheerful and insists on calling father 'Your Reverence', much to father's embarrassment and my amusement!

Have you heard about the Government rounding up aliens? An old harmless German couple here were taken away for questioning overnight by military police. He did wood carving and she kept a few chickens at their cottage in Sheep Lane. Everyone in the village was very shocked. A neighbour found their dog whining at the back door in the morning, poor thing, so is caring for him. It's rumoured they have been taken to a detention camp in Wiltshire. Shocking. I'm sure they are innocent.

But of course they may have been taken away for their own protection. There has been quite a bit of animosity in some quarters against German-owned shops, businesses, etc. There was even red paint daubed on a tobacconist shop in Taunton owned by Germans with the words 'Germans – OUT' written on the windows. The war is bound to produce these strong feelings in people. And did you hear, a village in Kent was bombed and people were killed! We are lucky to be living here in Somerset. At least we are a bit safer here.

Tom seems more reconciled to the fact he can't enlist now and is more cheerful, thank goodness. I am helping him smarten up 'Three Chimneys'. It had got a bit shabby over the years since their parents died, so it is looking much more the ticket now. He was very suspicious of women working on his land to start with, but now he can see they are doing a good job, he is happier! The women workers seem a very cheerful crowd. Also, the older men working as herdsmen are proving very useful.

Well, I must close now and hope to see you soon. I am dying for a ride on Bessie so we must definitely arrange a visit soon. I would love to see your room with its charming view over the hills.

Hope you're not missing your family and Bertie too much.

With love, your friend,

Lottie

THE RECTORY
18th October 1914

Dearest Bella,

It was so good to see you yesterday, even though only a flying visit!

You looked so well and very dashing in your trousers and your new short haircut! And you DROVE DOWN in Rupert's motor! Well, my stars, how game you are! But yes, I can see driving will be so useful to you. It must be so much easier to get to your meetings, etc. by car, if you can get the petrol, that is. Father was quite shocked by it all, I have to say, as he thinks motor-cars are nasty dangerous contraptions. But we have to move with the times, don't we? I really enjoy it when Tom takes me out in his motor (not often) – we seem to fly along!

And that is good news that Ronnie is coming home on furlough soon. I suppose he will only get the usual ten days, but it will be such a treat to see him. I have missed his cheerful face and joking demeanour.

We still have very few letters from Luke, although in the last one he did casually mention he had been promoted to Lieutenant, so good for him! He also said they were pushing towards somewhere (blanked out by censor) and conditions were atrocious. They have had heavy casualties in their Battalion. We had our first casualty from the village this week. We heard that Georgie Pullen, one of Tom's farm labourers, had died from injuries received in the Battle of Mons. He was only 19. We are all so sad about it, he was a lovely lad, smiling and energetic. Father went to see the family to comfort them with a prayer or two. They are all distraught but are proud that he died fighting the Hun.

As I mentioned, Tom seems much happier now and feels he is doing his bit for King and Country by keeping the farm going/planting crops, etc. He now has one whole field planted out with potatoes and carrots, to help the war effort. Also since 'Three Chimneys' has been re-furbished he is very proud of it and can't wait to show Luke when he comes home.

Well, I won't stop for more now. Don't work too hard, dear Bella and be careful how you drive on the roads. (Father is praying for you!)

Hope to see you again before too long,

Your loving sister,

Lottie

SECRET DIARY

20th October 1914

11 a.m. Am feeling rather upset as I've just had such a poignant meeting with a young woman unexpectedly. Went into church to take some dahlias from the garden for the ladies to arrange and while I was there I suddenly noticed a young woman in one of the pews, sobbing her heart out and kneeling in prayer. I didn't like to intrude while she was praying, but when she sat back in the pew with her head bowed, I went over to her and sat beside her, asking her what was wrong and could I help. After yet more sobs she told me she had just heard that morning that her husband, Jimmy, had been killed at Mons.

I was so shocked – she looked so young to be a widow, only about my age. They had been childhood sweethearts apparently and had only been married two months. He was just 20.

I didn't know how to console her, but asked her name and where she lived, putting my arm round her to comfort her. I also decided to give her the flowers I had brought, instead of leaving them to decorate the church and she seemed touched by this small gesture. She stood up as if to leave and I asked her if someone would be at home. "I've got to tell my mother," she said, sobs coming afresh. "And Jimmy's mother – they don't know yet. I don't know how I'm going to tell her! I was alone at the cottage when the telegram came. I ran to my mother's, but she wasn't there. I didn't know what to do, so I came here..." She looked distraught and confused as she dabbed at her eyes and clutched the flowers I had given her and we left St. Stephens together. She needs to be with someone who will take care of her, I thought.

So I accompanied her to her mother's cottage in Sheep Lane and after a few words with her mother I left them in their grief, feeling desperately sad. I vowed I would try and keep in touch with Sophie Speedwell, but the incident really upset me and brought home to me what an impact this war is having.

***6 p.m**. Have just returned from 'Three Chimneys' and am worn out! We have nearly finished re-furbishing the farmhouse and it has been a very worthwhile project, but a lot of hard work. I have had to go with Tom into Taunton on several occasions to help him choose material, carpets, furniture, etc. and my life is already so busy that it's difficult to fit in these extra trips. I don't mind, but he seems to take me for granted. Last week I had already devoted two mornings to giving him advice about furnishings, when he calmly mentioned he'd made an appointment with a decorating firm for the next day and wanted me to go with him to choose colours.*

I'm afraid I lost my temper with him at that point, something I rarely do. "No, Tom," I said, "I can't manage tomorrow or the day after. I'm busy with the Soup Kitchen and other things. I do have a life apart from you, you know. Oh, goodness, sometimes I think you just want a housekeeper, not a fiancée!"

And I rattled off angrily on my bicycle down Turners Lane. I was still in a bad mood once I got home and snapped at poor Mrs May when she said my ironing wasn't ready. Tom often seems to make me very tense and irritable these days, I'm sad to say. I decided to work off my anger by giving Bessie a good rub down and brushed her coat till it shone, much to Davey's surprise, but it made me feel tons better. And Bessie gave a little whinny of pleasure when I had finished.

Anyway, thankfully, the re-furbishment of Three Chimneys is nearly complete and we now have only the main sitting room curtains to consider. Have left these to last as I think they are the most important. Tom must have spent a small fortune on all this interior decoration, etc. and he has been more than a little secretive about it all, which is odd. He did say he had come into a small legacy but the way he has been spending money it must have been a very large legacy! For not only has he re-decorated and carpetted the entire house, but has had the roof re-thatched and a new bathroom fitted, the height of luxury!

The house has been alive with workmen, older men glad of the work, so a very busy time. It all looks very grand. But when I tried to probe him about where the legacy had come from, he just said 'a relative.' He seems particularly keen to impress Luke when he gets home from the war. He's got a real bee in his bonnet about it. He is, thankfully, leaving a few decisions until then. He wants to modernise the dairy equipment, also buy more cattle and more farm machinery, but is waiting for Luke's return when they can discuss it together. I am glad about that, as I feel Luke would definitely want a say in these things.

SECRET DIARY

21st October 1914

Had a little heart-to-heart with Mrs Bryant today, while waiting for Tom to come back from the fields. I was curious about the source of Tom's legacy. She says the uncle who left Tom the legacy was an older brother of Tom's father and he never married, so left more or less his entire estate in Scotland, including a substantial house and grouse moors to Tom, apart from a few charity bequests. Luke wasn't included in the legacy, as the uncle was a bit of a recluse and out of touch with the family. Maybe he thought Luke was still a minor. Mrs Bryant only knows all this as her family have 'looked after' the Trevithick family for over fifty years. She seems to think Tom is a little embarrassed by his sudden wealth, hence his reticence to speak about it. She was anxious to stress she doesn't normally 'gossip' about the master, but as I am his fiancée, she felt I was entitled to know the facts.

25th October 1914

Poor father is ill with influenza! The doctor has prescribed aspirin every four hours and instructed him to stay in bed and drink plenty of fluids and rest. The poor dear looked very sorry for himself, as I tucked him up like a child and drew the curtains across to shut out the rain. "You're my little sunbeam, Lottie," he murmured as I sponged his fevered brow with cooling lavender water. Then he obediently closed his eyes and sank back on the pillows looking quite exhausted. He looked so sweet and angelic lying there without his spectacles on, that I gave him a kiss on the forehead! I had also arranged for Elsie to light a fire in his bedroom, an unheard of luxury, but I believe it to be an essential part of father's cossetting.

Thank goodness we now have the telephone installed at home. I was immediately able to contact the Rector of the next parish, Revd. Snelworthy and ask if he or his curate could conduct Matins or Evensong for us on Sunday, also do a few home Communions for the very sick members of our flock. This is where we really miss Dudley Sims, for he could have so easily taken over from father and willingly.

It was my day for the Soup Kitchen as well and I really didn't think I could leave father at this time. It was bucketing down, so I hastily pulled on my mackintosh cape and dashed down to the Hall on my bicycle through the rain. There was Matilda with her severe-looking bob and voluminous overall, already setting up the tables, etc. and getting out the bowls and cutlery. Fortunately we had made the soup yesterday, a nourishing vegetable soup with pearl barley, and it only had to be re-heated. She quite understood my predicament and I felt perfectly happy leaving her in charge of the fast-growing queue forming outside. She is a dear and so capable! I'm becoming quite fond of my new chum.

Meanwhile, back at The Rectory, Mrs May was preparing hot lemon and honey drinks to soothe the sore throat and did suggest some left-over tapioca pudding to build father up. Thankfully I was able to dissuade her from this, as I thought it might finish him off!

* * *

Lottie is arranging some flowers in the big farmhouse kitchen at Three Chimneys the next week. She stands back and admires the tawny chrysanthemums with their ragged blooms, then places the earthenware jug on the window sill and the other china vase on the dresser. 'There, a splash of colour – makes it seem more homely somehow.'

Tom comes in with an armful of earthy carrots and a box of potatoes and puts them down by the door, Benny the dog following his master in. "Thought you might like these for your Soup Kitchen," he says gruffly, then notices the flowers as Lottie tidies up the detritus of leaves and stalks at the sink. "Oh, they look nice, thank you, dear."

Lottie smiles broadly. "And look at all those lovely vegetables! Thanks, Tom, that will be a big help."

Lottie's visits to Tom are now restricted to lunch or an afternoon cup of tea, like today and their Sunday walk after church. The vicar doesn't approve of his daughter being alone with Tom without a chaperone, so they have to abide by his strict rules and see each other only when someone else is present or when they are out together in public.

Lottie had hoped that Tom might take her to a concert or visit an art gallery occasionally like she used to do with Bella. But he doesn't seem interested in the arts and finds it hard to stir himself from the fireside in the evening, no doubt tired from his day working around the farm. Lottie loves Tom but she is finding being engaged to him is proving rather disillusioning. Tom's only hobby is fishing, a solitary occupation and one Lottie isn't interested in. So she finds when they're together they tend to look through family photos or take a stroll around the perimeters of the farm, along muddy lanes or the rough stubble of the fields, not exactly a stimulating exercise.

"Let's go into the parlour and have a cup of tea," Tom says, "I'm tired out."

They move into the sitting room where the faded worn curtains hanging at the window remind Lottie only too painfully they need to choose some fabric for new ones very soon. These are practically falling apart!

Mrs Bryant enters, bringing some tea-things for them and as Tom is putting another log on the fire in the big hearth, one of the older labourers suddenly puts his head through the window, which abuts the courtyard.

"Beg pardon, boss, we got a problem with the tractor on the top field. Can you come and take a look? Sorry to bother you an' that."

Lottie sighs and a wave of annoyance sweeps through her. This is always happening!

Tom gets wearily to his feet. "Excuse me, dearest, I must go and take a look, sort it out. Won't be long. You help yourself there." And he waves his hand at the tea and cakes on the table and goes out, accompanied by Benny running along behind him.

Seeing Lottie's disappointed face, Mrs Bryant gives a laugh and lifts the tea-pot. "Never mind, lovie. Let me pour you a nice cup of tea." She shakes her head. "The master is married to the farm, I'm afraid, Miss Charlotte, married to the farm."

Lottie gives a sigh, but makes no comment.

"And how's the Rector, any better?"

"He's still not right," Lottie replies, shaking her head. "The flu has pulled him down, but he'll soon be on the mend, I'm sure."

Mrs Bryant gives Lottie a cup of tea and cuts her a piece of cake, then picks up a photo from a pile on the table with a smile. "That's a nice one of Tom and his father," she says, holding it up to Lottie.

"He was about 5 then I think. Look at him, little pet!"

Lottie is puzzled. "Oh, *that's* his father?" She had seen another photo of Tom and Luke with their father and this man is not the same.

"Oh yes, that's *Tom's* father – but he died when Tom was seven and then two years later Mrs T married again, her husband's brother and after a year Luke was born."

Lottie nods. "Oh, I *see!* That explains a lot. That's why they're so different, I suppose. They're only half-brothers."

Mrs Bryant nods sagely. "Like chalk and cheese, I'd say."

A worried look crosses her face. "I wonder how Master Luke is getting on out there..."

Lottie flicks through the photo album rather too rapidly, as if trying to dispel unpleasant thoughts from her mind. "I pray for all the men out there every night. From the reports in the papers it doesn't sound good, terrible casualties."

Mrs Bryant shakes her head. "I shan't rest till he's back again. And you heard about young Georgie Pullen, I'm sure..."

Lottie nods. "I did. How dreadful for his poor family."

"Such a lovely young man, always had a laugh and a joke with me, he did..." Mrs Bryant says, sniffing hard. But then she lifts the tea-pot with a brave smile. "But, life has to go on, so I'll top the pot up, miss, that's what I'll do, top up the pot." And she moves briskly to the door, her long skirt swishing against the table and causing a photo to flutter down on the carpet.

Lottie picks it up. It's a recent photo of Luke, a good likeness in his riding clothes, with his horse, Rufus, by the stable, taken in the summer. She gazes at it for a moment, a smile on her face, then slips it inside her handbag.

Chapter 8

NOVEMBER

SECRET DIARY

7th November 1914

Father has now fully recovered from his influenza, thank goodness, so at last I can resume my normal duties. He was in bed for three days and then seemed very weak and exhausted for another week after that, so Dr Witherspoon prescribed a bottle of Wincarnis tonic to aid his recovery. We were grateful to the Revd Snelworthy for 'loaning us' his curate, Revd Peter Smith, who filled in very helpfully for us. I have heard people say he is a 'conchie', (I think that's what they now call a conscientious objector) but he seemed a pleasant enough young man and was almost flirtatious with me at times. But as soon as I mentioned my fiancé and flashed my ring he went quite pink with embarrassment and never spoke to me again!

Tom has been badgering me to help him choose material for the sitting room curtains and to-day I am going to 'Three Chimneys', as a gentleman from Bentalls Department Store in Taunton is coming to show us some samples, to save us the trip into Taunton, also measure up for us. We have put so much business their way lately that I think it is long overdue! Tom is anxious to have the house all finished in time for Christmas, as we are hoping that perhaps Luke may be able to come home on furlough about that time. He is certainly due for some leave.

8th November 1914

I have to set down the events of yesterday. I rode over to 'Three Chimneys' on Bessie for a change and Tom and I were in the sitting room in the afternoon, looking through the big swatch of curtain fabrics and trying to decide between a green velvet or a striped pink silk. Tom was holding the green velvet up at the window against the wallpaper for me to see and I had just said: "Oh, the green velvet, I think, don't you?" when through the window I suddenly caught sight of a red bicycle rattling through the five-bar gate, scattering the chickens as it came into the courtyard.

My heart stood still. It was the dreaded telegraph boy in his distinctive dark blue uniform and jaunty pill-box hat. Benny ran up barking at him as he came to the door. I pointed to the window and stuttered out: *"Look, Tom, a wire..."* I could hardly speak and my stomach tightened in fear.

Tom's face paled and he went swiftly to the door, muttering to me *"Don't you worry now, Charlotte..."*

My heart began to thump wildly and I felt I couldn't move. The gentleman from Bentalls sat down abruptly and fiddled with his hat, looking rather embarrassed to be present at such a delicate moment.

Tom came back holding the yellow form he had torn open and I held my breath until he spoke.

"He's all right, thank God!" he said, *"but he's been injured and invalided out, discharged unfit for further service. He's in the military hospital at Taunton."* And then he added: *"He's been made a Captain, it's Captain Luke Trevithick now."* He looked really proud when he spoke.

I suddenly felt very emotional and mixed-up. Tears pricked at my eyelids. I was so relieved to hear Luke was alive and back in England, but very anxious to know the extent of his injuries. *"How is he, do they say? How badly is he injured?"*

Tom shook his head. *"They don't say. But I must get over there straight away."* He took out his pocket watch. *"It's 2.30 now. If I hurry I could be over there within the hour. I'll take the car."*

He hurried upstairs to change his clothes and I dismissed the gentleman from Bentalls as politely as I could. Choosing furnishing fabrics had all at once become rather insignificant.

Riding home, as I trotted gently along the lanes, now clad in a carpet of tawny autumn leaves, my thoughts were in a turmoil, as I reflected on the news – it was a mixture of relief and anxiety. Let's hope the news will be good, I thought. These thoughts were quickly dispelled by *more practical matters, however, once I got back to The Rectory. I found that Mrs May had retired to bed with a sick headache, so I had to knuckle down and cook the dinner for us all. The meat was already cooking in the slow range oven and Mrs May had been intending to make a pie for us, but I'm no good at pastry. So Elsie and I prepared a few vegetables, put them in with the meat and turned it into a tasty stew. I'm not quite at home in the kitchen, but with Elsie's help and her cheerful banter, we produced a meal of sorts between us, so it was I suppose a welcome distraction.*

Later in my bed I said my prayers fervently, praying to God that Luke has not been too badly injured. I knew some of the soldiers returning from the Front often suffered horrific injuries, were blinded or had to have limbs amputated. Tom wasn't yet on the telephone at the farm, so I hadn't heard from him when he returned home from the Hospital. He obviously didn't think to call in at The Rectory to let me know.

I blinked back the tears as I fell into a fitful sleep. "Please God, make Luke completely better. Don't let him be maimed, please God, don't let him be maimed." I had never prayed so hard in all my life. I am beginning to realise how much Tom's brother means to me.

THE RECTORY
12th November 1914

Dearest Bella,

Just a few lines to thank you for your brief note. So pleased to hear Ronnie is now home for a few days. No doubt I shall see him about the neighbourhood soon. Am looking forward to seeing you when you come down on your weekend visit. Quite understand you wish to stay with the Posts in the circumstances.

You may have heard from the Posts that Luke is now back, having been invalided out. He is in the Military Hospital at Taunton with an eye injury (shell splinter, but sight mercifully saved) and a complicated leg fracture (still in splints). It was badly set in the field hospital apparently and will leave him with a permanent limp. But anyway he is alive, that's the main thing, so is counting his blessings. I haven't seen him yet (have been so busy with the Soup Kitchen) but Tom has visited a couple of times on his own. Luke is apparently much quieter and still quite weak and poorly, so can't cope with long visits, but he has asked after me (and you) apparently, so I feel I should go soon.

I was wondering whether I could ask you a favour? Could you spare the time to accompany me to hospital to see Luke when you are here? It sounds awfully silly but I suddenly feel very shy of visiting him on my own, don't know why, and Tom is too busy. Don't laugh, but I think I need my big sister there to bolster my confidence! And I know he would love to see you.

If you could spare the time while you are down here, it would be spiffing, but don't worry if not, I expect I'll manage somehow, he's not an ogre, I know. But he still makes me nervous.

Looking forward to seeing you at the weekend,

Much love from your silly sister,

Lottie

SECRET DIARY

18th November 1914

Visited Luke in Hospital today, find it hard to describe my feelings, but I will try. Dear Bella was, thankfully, beside me as we arrived at the big Military Hospital and found the ward. It was frantically busy everywhere, the wards packed out with casualties, the nurses and VADs scurrying to and fro with their usual calm efficiency. The nurse waved us towards his bed and my courage almost deserted me when I first saw him. He turned his head as we approached and looked so young and somehow vulnerable, I could have wept.

I felt so shocked at the sight of him – his thick dark hair had been closely cropped (due to lice infestation in the trenches) and his left eyelid was drooping down with a vivid red, raw scar running across it. Tom had not mentioned about his hair, but it made him look so different.

His injured leg was protected by a large cradle under the bed-clothes. He was pale and drawn, so unlike his usual demeanour. I suddenly felt shy and tongue-tied and my heart began to beat erratically.

But dear Bella was marvellous as usual. She sailed towards the bed smiling broadly, her heady perfume wafting over the pristine starched sheets.

"Luke, darling!" she cried, and thrust a bunch of flowers in his hands. "How lovely to see you – handsome as ever and I love your new haircut!"

I noticed that all the young men in the ward were now turning their heads and gazing interestedly at Bella, as she hugged Luke and called for a vase for the flowers. I heard the phrase 'Absolute corker!' murmured more than once as we passed through the ward. She must have seemed like the angel of mercy and Lily Langtry rolled into one, deprived as they had been of female company for so long.

I pulled up some chairs for us both and Luke managed a wan smile, obviously pleased to see us, despite his gaunt appearance.

"Thanks for coming, girls, lovely to see you both." I sat on the edge of my seat, clutching the box of chocolates I had brought for him. "Hallo, Lottie, nice to see you."

I smiled and offered my burning cheek for a token kiss and held out the chocolates. "Hallo, Luke," I mumbled, "welcome home. These are for you. Sorry I couldn't send you any stew. Did you get the socks?"

What a stupid thing to say! I felt so awkward and gauche, I blushed and looked down at my shoes.

Luke shook his head and laughed. "Not yet, but thanks for sending them."

Bella got up and plumped up the pillows behind Luke's head. "You are well out of it, my dear, you've done your bit. But I hear congratulations are in order. Promoted to Captain, I hear, and now the D.C.M., am I right?" She kissed him on the forehead. "You are a very brave boy, we are very proud of you, aren't we, Lottie?"

I nodded dumbly and murmured my congratulations. The

Distinguished Conduct Medal. This was something else Tom had not mentioned. What an honour! Luke had been awarded this, I learned later, for outstanding bravery at Ypres when he had brought in wounded men in the face of enemy attack and had even gone back for more men when wounded himself in the eye, only to have his leg shattered by another shell attack. Why hadn't Tom told me? I felt deeply hurt that I hadn't known about it before I had come.

Luke asked after Ronnie Post, so Bella told us news of him and how he was going to address a meeting of Scouts while home on furlough. He's had a tough campaign, she said, he needs a break. She then described what it was like in London at the moment. The railway stations are so busy these days, she said, with hospital trains constantly arriving, bringing the injured from the Front, and a line of ambulances taking them to hospital. With a mischievous smile, she then had us in helpless giggles as she described a lovey-dovey socialite couple she had met at a country house party recently.

"They called each other Flopsy and Boo-boo..."

"Sounds like pet rabbits!" put in Luke, smiling.

"They referred to each other in the third person all the time," Bella said, "it was quite bizarre. He would say 'Flopsy loves Boo-boo so much' and she would reply: 'Boo-boo thinks Flopsy's a perfect poppet.' Sounded really hilarious but rather coquettish to me. But I knew Bella was only being entertaining, to raise Luke's spirits.

All at once Bella suddenly stood up and bade farewell, to my surprise, saying she needed to speak to the doctor. She gave Luke a kiss and swept through the ward to appreciative whistles from the young men. Bella of course completely ignored this, being used to such attention. Immaculately dressed as usual in a jewel blue coat with matching hat trimmed with ostrich feathers, which set off her flaming hair to perfection, she paused at the door on her way out and flashed a brilliant smile at us: "I'll see you outside, Lottie, in about five minutes," she said, "we mustn't tire Luke out..." My heart swelled with pride as she disappeared down the corridor – how I loved my dear bossy stylish sister!

Luke smiled and sank back on the pillows, obviously drained of energy. "Same old Arabella, in my present state I find her quite exhausting!" And his dark eyes met mine for the first time. "Thanks for coming, Lottie, it's cheered me up no end. I needed cheering up…"

He placed his hand over mine, as it rested on the coverlet and it gave me quite a shock. A strange feeling ran through my body, that thrilling feeling I remembered from our dance together. Why didn't I feel like this when Tom touched me, I wondered? Was this what Bella had tried to tell me?

I suddenly felt very aware of being alone with Luke, as he sat up in bed in his pyjamas. The other patients didn't exist. The dark hairs on his chest were just visible where the collar was open, his voice was deep and he was so close.

"It was pretty bad over there, I hear…" was all I could say.

Luke nodded. "Can't talk about it. We were just sitting ducks, cannon fodder. I'm damned lucky to be here at all, I can tell you. Most of 'em weren't so lucky. Anyway, changing the subject, I hear as soon as my back is turned my brother has come into a vast amount of money, is that right?"

I nodded and smiled. "You won't recognise the place. It's looking very smart. But he wants your advice about a lot of other things," I added.

"Dear Lottie," Luke said, squeezing my hand, "so diplomatic as usual." He held my gaze. "I thought about you quite a bit, you know…"

I blushed and released my hand, feeling embarrassed again. "I'm so glad to see you back again safely, Luke." It was all I trusted myself to say. I realised I'd been thinking about him, too, and far too much lately. I suddenly felt guilty that my future brother-in-law had occupied my thoughts so much. My emotions were very churned up.

But now he was back, our relationship seemed to have changed. Luke seemed to have lost some of his brashness. He had a new maturity about him which belied his age. He was quieter and more intense than he had been. We chatted a little about the farm and local matters, but he was not so voluble as he had been previously.

You could tell from his eyes he had suffered pain and anguish. He had experienced first-hand the terrible slaughter of young, untrained men and was only too aware of the useless futility of it all. He had gone to war a boy and returned a man. It was trite, but it was true.

I felt it was time to leave and stood up, smoothing down my coat and gathering up my handbag. I gave him a light kiss on the cheek. "Bye, Luke, I must go now and find Bella. Hope your leg will soon be better."

He grinned up at me. "Don't worry, Lottie, I'll be chasing you up the driveway again any day now."

I giggled at the memory. "Luke! How much longer do you think you'll be here?"

"Oh, a few more weeks, maybe..."

I paused at the end of the bed, pulling on my gloves. "I'll come again in the week with Tom, if you'd like me to..."

"I'd prefer you to come without Tom, but if you insist..."

My heart fluttered beneath my coat, shocked by the realisation that even before I'd left him, I was longing to see him again too.

"And don't forget, Flopsy loves Boo-Boo!" *he called out in jest as I took my leave. I giggled again and shook my head at him as I went through the door.*

I almost floated down the antiseptic, polished corridor to meet Bella, a smile on my lips, my thoughts and heart racing. I felt keyed up with the excitement of seeing Luke again. I was so relieved he was home again and that he hadn't been too badly injured.

But that nagging, uneasy thought kept returning to me again and again, as I went out into the cold November air. It was a thought so alarming I hardly allowed myself to think it. I had contemplated speaking to Bella about it but decided against. It was too private, too important.

Had I made the most dreadful mistake? Could it be I'd become engaged to the wrong brother?

* * *

Lottie is conducting one of her weekly Sick and Poor visits with Mrs Post. They have already gone to two cottages in Sheep Street and are now about to visit Mrs Priddy in Oak Cottages, mother of Bennie the deaf mute and three other children under five. Mrs Post has told Lottie how caring Mrs Priddy is to her disabled son. "She has learnt the deaf and dumb sign language and taught it to Bennie, so that she can communicate with him. Isn't that wonderful?"

Lottie nods, thinking that perhaps she ought to learn it herself to help more deaf people in the parish.

Faithful Mrs Post has been accompanying Lottie on her visits for several months now and Lottie has grown to depend on her for her sensible judgement and wise counsel, when they are faced with difficult families.

It's raining as they knock on the door, noticing the peeling paintwork on the windows, the worn thatch on the roof and unswept path covered in leaves and debris blown from the trees. 'Another cottage owned by Squire Madely,' Mrs Post mutters to Lottie as they wait in the porch. Squire Madely had been reported to the Parish Council as a notoriously bad landlord. He had been spoken to and warned by Major Post, but the bad practices still continued.

The door swings open and Lottie is surprised to see quite a young woman standing there, if care-worn and tired-looking, a grizzling baby on her hip. She had imagined Mrs Priddy would be an older woman, as the mother of four children, for Bennie is at least 8 or 9. She must have married young.

"Come in," she says, dropping her eyes and apologetically picking a few items littering the porch and stuffing them in her overall pocket. She indicates a worn armchair, its seat cushion sagging almost to the floor. "Take a seat, ma'am." Mrs Post sits down with a smile. Mrs Priddy pulls up a wooden stool for Lottie who perches on it awkwardly.

"May I get you both a cup of tea, ma'am?" Mrs Priddy asks. Mrs Post shakes her head. "Thank you, but no, we have quite a full list today."

"And how are the little ones, keeping well?" Lottie asks.

One of the children climbs onto her mother's knee, a pretty child with dark curly hair and a dimple when she smiles. "This is my Gladys May, she's five," the mother says proudly. "They get a few coughs and colds, but no too bad, thank you, miss."

There is a damp, smoky atmosphere in the room, due to nappies drying on a clothes horse by the meagre open fire. Lottie can't help also noticing how thin the mother is – her collar-bones are protruding sharply and she is very pale with dark circles under her eyes. "And you yourself – are you all right?"

Mrs Priddy nods and gives a weak smile. "I'm no too bad."

Mrs Post pats the baby crawling on the floor. 'You know there is a free weekly surgery in the Village Hall on a Wednesday where you can get advice from the nurse – I hope you take the children along if they're not well. You can also get free milk for the children and of course Miss Charlotte's Soup Kitchen is held there three times a week.'

Lottie looks around the small crowded room, noticing it is clean if not tidy. "And where's Bennie to-day?" She suddenly realises the deaf-mute boy is missing. "He's having a little sleep, he did'na sleep too well last night. He frets for his pa."

Mrs Post nods. "At the Front?" But Mrs Priddy shakes her head. "Rejected for enlistment, flat feet. He's working in the munitions to make a few bob, ma'am."

Lottie is horrified. "So how often does he come home?" She knows most of the munitions factories are in Birmingham and Manchester and it's dangerous work. Mrs Priddy shrugs. "When he can – once a month if we're lucky."

Mrs Post stands up and reaches into her bag and Lottie follows suit. "Here are a few clothes for the children, my dear, hope they fit."

And Lottie then delves into her capacious bag. "Some apples for the children," she says with a smile, "and one for Bennie, too. And the vicar has sent these lovely coloured texts for them too."

Mrs Priddy's eyes fill with tears. "Thank you kindly, ladies, I'm that grateful."

She turns to the children. "Say 'thank you' to the kind ladies now." The children mumble their thanks and begin biting on the apples.

"We have to go now," Lottie says and Mrs Priddy opens the cottage door for them. "God bless you and your family," says Mrs Post as she goes out.

Lottie is suddenly overcome with pity for this poor young woman and her brood of children, coping on her own in difficult circumstances. She touches Mrs Priddy lightly on the shoulder. "How do you keep going?" she asks in wonderment. Mrs Priddy smiles. "I believe in God and follow my heart, miss," she says simply.

Lottie is quite overcome. "May the good Lord take care of you, Mrs Priddy, you are a brave soul," is all she can manage to say before she leaves.

And as Lottie goes on to the next cottage with Mrs Post she thinks of her dilemma with Tom and Luke and ponders: that's not a bad philosophy to pursue in life. I already believe in God. But now maybe I should start following my heart.

Chapter 9

DECEMBER

THE RECTORY
4th December 1914

Dearest Bella,

Hope you enjoyed your brief visit down here to see Ronnie. It was lovely to see him again, although I agree with you he did look rather tired and strained. His talk to the Scouts was particularly poignant, I thought. All those young faces looking up at him, so eager and respectful, and Ronnie looked so smart as always in his dark green uniform of the Royal Somerset Rifles. I thought that, knowing his true feelings, he was very restrained in his criticism of the top echelon of the military and current tactics deployed. No doubt he didn't want to destroy the boys' unstinting patriotism. Let us pray to God that this terrible war ends soon and that these young boys don't eventually join the ranks of the 'cannon fodder' in Europe, as Luke would put it.

What fun we all had playing croquet! The Manor House lawn has never heard so many shrieks of laughter, I'm sure. And thanks once again for coming with me to see Luke. He is making good progress and is now hobbling round the ward for a short time on crutches, so Tom and I are hopeful he will be home for Christmas, if not before.

Luke has heard now about his medal ceremony (what an honour!) and it will be held in Taunton on Friday, 21st December. Is there any chance you could join us, if not for the ceremony then at 'Three Chimneys' for a special dinner we are putting on afterwards in honour of the occasion? The ceremony is at 2.30 p.m. at the Army base of the West Country Fusiliers and after a little tea and social gathering we can return to Tethercombe for dinner at about 6.30 p.m. or soon after. Do hope you can come, as it wouldn't seem the same without you. Also, confidentially, Bella, it might keep the peace between Tom and Luke, as they are already bickering when they start discussing proposed improvements around the farm, etc. They are like chalk and cheese. I find it difficult at times knowing whose side to take, so a bit of moral support from you would be wonderful!

Am assuming you will be coming home for Christmas? Father is expecting it I know. Mrs May is up to her elbows (literally) in the Christmas baking, so there will be plenty of goodies to eat. Why not come on the 21st and stay over for Christmas? You need a decent holiday, as you are working so hard. Do hope so, as father has already said he expects me to remain at home on Christmas Day and not spend it with Tom, so I hope that there will be at least three of us at the festive table, if not four, as indeed father has said he may yet invite Aunt Hilda. I told him to be quick, as I have a feeling she leads quite a busy social life up there on the quiet, am I correct?

And of course Father may decide to invite some 'stray lambs' to join our flock – do you remember one year he asked old Miss Featherstone along and she promptly went to sleep after two glasses of sherry?!

Anyway, think about it and let me know, but do hope you can come on the 21st. Don't work too hard.

With best love from

Your loving sister,

Lottie

SECRET DIARY

22nd December 1914

8.00 a.m. What a day we had yesterday! I was too exhausted and upset to write my Diary last night so am doing so now, before I embark on typing Father's Christmas Day sermon. The poor dear is getting all of a dither as his Big Day approaches, so am doing my best to try and support him.

Luke's ceremony at the military base went very well – the Army conducts these occasions with such precision and finesse. There were several men being presented with medals by the Brigadier, including five D.C.M.s and a special posthumous bravery award which was given to a young widow, on behalf of her late sergeant husband. Very moving, as she stood there so brave and dignified, with her young son. And Luke looked so smart in his uniform. He was using a stick to help him walk, but did very well.

It was a cold, raw day and as we drove home in Tom's motor it started snowing! I was warmly clad, with my hat securely fastened with a warm scarf and a tartan blanket across my knees, but Tom was driving very slowly due to the atrocious slippery conditions and we were all frozen to the bone by the end of the journey.

Darkness had now fallen and we were glad to reach Tethercombe and see the lights of 'Three Chimneys'. I was relieved to see that Bella had arrived from London safely in Rupert's car. She is such a brick to drive all that way in this weather. It was so cold the frost was already forming on the windows making patterns, as we entered the house.

A roaring log fire greeted us in the sitting room and we gathered round it gratefully to warm ourselves, as we sipped sherry before dinner. Benny gave us an enthusiastic welcome and then happily settled himself down in front of the hearth, making snuffling noises. The new green velvet curtains looked very smart and the Christmas tree (decorated by me the previous day) added a festive touch, also a big bough of holly by the window, bright with berries.

Bella hugged us all and asked after Luke's health, then casually mentioned she'd had a minor accident at Salisbury on the way down. She'd apparently put the car in a ditch when another car had overtaken her too closely. But, with the luck that only Bella seems to receive, she'd then been helped by an army truck full of soldiers who stopped and with many shouts of laughter had physically lifted the car out of the ditch and cranked it up again for her. Although shaken up a little, she went on her way, grateful for the help. Bella then wanted to hear all about the ceremony and see the shiny new medal, now pinned proudly on Luke's smart brown jacket. She asked him to say a few words.

Luke was I felt very modest in his little speech, saying he thought he had been chosen to represent those soldiers who had paid the ultimate sacrifice or whose service had gone unrecognised. He didn't mention at all the act of bravery at Ypres for which it was awarded. He was glad to see his pals again today and felt very honoured, he said, though I knew he was deliberately underplaying it so that Tom wouldn't feel he had been deprived by not enlisting.

But Luke was in top form and as he relaxed with a drink began flirting with Bella, asking after Flopsy and Boo-boo and her other friends and their activities. Bella was looking stunning as usual in emerald green and her eyes were shining as she responded readily to Luke's chatter. It was good to see Luke back to his old self, but was that a twinge of jealousy I felt at this? Maybe, for witty banter was as scarce as hen's teeth between Tom and I.

I had changed into my new red velvet dress with the lace collar (bought with Aunt Hilda's Christmas money) and also I was wearing again the beautiful string of pearls Tom had given me for my birthday. Tom never gives me any compliments, so it was very special to me when Luke held me at arm's length and declared: "Lottie, you look scrumptious, good enough to eat!" He then stole a quick kiss under the mistletoe from me as the custom permits, while Tom was busy stoking the fire.

Mrs Bryant served a delicious roast pork dinner on their finest Wedgwood bone china dinner service – the table looked magnificent, set with silver candelabra and crystal wine glasses and a fine Honiton lace table-cloth. I had arranged a centrepiece of hazel-nut catkins and trailing ivy in a crystal bowl, which looked delicately lovely in the soft candle-light from four tall white candles. I was delighted by the dessert – Charlotte Russe, served with peaches – which Tom had suggested, much to my surprise, as a thank you to me for helping him with all the refurbishment of the house and it was declared delicious.

However, I learned later from Luke that it wasn't Tom's idea at all, but Mrs Bryant's, but Tom had been quick to take the credit for it.

Bella had brought along some special French burgundy wine for the occasion and we were all feeling nicely mellow, although Tom had been on the whisky all evening, to warm himself up, he said, which worried me somewhat.

He had been annoying me since we returned with several cutting remarks and caustic comments directed towards Luke, but I didn't want to cause any trouble so said nothing. Mrs Bryant had served the coffee and departed for the night. Luke was pouring the port for us all when Tom stood up rather unsteadily and raised his glass:

"I'd like to propose a toast — to my brother, the hero!" he said in a sarcastic tone. "Thinks he's the big hero, anyway, sitting there in his smart uniform. Got himself some Blighty wounds, oh yes." Luke gave an incredulous gasp at this untruth. Then Tom continued: "Comes back here with his medal and his limp. Gets all the girls round him that way..."

I thought he was joking at first but then I could see he was perfectly serious and I glanced at Bella, horrified. "What are you saying, Tom? Don't spoil the evening..." I pleaded. Bella glared at him and shook her head. "It's the demon drink talking..." she said.

"Weren't in it for long, though, were you?" Tom carried on. Bella and I both simultaneously gasped at such an insensitive remark.

"...longer than you," Luke countered, obviously angered by his sneering comments.

Tom jabbed his finger at Luke. "That's it, mock a sick man, put your spoke in. Well, someone has to keep the home fires burning. You deserted me pretty quick to cover yourself in glory, didn't you? But as it happens I've done quite well for myself without you..." he waved his hand around the room indicating the new furniture and furnishings.

Luke stayed perfectly calm and blew a smoke ring from his cigar. "...not through any effort on your part, I would remind you, brother," he said icily.

At this Bella rose from the table, her face immobile. "If this is going to develop into a family row, I think we should leave now, Lottie..."

But I could bear it no longer and stayed in my seat. I turned to face Tom. "I think your behaviour is quite despicable, Tom. Luke has fought bravely in the war and was awarded a medal for it. You should be proud of him. Why, I do believe you're just jealous – you took your time telling me about it, didn't you?"

I stood up, really angry now, my hands trembling against the table and continued: "Well, I should like you to know that I am proud of your brother, even if you're not, Tom Trevithick and you'd better change your attitude or – or I just might want to change my mind about... certain things..."

With that I ran from the room, sobbing, and Bella followed me. We collected our capes from the hall-stand and left hurriedly, just murmuring our apologies and thanks to a solicitous Luke on the way out. We could hear the brothers raising their voices in anger as we hurried to the car.

I felt really upset by the row but glad I had supported Luke against Tom. It's about time I started saying what I feel. These days I seem to agree with Luke more than Tom, which is rather disturbing and only increases those nagging doubts. I have tried to push them from my mind, but they keep returning, now Luke is back.

THE RECTORY
28th December 1914

Dear Amy,

Just a few lines, hoping you arrived home safely yesterday. I was quite worried about you as I saw the bus disappearing down the snow-covered road into the swirling mist. The weather conditions were so bad here that I dreaded to think what they were like in hilly Porlock. It looks as if it is setting in for a few weeks now, unfortunately. It was very good of you to come to us for Christmas at such short notice, but do hope your parents are now recovered from their indisposition. I was glad Tom and Luke were able to join us for drinks after Matins, not to mention our impromptu snow-ball fight on the way back from church!

Father doesn't go in for a lot of fancy decorations in the house at Christmas time, but the tiny tree looked quite sweet in the window, I thought, with our tinsel 'icicles' and silver bells and the star on the top.

I really enjoyed your company and it was exciting to see the Dulverton Hunt go off on Boxing Day in their red jackets, with the hounds and the hunting horn, wasn't it? I loved your fur hat and mittens and your stylish new boots.

It was so disappointing that Bella was called back to London unexpectedly on Christmas Eve. I haven't yet heard from her, but imagine it must have been some very urgent work she was required to do. This does happen from time to time. I was glad Matilda Rowntree was able to join us for Christmas dinner. She is quite a character and surprisingly good company once you get to know her, don't you think? But she certainly doesn't suffer fools gladly. She keeps them all in order at the Soup Kitchen.

I hope you understood why father was a bit quiet and grumpy. He is, of course, so busy at Christmas-time and he was particularly disappointed that Bella couldn't stay over the festive period. He had been so looking forward to seeing her. He wasn't very happy about the church attendance over the Christmas period either, but he has to accept that people find it difficult to 'turn out' in these dreadful weather conditions, some of them coming in from out-lying hamlets under deep snow.

Anyway, I enjoyed the Carol Service on Christmas Eve and hope you did too. All the stalwarts were there, thank goodness. And I was glad to see Sophie Speedwell (the pretty young war widow I pointed out to you) there with her parents and her sister. I heard from Mrs May that she is back at her job at the baker's as a pastry-cook now which is a good thing and also I've seen her at our Prayer Meetings occasionally. Sophie was apparently heartened recently as she heard from a corporal in Jimmy's regiment that Jimmy had been sharing a joke with the lads when he was killed by a sniper, so at least he went with a smile on his face. This gave her some comfort. The Misses Tiptree (who live near her parents where Sophie is living, now she has left her lodgings) seem to have taken her under their wing. As neighbours the twin sisters saw her grow up and remember seeing her as a radiant bride at the hastily arranged wedding back in August, before Jimmy went to the

Front. And now they are doing all they can to help her recover from her sad loss, popping in with home-made cakes and little things they have made. Dora and Ida are very sweet old ladies, so caring. Everyone in the village is standing behind those who have lost someone at the Front, looking out for them in these sad and needy times. Neighbours give vegetables from their allotments or a pot of stew to poor families. The war is fostering a very good community spirit.

The choir was in good voice, too, wasn't it? leading the congregation in all the familiar carols – singing 'In the Bleak Mid-Winter' seemed particularly appropriate, didn't it?! It was so stirring to see the servicemen in uniform looking so smart as they took the collection. And very poignant and sad to hear father read out the names of the local soldiers who have fallen at the Front in recent weeks, before he said the Blessing. The muffled bells were tolling sombrely overhead as he spoke.

The news of the dreadful incident up north before Christmas, when German warships gunned Scarborough and Whitby causing many fatalities has shocked us all. We are all praying fervently that this terrible war will soon be over.

Thanks so much once again for the lovely Christmas gift. The scarf and gloves you knitted are just what I need in this weather and I love the colour red in the winter.

So sorry to hear the news about Richard being injured and do hope he will be brought home soon, so that you can visit him. This dreadful war seems to drag on and on with no end in sight. It is a real test of faith for us all. I shall have to leave my ride over the moors until the weather has cleared now, but one thing spring will soon be on the way, once we get into the New Year.

I will close now and wish you a very Happy New Year, dear Amy, and hope the news is good of Richard and that Bertie is faring well too.

With much love from

Your affectionate friend,

Lottie

***

"Behind you, behind you!" All the children in the audience scream and shout as the Fairy Godmother and Buttons chat on stage. And Lottie, Polly and Clara all join in the laughter as the Ugly Sisters are chased off the stage to much applause.

Polly and Clara had appeared yesterday at The Rectory with tickets for the pantomime 'Cinderella' now performing at the Empire Theatre, Taunton. Local authorities had decided to keep theatres open for the moment, to keep up morale and it was proving a popular move. Clara is taking her small niece, Rose, for a Christmas treat and Lottie had eagerly accepted the invitation.

The matinee show has been terrific fun and they have all enjoyed it immensely, passing a box of chocolates along the line between them now and then. The music is cheerful and the bright costumes are wonderful to see. And the young lady playing Cinders is just so pretty and has a lovely soprano singing voice.

The girls had muffled themselves up for the car journey as the weather was bitterly cold with snow still on the ground. But Clara had whisked them through the frosty country lanes in no time at all, while chattering on about the latest Charlie Chaplin film she had just seen at the flicks.

And they were soon gathering in the warm brightly-lit foyer of the theatre. Elegant palms in brass pots decorate the plush velvet draped entrance hall which is thronged with families enjoying the outing. There is a distinct lack of young men, Lottie notices, although there are a few servicemen smartly dressed in uniform relaxing on their leave. Rose, Clara's 6-year-old niece has been jumping up and down with excitement as they file in to take their seats in the stalls.

Lottie had only once before been to a pantomime years ago when as a child Aunt Hilda had taken her and Bella as a Christmas treat. Father doesn't really approve of stage shows and theatricals and Lottie's memory is pretty hazy. But she does remember she had thoroughly enjoyed it, the two sisters laughing fit to bust at the antics on stage and full of wonderment at the whole colourful spectacle before them.

The ballroom scene with the golden coach bringing Cinderella to the ball is magnificent with Prince Charming (played by a young woman) dancing the night away with her, despite the Ugly Sisters vying unsuccessfully for his attention.

And as the clock strikes midnight the golden coach turns into a pumpkin in a puff of smoke. "How did they do that? Where's the coach gone?" cries Rose in bewilderment and poor Cinders runs off, leaving behind her glass slipper and her lovely ball gown turns to rags.

The pantomime comes to its happy conclusion with Prince Charming fitting the slipper onto Cinderella's dainty foot and all the cast appear for a triumphant finale on stage.

The girls leave the auditorium happy and exhilarated and Rose clutches Clara's hand while skipping along happily beside the girls. In the foyer they all button up their coats, don their hats and gloves and wind their scarves tightly round their necks, before emerging into the frosty evening air.

Lottie walks along beside Polly stepping out briskly chatting happily about the show, discussing the costumes and the ballroom scene. The street is crowded with families leaving the theatre and making their way towards buses and cars parked nearby. There is a rush to board a crowded tram.

The traffic begins to pile up behind the tram in the narrow street and Lottie suddenly realises she recognises a car – it's Tom's Tin Lizzie passing slowly nearby. And then she sees Luke is driving it and notices he has a lady passenger beside him, chatting away. And yes, now she recognises the young lady – it's Victoria, her chum from the beach outing. Well, what a surprise! The car goes slowly ahead of them, before Lottie can point out Victoria to Polly, but she tells her, nonetheless. Lottie didn't realise that Victoria even knew Luke – she is frankly amazed. Polly, however, is not too surprised, as of course she doesn't know Luke. "Oh, Victoria seems quite popular with the young gentlemen," she says airily, "she goes out with quite a few different people…"

Lottie stares ahead as Luke's vehicle is swallowed up in the busy traffic and they walk towards the side street where Clara's car is parked.

Yes, she's had a lovely outing, she has really enjoyed the show, but seeing Victoria so unexpectedly with Luke has sent a jealous pang through her heart. And once she arrives home and climbs into bed, Lottie has to admit that she can feel the green eye nagging at her, when she recalls Victoria talking to Luke so animatedly and gazing up at him with a rapturous smile.

Chapter 10
JANUARY

SECRET DIARY

10th January 1915

Have just had an unexpected encounter with Luke and so must record the details. I was tired of being cooped up in the house during the bad weather. Several of my usual activities had been cancelled due to the dreadful conditions, Tom was away looking at investment properties in Devon, (just as well as we were barely on speaking terms after the row at dinner). So I was itching to get some exercise. The snow had now cleared, the thaw was definitely setting in, so after lunch I decided on the spur of the moment to saddle up my chestnut mare Bessie and go for a brisk ride on the moors.

Father doesn't like me riding on the moors, particularly in winter as there are known to be treacherous bogs here and there. But I skirt the hills and stick to the well-used tracks, so feel I am perfectly safe and love the freedom of the moorland. When I set out from home the sky was clearing and some weak rays of sunshine were endeavouring to penetrate the leaden clouds. I did think of taking my sketch book with me to capture the trees and wild ponies on the moor, but once I felt the raw wind against my cheek decided against. The trees have such a stark beauty in winter I would love to make some sketches of them.

I had a good gallop as far as Tor Point, admiring the purple heather which was giving a splash of colour in the January gloom, then to my dismay I saw a mist beginning to form ahead on Dunkery Beacon, so thought I should turn back. I had enjoyed the ride and the fresh wind had whipped colour into my cheeks. I felt like Lorna Doone riding over the moors for an assignation with John Ridd! There is such a wild beauty on Exmoor it refreshes one's soul, hearing the call of the curlews, seeing the rushing streams, the ferny gullies, and catching sight of a hare or some red deer occasionally. After a couple of weeks inside the house, I felt invigorated and refreshed.

I was well wrapped up against the cold in a thick tweed riding cape, my long brown woollen skirt and had my riding hat tied on with my new red scarf, plus thick gloves, of course. So I was well protected.

As I criss-crossed the granite boulders on the moor I suddenly spotted a familiar black stallion tethered to a tree ahead of me. Rufus. My heart missed a beat. And, yes, there was Luke beside him, his tall figure muffled up in a capacious mackintosh cape and husky sweater. I suddenly found it hard to breathe and my heart was beating erratically. He seemed to be scanning the moors, looking around, holding his hand up to his forehead.

He looked round as I approached and gave a wave. "Why, it's the beautiful Miss Carr!" He gave a mock bow. "Didn't expect to see you out this way to-day. Happy New Year to you!"

I grinned down at him, then slid down onto the bracken. "Thank you, and to you! I just had to get out of the house. I've been stuck inside for two weeks due to the bad weather." Our two horses, Bessie and Rufus, were now nuzzling each other in a friendly fashion, their breath white in the cold air. "What's happening, what are you doing out here?" I asked curiously.

"One of our ponies escaped from the paddock – I went after her – kept her in sight for a while, now she's gone…" he shrugged, "I expect she'll come back."

"And did you have much damage from the storm the other day?" I queried. There had been a big blizzard the previous week, with torrential sleety rain and high winds, causing many trees to come down and branches torn off.

Luke was about to reply when the sound of a stray bleating sheep nearby made him turn his head sharply. For a moment he seemed distracted and stood transfixed, then recovered himself. "What is it?" I asked, for I could see something had unsettled him.

"Oh, nothing," he replied, avoiding my eyes. But when I pressed him he explained to me that when he was in France all those months ago, he had seen a regiment of new French recruits passing their superior

officers, as they marched through the village. Luke looked at me strangely. "They were all bleating like sheep to indicate they were going like lambs to the slaughter. I will never forget it. It's haunted me ever since. And we all knew we were next in line. So, every time I hear sheep now it turns my stomach… But," he gave a resigned sigh, "I have to live with it, I'm a farmer!"

I touched his arm and shook my head sympathetically. "Luke, how dreadful!" I murmured, but I was thinking: what an unnerving experience for him. I could empathise with him completely about this, remembering how I still felt about the muffled church bell tolling at mother's funeral, two years after her death.

But I was amazed at the change in him. Was this the conceited, womanising young boor I had known six months ago? He had now developed into a mature and sensitive grown man, irrevocably changed by the events at the Front.

But then Luke noticed me shivering and pulling my cape around me. "You'll get chilled to the marrow standing here – it's so high here, and the mists can come down very suddenly." He rubbed his hands and gave a sudden grin. "How about we go back to the farmhouse for a cup of tea to warm ourselves up? The old chap is away at the moment, as you know, but Mrs Bryant is there today, so never fear, you'll have a chaperone." I readily agreed, I was frozen and it seemed quite an adventure for me to go back to 'Three Chimneys' with Luke when I knew Tom was away, though I suspected father wouldn't approve.

We re-mounted (Luke had some initial difficulty, with his injured leg still heavily strapped) and set out together, our horses trotting along the springy turf, picking their way skilfully up the steep slopes in between the boulders scattered around the moor. By the time we reached the ancient clapper bridge at Tarr Steps, we saw the river was already running pretty high, skimming the stones as we rode our horses through the ford. A thick mist descended quickly, swirling around us and blotting out the surrounding landscape completely, until visibility was restricted to a few feet.

Luke came alongside me on Rufus and put his hand on my shoulder. I narrowed my eyes against the driving rain, peering out from the scarf shielding my face. The rain was being whipped around almost horizontally now and the wind was whistling through the bare trees at a frightening pace. "I'll lead the way," he shouted above the noise of the wind and the rain. "I know somewhere we can shelter near here."

I followed Luke's stallion as he made his way down a sodden, muddy track, passing a group of wild ponies huddling together under a tree sheltering from the storm. Then I suddenly saw the dark shape of an old building loom up out of the mist. We tethered our horses to the tree and Luke pushed open the door. We both stepped thankfully out of the storm into the hut.

It was a dilapidated old shepherd's hut which had been empty for years, and now used to store supplies of fencing timbers and wire. It was dank and musty, the roof was leaking at one end, with rain water dripping down the wall. But it was somewhere to shelter.

We peeled off our soaking wet clothes and stood looking at each other, the rain still dripping from our hair and noses. Luke's hair had now grown back to its normal length and was plastered flat to his head like a monk. I removed my sopping wet scarf and my riding hat, then shook my hair now formed into tight wet golden ringlets. I had to say it. "You do look funny, Luke!"

"Oh, thanks," he replied in mock anger, "is that all the thanks I get for rescuing you from the storm?" We both laughed at the sight of each other.

"What a wild storm!" I said and took off my shawl and began rubbing my hair with it. "Here, let me dry yours too, or you'll catch your death of cold." I faced Luke and began rubbing his wet hair vigorously with my woollen shawl. "Your hair has grown back well," I remarked. "M-m, the shawl is still warm from your body," Luke murmured in a low voice.

We were very close, when he suddenly put his hands on my shoulders and kissed me full on the lips. "Lottie, oh, Lottie! Your eyes are sparkling like violets after rain..." His words were stirring my soul, but I had to be strong, so pulled away from him, blushing profusely, taken by surprise. He just smiled at me and kissed the end of my nose. "Forgive me, couldn't resist that" – he gestured helplessly – "that's a 'thank you' for defending me the other night at dinner, when the old chap was being so rude about my war service."

I nodded. "How are things between you and Tom now?"

Luke gave a hollow laugh. "Not the best. We row all the time, mainly about money. Now the question of my inheritance has come up..."

I was puzzled. "Oh...?" I knew Luke was turning 25 in May.

"I was a child of 10, you see, when my parents died. And so Tom inherited the farm and assets as the eldest son, despite only being my father's step-son. They specified in the will I was to receive my share when I was 25. But they didn't exactly spell out what percentage, it was left to Tom's discretion, unfortunately. It should have been put in Trust for me or something."

"And now he's being difficult about it?"

Luke nodded and gave a wry smile. "My brother is not exactly known for his generosity. He thinks he can get away with giving me a small lump sum, a rise in wages and some shares in an Australian gold mine... now defunct."

I gasped. "But there must be some legal recourse you can take...?"

"M-m, I'm just doing that at the moment. My pal, George, at Porlock has a brother who's a barrister in London. I'm going up to see him soon to see if I have a case for claiming my true share."

I was really troubled by this news. No wonder the two brothers were at loggerheads with each other! I suspected Tom was a bit parsimonious, but did expect him to do the right thing by his brother over such an important thing as his inheritance, especially as he had recently received a further legacy from his uncle. I shook my head. "Fancy Tom treating you so badly. I'm so sorry." But then I smiled up at him. "Well, I wish you the best of luck, Luke. But it must make life difficult living together there at Three Chimneys."

Luke agreed. "It's going to come to a head soon, I can feel it. Anyway, my pal, George, has said I can go over there, if things get too *desperate."* There was a brief silence between us and Luke put a match to some kindling in the wood stove. *"Let's see if we can warm this place up."*

I began to think now would be a good time to ask Luke about the childhood incident long ago – put the record straight, as it were. I gave a nervous laugh. *"You'll think me funny, Luke, but can you tell me something. That incident at the party all those years ago. What was it all about? Why were you so rude to Bella and I that day? I know you were only a child but, well, it seemed so – uncalled for, so out of character, now I know you well."*

Luke gave me a quizzical look. *"Hey, that's going back a long way. Hang on, I was only 10 at the time! You don't still bear me a grudge about it, do you?"*

I met his gaze and shrugged. *"All I know is what Bella told me. I only have vague memories of it – I was only 4 at the time! I just remember dressing up in our party frocks, bows in our hair and being taken to The Grange for Lucy Pemberton's 10th birthday party, playing games, having a lovely tea and so on. And then a shouting match broke out between you and Bella. And she was yelling: 'That's horrid and cruel, you're a nasty boy, Luke Trevithick. Come on, Lottie, we're going home.'* Lottie shook her head at the memory. *"Bella was only 8, but naturally she objected to anyone calling her mother a cripple and her father a dimwit."*

Luke shifted uncomfortably and dropped his eyes, but I continued. *"She thanked Lady Pemberton politely and apologised for leaving, grabbed my hand and we ran home. When I asked her what was happening, Bella said our family had been insulted and we had to leave. I didn't even know what it meant. We never told mother and father the full story, we didn't want to hurt them. Bella came up with some tale about me falling over, even though there was no graze and I wasn't crying."* I laughed and shook my head. *"Lies fell off Bella's lips like drips from a honey-pot in those days. She was very inventive."* I put my head on one side reflectively. *"I think we were particularly upset because father always taught us to be kind to people, whatever we thought of them, particularly if they had afflictions. Mother went to see Lady Pemberton the next day to apologise for our behaviour and try to find out what had caused it, but Lady P could shed no light on it – she hadn't heard what was said – and it was dismissed as a childish argument.'*

Luke leaned against the table, arms across his chest, an enigmatic look in his eyes. "I was very mixed up, Lottie, at the time. Bella was right, I was a nasty child. But you have to remember my parents had just died within 3 months of each other, a big shock. Tom was doing his best to look after me, but he was a young man of 20, trying to run the farm, go out with his pals and was walking out with a few girls then. He didn't want to act as nursemaid, as you can imagine. So I was left with Mrs Bryant a lot of the time and any other female they could find. I got in bad company at school. Consequently I became a bit aggressive and resentful. I think I took it out on anyone who seemed to come from a stable happy family. Quite simply, I was jealous."

Luke held up his hands. "Well, Lottie, for what it's worth, I apologise now for my bad behaviour, 15 years after the event. I'm sorry it caused you and Bella so much distress." He shook his head. "And it's ironic I should call your mother that offensive name, because," Luke touched his leg, "now who's the cripple? I've got my just deserts, you could say."

I winced and patted his hand. "No, no, but apology accepted. I understand now. It must have been such a terrible time for you, to lose both your parents suddenly at that young age, shocking. I don't think we knew about it until much later on. Father was away. I don't think he conducted the funeral services. Our paths didn't cross, did they?"

"Until now." Luke came forward as if to hold me. So to distract him (and myself!) I decided to change the subject. I had suddenly remembered seeing Luke in Taunton after the theatre with Victoria in Tom's car and thought I would ask him about it.

"Anyway, changing the subject, are you still seeing Victoria Mansfield?" I asked, somewhat awkwardly.

Luke raised a quizzical eyebrow. "Seeing her? I'm not exactly seeing her, but why...?"

I shrugged, feeling rather embarrassed to have mentioned it. "I happened to see you with her in Tom's car in Taunton last week when I went to the theatre, that's all, I didn't realise you knew her. I was at school with her, nice girl..."

Luke gave a guffaw as if seeing the light. "Oh, I see! Now, don't get the wrong idea there, Lottie. I'm not 'walking out' with Victoria, she happens to be a relative of Mrs Bryant, our housekeeper and I offered to teach her to drive, that's all..."

"...but you were driving," I insisted.

"Correct." Luke gave me an old-fashioned look and continued patiently. "If you must know, Miss Carr, I was giving her a driving lesson, she lives near Taunton as you probably know, then we realised we'd somehow wandered into the centre of Taunton and the traffic was getting a bit busy, so I took over when Victoria got a bit flustered – that's what happened. Happy now?" he teased.

I suddenly felt instantly relieved and could have shouted out loud with joy. Instead I had to restrain myself and merely reply: "Oh, I see! Oh well, good for you. Sorry, I didn't mean to pry." I felt contrite at once, but was glad I knew what the situation really was.

He turned away and limped into the small scullery at the back of the cottage. "Now, let's see if I can make us a warm drink. We keep a few things here just for emergencies like this. These Exmoor mists are notorious." A small fire was now flickering in the stove, and Luke opened a tin of milk and poured it into a battered old saucepan. I fetched a couple of tin mugs I saw in the cupboard. "This should warm us up," he said smiling.

But I was still feeling so cold and began to rub my hands and arms together to keep warm. Only wearing a light woollen jumper, I then began to shiver involuntarily, my teeth chattering. Luke came and sat next to me on the bench. "You're frozen, Lottie. Let me warm you up by the fire". And he put his arms around me, hugging me to him.

But I felt it was not seemly and pulled away. "No, Luke, it's not right."

At this Luke laughed aloud at me. "Not right for me to warm you up when you're feeling cold? Don't be so silly, Lottie. You don't want to catch pneumonia now, do you?"

I was very torn. I wanted to be warmed up, of course, but it didn't seem proper to me for Luke to hold me like this. And, if truth be known, I didn't trust myself, now I was alone with him.

I gave a wan smile as we sat in front of the meagre warmth from the fire. "Must admit, I am feeling cold…"

So he massaged my frozen hands and rubbed my arms. He hugged my body to his and we clung together. His lips were temptingly close and his body so warm and vibrant. I began to experience those magic feelings I'd felt before, when we'd danced and again in the hospital. It was as if we were drawn together by an invisible cord. My lips were crying out to respond and kiss him properly, but after a minute or so I moved away decorously, reluctantly forcing myself to resist him. Gradually the circulation was restored in my body and then we did little running steps on the spot together, holding hands and laughing.

I suddenly noticed the milk was coming to the boil and rescued it, stretching across him to do so. As I put the saucepan down Luke caught my hand. "I'm becoming very fond of you, Lottie," he murmured, gazing into my eyes, "you know that, don't you. Thinking about you at the Front was the one thing that kept me going. I care about you, I…"

But in my heart I knew it wasn't right. It wasn't fair to Tom. Whatever the state of my relationship with Tom, I was still wearing his ring. I had to resist him. So I turned and went to the window. "You mustn't say that, Luke, it's not right. I'm engaged to Tom. Look, it seems to have stopped raining now, we must go back soon…"

Luke gave a deep sigh and slopped the milk as he poured it into the tin mugs. "Oh, Lottie, Tom doesn't deserve such loyalty. I hope you know what you're doing."

Once I got home and thought about it, I wasn't sure that I did. And the memory of that unexpected kiss and those magic feelings remained with me as I drifted off to sleep.

Private

THE RECTORY
18th January 1915

Dear Amy,

I am writing to ask you a big favour. We have known each other all our lives and I hope that you trust me. So I hope you will accept what I have to say in good faith. But I will quite understand if you feel you cannot help me, as I know you are a person of high principles.

I am in trouble with my father. He called me into his study last week and said someone (person unknown) had made a complaint about me, although I would call it gossip and am surprised father listened to it. He really lectured me, saying I had to set an example in the community, that my behaviour should be impeccable at all times. I should remember I am engaged. He even quoted the Bible at me – that bit from Isaiah 'we are the clay and Thou art our potter', do you know it? He made me feel most uncomfortable.

He said I had been seen riding on the moors with Luke Trevithick during a storm (on Thurs. 10th Jan. p.m.) and that we had gone into a hut together and stayed there for at least an hour with the door closed.

At this point I acted extremely foolishly. For I panicked and told a lie. I said that yes, I had indeed gone riding on the moors that day, but I had gone to see you at Porlock. Would you vouch for me, dear Amy, should father not believe my story? I am truly sorry to involve you in this sorry tale.

The truth is that yes, I did go riding on the moors and happened to meet Luke T. purely by chance. A storm then blew up and we sheltered in an old hut near Tor Point. But it was a completely innocent encounter and all we did was talk to each other, and Luke made us a milky drink to warm us up and we lit a fire to dry our clothes. Please believe me, this is the truth.

Why on earth I didn't say this in my own defence to father when he questioned me, I don't know. I suppose I felt embarrassed by the accusation and just impulsively said the first thing that came into my head, and having said it, of course I couldn't retract it.

Hope you will understand the difficult position I find myself in, dear Amy. I don't think for one moment father would feel the need to speak to you, as I'm sure he trusts me to tell the truth. But anyway, I thought I should let you know the situation between us. I am truly mortified and so angry with myself for telling an untruth.

I am also very sad that my relationship with my father is now at a very low point.

If you could reply quickly I would appreciate it.

Yours ay,

Lottie

* * *

"Well, thank you for asking me, Matilda. I really enjoyed it. See you next week, bye!"

The car goes off down Church Lane and Lottie hurries up the drive-way, pulling her scarf round her neck tightly against the bitter wind.

She has been to a Mozart concert at the Town Hall in Taunton with her Soup Kitchen chum, Matilda Rowntree.

When Matilda had come round out of the blue and said she had tickets to go with two other friends, Lottie had jumped at the chance. She was desperate to leave the house and see some other people. Relations between herself and father were as frosty as the weather outside, after the recent dressing-down she had received from him.

The concert had been excellent, with older retired musicians from the Exeter Symphony Orchestra performing the Eine Kleine Nachtmusik and a local ladies choir singing some unusual 18th century madrigals after the interval.

But the Town Hall had not been heated adequately on what was a very cold afternoon, a lot of people preferring to sit in their coats. Lottie now feels rather chilled and is glad to see a roaring log fire in the sitting room fireplace. The oil lamp has been lit and is casting a welcoming warm glow over the room. Electric light has now been installed at The Rectory, but the Rector still likes to keep a few oil lamps about the house. Mrs May greets her with a smile and a freshly brewed pot of tea and a plate of home-made scones set on the table by the fire. Pussy Carr stretches and purrs on the rug to greet her and Lottie fondles her tabby coat.

"There we are, Miss Charlotte, a nice cup of tea to warm you up! I'll leave it with you. Was it a good concert?"

Lottie settles down in an armchair and then starts to pour the tea. "It was excellent, thank you, Mrs May, I really enjoyed it. Is father in his study?" she asks.

"Yes, miss. He's got a visitor, that Colonel Carruthers again. I took them some tea there earlier…"

Their conversation is interrupted by a distant knocking noise coming from the back of the house. Mrs May looks a little startled. "Oh, who can that be at this time of day? Excuse me, miss, I'll go and see who it is."

And she goes off down the hall to the kitchen. The Rectory is a typical Victorian house with lots of draughty corridors and ill-fitting sash windows. But Lottie is warm by the fire as she sips her welcome tea and nibbles on a scone.

Mrs May reappears in the doorway, her face shocked and serious. "Can you come, Miss Charlotte? I'm sorry to disturb you when you're having your tea, but she's asking for you…"

Lottie puts her cup down and looks up. "What is it, Mrs May? Who's at the door?"

Mrs May's eyes begin to fill with tears in her homely face. "It's Mrs Priddy, miss. There's been a terrible accident, it's her husband. There's been an explosion in the munitions factory…"

Lottie rises to her feet, instantly alert and shocked. "Oh no, how terrible! How absolutely ghastly, that poor woman!

I'll come and see her at once. Has he been injured, what does she say?"

She hurries down the corridor with Mrs May towards the kitchen. Mrs May bites her lip and lowers her voice. 'Constable Perkins came to tell her the terrible news, miss, cycled round on his bike, he did. She's asking for some money, miss. The authorities want her to go up to Birmingham and see him in hospital, he's been that badly injured. But she's got no money in the house, poor soul. Her husband was due back tomorrow.'

Lottie enters the big warm kitchen, Elsie busy at the sink preparing vegetables, a big kettle on the hob singing away. Mrs Priddy is sitting at the table sipping a cup of tea, staring blankly ahead. She gets shakily to her feet when Lottie appears, her face pale and drawn, her hair awry, a thin shawl pulled round her shoulders.

"I'm that sorry to disturb you, Miss Charlotte..." she begins, but Lottie interrupts her, putting her arm around her bony shoulders.

"Mrs May has told me all about your husband's accident, Mrs Priddy. I am so sorry to hear about this. I want you to sit down and drink your tea," she spoons more sugar into it, "lots of sugar will help and Elsie, give the lady some hot buttered toast and a nice piece of fruit cake to go with it."

She turns to Mrs Priddy again, bending over her solicitously. "I'm going to speak to my father now and he will give you some money for the journey. But," she pauses, puts her head on one side, thinking. "I think the Red Cross should be helping out here and I know just the person who could arrange it.

"I'll telephone Matilda. I'm sure they will take you to Birmingham when they hear the circumstances. I don't like to think of you travelling on your own on public transport, after the shock you've had." She clicks her tongue. "It's quite appalling the factory did not provide a car for you."

Lottie pats Mrs Priddy's shoulder. "I'll go and see father now – oh, what about your children? Is someone looking after them?"

Mrs Priddy nods, a faint smile crossing her face. "My neighbour at No.2 has took them, miss, everyone is being that kind," she shakes her head, "I'm that worried…"

Lottie disappears and reappears after five minutes or so, bustling into the room carrying a small bag and a thick winter coat. "The vicar sends his sympathy to you – he regrets he can't see you just now as he's busy with a visitor, but he is providing you with this money from Church funds and he will of course be praying for you."

Lottie gives Mrs Priddy the small bag and the coat, also some folded bank-notes and small change. "I've packed a bag for you with some essential change of clothes and I want you to have this old coat of mine, it's very warm and you will need it for the journey, it's a very cold day."

"Thank you, miss, I'm that grateful."

"Nonsense, it's nothing, now I'll just go and telephone Miss Rowntree."

Thank goodness for the telephone, Lottie thinks as she hurries down the hall.

She returns after 10 minutes smiling and looking quite relieved. "It's all arranged, I've spoken to Miss Rowntree. The Red Cross are sending someone to pick you up and they will take you to Birmingham by car to see your husband at the hospital. They will arrive in about half an hour."

Mrs Priddy looks amazed and bewildered at all the attention. "All the way to Birmingham in a motor car?" She shakes her head. "That will be just the ticket. Thank you miss for your kindness."

"Now I don't want you to worry about your family," Lottie says to Mrs Priddy, glad to see she has eaten some toast and cake. "I will personally go and tell them what is happening and make sure all is well with the children."

After half an hour a sound of a horn and there is the Red Cross van in the drive-way. Lottie sees Mrs Priddy into it, instructing the driver of the destination. She hugs her and gives her a smile. "I do hope you find your husband's injuries are not too serious. We will all be praying for him in the parish. Come and see me when you get back and let me know.

Best of luck, goodbye!"

And as she watches the Red Cross van disappear down Church Lane, Lottie reflects soberly: "Phew! And I think *I've* got problems!"

Chapter 11

FEBRUARY

THE RECTORY
4th February 1915

Dear Luke,

I need to see you urgently. Will explain when we meet. Please come on Tuesday evening, 10th February, at around 7.00 p.m. as father will be out. Am typing the envelope so that Tom won't be suspicious.

With love,

Lottie

SECRET DIARY

11th February 1915

'Oh, what a tangled web we weave, when we practise to deceive!'

I have to record the events of yesterday, all getting more complicated by the minute.

After I had written my letter to Amy and received one back from her, agreeing to provide me with an alibi, I realised that I needed to explain all these happenings to Luke, to keep him au fait with current events.

I suddenly felt guilty that by denying being with Luke on 10th Jan. I had somehow implicated him in being with someone else in the hut. I didn't quite know how he would take this.

I felt nervous and restless all the afternoon until father went out about six o'clock, to meet someone in Taunton for a business dinner. I tried to settle to do my hassocks, then attempted to do some knitting, but kept jumping up and down going to the window to see if there was any sign of him. The bell-ringers were engaged in their usual Tuesday evening practice, which was driving me mad. They seemed particularly loud and discordant, as they went up and down the scale next door.

I had told Mrs May I didn't want any dinner, as I didn't feel well, so she said she was going to her room and Elsie had gone out earlier. But as the church clock struck seven o'clock, I could still hear Mrs May tidying up in the kitchen which made me very fidgety. However, she eventually trudged up the stairs with her creaking knees and then ten minutes later the doorbell clanged and I rushed to the door, expecting Luke.

Imagine my surprise when I opened the door. There stood Bella and Ronnie! I hadn't seen Bella since Christmas Eve and we had received no word from her and our phone messages to Aunt Hilda had been ignored.

I was totally flummoxed, especially as I could hear a clip-clop in the lane and then could see Luke's horse, Rufus, approaching as I let Bella and Ronnie into the hall.

I felt very flustered, but recovered myself and remembered my manners. I offered Bella and Ronnie a drink and they sat down. Ronnie's gaunt, pale appearance shocked me. He didn't look at all well, had lost weight, his clothes were hanging off him. But they were obviously in high spirits, laughing and joking together. Ronnie bowed and doffed his hat, his fair hair falling over his forehead as usual. And Bella presented me with a huge bunch of early daffodils, as an apology for her being so remiss and not getting in touch with us all recently.

She still didn't say what she'd been doing, but then she gaily flashed her left hand at me, adorned with a sparkling diamond ring, and announced she and Ronnie had just become engaged to be married!

I was just about to give my congratulations, when the doorbell jangled again and of course I knew it was Luke. How was I going to explain what he was doing here, without Tom?

As I hurried to the door, a plan began to form in my mind. And I greeted Luke loudly with "Oh, Luke, thanks so much for coming round. But before you go and look at Bessie (Luke looked slightly bewildered) come and say hallo to Bella and Ronnie. They've just arrived and, guess what, they're engaged to be married!"

Luke took it all in his stride and gave his congratulations to the happy couple, chatted for a bit about the war situation and then said to me, looking at his pocket watch, "Well, can I see this lame mare of yours now, Lottie? I have to be in Dunster by eight o'clock."

Bella looked concerned. "Oh, has poor Bessie gone lame, Lottie?"

"Not sure what's wrong at the moment, she's a bit poorly, stiff in her hind quarters, off her feed," I mumbled.

Luke took charge and hustled me out of the room. "Excuse us, we won't be long…"

"Luke's got a magic touch with horses," I cried trying to smile and appear relaxed, as I grabbed my shawl.

We hurried to the stables and went to Bessie's stall. Luke leaned his tall frame against the stable door and folded his arms across his chest. "Now, young lady, what's this all about? There's nothing wrong with Bessie, I'm sure?" But his eyes were twinkling (at that stage).

My heart was in my mouth as I explained the situation, feeling very embarrassed about it all and when I had finished Luke looked sharply at me, then turned his head away, as if deeply hurt.

"Oh, so I have to pick up the pieces, do I, so that your reputation remains intact?" His voice had a hard, sarcastic edge to it.

I was taken aback by his response and stuttered my apologies once again for my foolishness.

"Why on earth didn't you just tell the truth, you silly girl?" he berated me. "Nothing happened in the hut, you know that full well. You had done nothing to be ashamed of and neither had I." He gave a hollow laugh. "In fact, I needed a medal – I was being so restrained!" He shook his head and started to walk away. "Women! I'll never understand them." He started limping up and down the stable courtyard. "So now I have to invent some mythical woman I was in the hut with, in case I'm asked, is that right?" He cast his eyes up to the dark night sky, frosty bright with stars. "Ye Gods, I don't believe this!! As if I didn't have enough to deal with at the moment as it is." He moved away from me, eyes flashing, obviously very angry.

Then he turned back and gave a parting shot. "Oh, and by the way, I'm not living at 'Three Chimneys' anymore, I've had a big row with Tom and we've parted company. I'm staying at Porlock with George. Not that that will interest you, I'm sure. And," he came up close to me again, "can I give you some advice, Miss Carr, I don't know why you're continuing to be so loyal to Tom, because I have to tell you he's certainly not being loyal to you..." Luke's dark eyes were mocking and intense.

I looked questioningly at him, my heart jolting uncomfortably. "What on earth do you mean?"

"Have a look in his top chest of drawers in his bedroom, at the back," Luke said. "You might find something of interest there. He's got this ladyfriend, if you can call her a lady, across the border in Devon – he's known her for years, his 'bit of rough' I think they call it. He doesn't go there to hold hands, let's put it like that." And he hurried away from me in his awkward gait round the side of the house where Rufus was tethered.

Steadying myself against the stable door, I tried to absorb this shocking information. I shivered in the cold night air and pulled my shawl around me more tightly. I didn't believe it, it wasn't true – Tom wouldn't be unfaithful to me, surely? I couldn't believe he would deceive me in this way. But a seed of doubt had now been cast in my mind and I vowed to investigate Luke's claims next time Tom was out.

Meanwhile, I had other problems to address. My mind was whirling with conflicting emotions. I was in tears now, stung by Luke's reaction, but desperately tried to compose myself before going back in the house to face Bella and Ronnie, ecstatically happy and certainly not expecting me to be in floods of tears because of Bessie being lame.

But I couldn't hide my moist eyes from Bella for long. Once Ronnie had tactfully left, saying he had to see his parents at The Manor House, Bella faced me on the sofa and put her hand on my shoulder. "Come on now, Lottie, what is it? What's the trouble? Is it to do with Luke?" I decided there and then I would only tell her about the moors problem and say nothing at all about the terrible revelations about Tom. That was too private, too new.

When I heard Bella's sympathetic familiar voice and saw her green eyes searching my face, I nodded and crumpled up. Bella was very sharp. She knew Luke hadn't come to look at Bessie.

When I had finished and started weeping again, I ended by saying: "So what should I do, Bella? I'm in such a mess!"

She took my hand and patted it. "Do what you've always done in your life, Lottie. Tell the truth."

"But I..." I began, but she carried on.

"Go back to father. He's not an ogre, he's your dear father who loves you. Tell him you made a big mistake and tell him the truth, what really happened that day. You did nothing wrong." She laughed suddenly. "You didn't, did you, Lottie?" I shook my head and she continued. "And then tell Amy and Luke what you've done."

I sniffed and dabbed at my nose with a handkerchief. "I feel so foolish. I've told lies and involved other people, I feel dreadful about that..." Bella looked at me oddly. "A lot of people tell lies now and then. Sometimes they have to..."

I knew she was referring to herself and her secret war-work. "Where have you been these last six weeks, Bella?" I asked, "Can you tell me?"

She shook her head, but there was a flash of recognition between us as she realised that somehow I knew about her secret work. "Not yet, Lottie, not yet. I'm sworn to secrecy. But I'll tell you one day, promise, when we're old and grey."

I was suddenly fearful for her safety. I had a horrible dread that she had gone to France over Christmas. "But you're not a spy, are you, Bella. You're not doing espionage work..." I was willing her to deny it.

She was silent and refused to meet my eyes. I didn't press her on the subject. I had to respect her decisions. I knew my sister was a strong character and I had to trust her judgement. She would tell me when she wanted to and not before.

Then she got up and began to tidy up the room, collecting the glasses from the side tables. "Let's have a cup of tea, shall we? And a sandwich or something. I'm starving. I never did have any dinner." And nor had I, I suddenly realised and we went to the kitchen to see what we could rustle up.

12th February 1915

Have not been sleeping well after the row with Luke, tossing and turning, going over things in my mind, chastising myself for handling the matter badly. Can't believe I have fallen out with him! It's all due to my own foolish behaviour! Cried myself to sleep last night, all the time praying to God we will resolve it soon. And as for the news about Tom, I can still hardly believe it! But it's there, nagging away at the back of my mind. I hope to investigate it soon, when the opportunity presents itself.

Very sad to report that Mrs Priddy's husband died yesterday. I heard the news from Matilda via the Red Cross and immediately went round to Oak Cottages to convey my sympathy and condolences to poor Mrs Priddy and take some flowers. Her husband had been horribly injured in the explosion, so it was a blessed relief when he died, I believe.

His widow was obviously beside herself with grief and I vowed to keep in touch with this brave woman. And make sure she receives a decent pension or compensation from the armaments factory to provide for herself and those four children. Father says the owners of these munitions factories are making a fortune out of them, so I feel it's the least they can do. Everyone in the village has been completely shocked by the tragedy and Mrs Post is collecting for a fund to help the family.

14th February 1915

Went into Tom's bedroom today and found what I was looking for. It's particularly ironic that today is St. Valentine's Day and Tom has totally forgotten it, but it doesn't really concern me now. I'm past caring about him. I did half wonder whether Luke might send one, but after our recent row, it's most unlikely.

It was very gloomy in there, his parents' heavy mahogany Victorian furniture dominating the room with a hideous red flock wallpaper which he had chosen himself when we were decorating. I felt guilty to be in there snooping about, even though I had a legitimate excuse to be in the house alone. (Tom had asked me to see in some new furniture being delivered, as Mrs Bryant had suddenly developed raging toothache and so was at the dentist and Tom had gone to Taunton to see his solicitor.)

I opened the top drawer of the chest-of-drawers and began to search through the papers and items there. A sheaf of ancient receipts, a few cuff-links, a pair of nail scissors, an old pipe – and then right at the back as Luke had said in a manila envelope, a bank book. It wasn't his usual bank but an unfamiliar one in Dunster. I opened it up and saw figures dating back 10 years or more, regular standing orders, monthly payments being sent to an address in Tiverton, Devon to a Miss Daisy Penhaligon. The balance was in four figures and there were deposits too, every few months, with recent dates. I felt disbelieving at first, looking for another explanation. I knew he had investment properties in Devon, cottages rented out, but this was different – not rent coming in, but payments going out.

I leafed through the bank book scanning the figures and as I did so a small photo fell out from a pocket in the back of the book. I picked it up and stared at it in disbelief. It was a faded snap of a buxom young woman holding a baby and underneath was written in Tom's handwriting 'My Daisy and William, 1903'. I was astounded. He had a child by this woman, this common village woman in her common clothes, standing there so brazenly, her chin raised so insolently! I felt a growing anger rise inside me. Daisy had obviously become pregnant by Tom and he had set her up in a cottage in Devon and was supporting them both. Now I knew why he never wanted me to go with him when he went to Devon and why, perhaps, he was such a penny-pincher. It was suddenly very clear to me.

When I thought of my total loyalty to Tom since our engagement, despite my growing attraction to Luke, I felt furious. And I could understand now how Luke had become so frustrated and had finally decided to tell me when he lost his temper.

I went to the window and looked out, a familiar scene with a girl feeding the chickens and the herdsman bringing the cows in for milking, but in my anger I barely saw them. I felt humiliated and used, but also desperately hurt. Tears sprang to my eyes and rolled down my cheeks. I had genuinely thought that Tom had loved me, loved me for myself. But no, he had obviously decided he needed a respectable wife, particularly when he came into money and who more respectable than a rector's daughter? And to think I had remained with him so loyally, even though at times I found him dull, mean and undemonstrative. I had helped him re-furbish the house, giving my time and advice so freely...

The sound of a noisy engine chugging up Turners Hill suddenly interrupted my thoughts and as the big blue van trundled through the farm gates into the courtyard, I knew I had to leave this room right away.

I hastily put everything back in order tidily and closed the drawer and padded quietly down the stairs. I felt totally betrayed and knew that Tom and I had finally come to the end of the line.

THE RECTORY
15th February 1915

Dear Amy,

My dear faithful friend! Thanks so much for standing by me in my hour of need. You are a real brick! But I am so glad that father didn't after all need to verify my story with you. I know it would have put you in such an embarrassing position, but I want to thank you for promising to provide me with an alibi, anyway.

Well, I am glad to report now that I have at last had a heart-to-heart with father and he now knows the full, true story. Bella happened to come home a few days ago (she is engaged to Ronnie!) and she advised me to tell father the truth, as I seemed to be getting myself in a big muddle and upsetting everyone, including myself!

Father was a real poppet and, although he was initially shocked that I had lied to him, he nevertheless has now accepted my story and said we will speak no more about it. He still refuses to tell me the name of the person who spotted us on the moors, but it is of no consequence to me now. Whoever it was they were indulging in idle gossip.

I am so relieved, as I hate to be 'out of sorts' with my nearest and dearest, including you! You are a dear friend to me, Amy, and I value our friendship more than I can say.

Once the spring weather arrives in a few weeks I will definitely ride over the moors (we are on the telephone now, (Tethercombe 218) if you can get a message to me) and see you at Porlock. Let me know a suitable day and we could walk into Porlock village and have a cup of tea together at the little tea room there. I shall look forward to hearing from you.

With much love from

Your loving friend, Lottie

SECRET DIARY

18th February 1915

Have had a rather chaotic day. I decided to have it out with Tom, even though it goes against my nature, as I'm strictly non-confrontational. But after my discovery in Tom's bedroom, with its startling revelations, I had spent another sleepless night, pacing about in my room. And I knew I had to confront him and break our engagement. I was shocked rigid by the realisation that Tom had been deceiving me all along, that he was a father to a 12-year-old boy and that he was still seeing this woman on a regular basis. I could still hardly believe it. The effrontery of it all astounds me.

I long to remove my ring, but am keeping it on for appearance's sake. So I had asked him to come round this morning, saying I had something important to discuss with him. I was in the kitchen when he arrived earlier than arranged. I was so nervous about it I had decided to help Mrs May make some biscuits to give myself something to do. Mrs May showed him into the back parlour and gave him a cup of tea, while I tried to pull myself together. I put my head round the door, forcing a smile. "I'm just doing something at the moment, won't be long." Tom grunted and I returned to the kitchen.

At that point there was a ring at the front door and after Mrs May had answered it she came back to me, now busy stamping out biscuit rounds.

"There's a group of young girls arrived, Miss Charlotte, asking for you…"

I stared at her. "Asking for me?"

"Yes, miss, something about the G.F.S. and art classes…"

I thought quickly, then clapped my hand to my mouth. Glory be! I suddenly remembered I had organised for them all to come to-day to do some sketching and drawing, as they were off school for half-term. My heart went pit-a-pat. With all the drama of the past few weeks I had completely forgotten all about it! Now I had nothing planned or organised for them and no provisions in, but – thank goodness for the biscuits now baking in the oven! And I was sure Mrs May had a fairly good store cupboard in the larder, despite the war restrictions, as she was so thrifty. She bought cheaper cuts of meat and then cooked them very slowly. Potter grew all our own vegetables in the kitchen garden. Jars of home-made jam and marmalade and bottled fruit were lined up expectantly in the pantry, so she was well-prepared.

Gathering my wits, I took over the situation, asking Mrs May to provide refreshments later on. "Sorry about this, Mrs May – it completely slipped my mind! Have you got enough provisions?" She nodded very calmly, as if a group of six girls turned up every day demanding tea and biscuits. "Show them all into the back dining room, can you please?" I thanked God that father had gone out, as he was not good at dealing with unexpected situations. I hastily removed my apron and washed my floury hands at the sink.

The girls filed in, muffled up in their hats, coats and scarves and began taking them off and piling them up on a chair. The parent disappeared, saying she would call back later. Bracing myself and desperately trying to think whether I had enough art paper and pencils and crayons for them all, I popped in to see them. A meagre coal fire was burning in the hearth and the room felt distinctly chilly. "I shall *have to tell Elsie to bring the oil stove in," I thought. I also suddenly noticed how shabby the upholstery on the furniture was looking, but was sure it wouldn't bother a group of young girls.*

Emma, a slim little waif of 8 or 9, gave me a big enthusiastic smile, so trusting with her big blue eyes and Lily — the only one with a smidgen of talent amongst them — wiped her nose on her cuff and stared at me truculently. The others were all looking around in awe at the lofty formal room with its heavy mahogany furniture and pictures of Jesus and lowing cattle on the wall. They all looked up as I came in, their eyes fixed on me with such hope and expectation. How could I turn them away? "Hallo, girls!" I beamed. "Lovely to see you. Sit yourselves down and I'll be with you soon." The grim thought of my unfaithful fiancé awaiting me in the back parlour gnawed away at me. "I've just got to speak to another visitor I have here to-day — won't be long."

I hurried down the corridor to see him. I would have to put him off or make up something, I thought wildly. There was no way I could speak about our engagement now, not hurriedly like this. I cursed inwardly as I had been mentally preparing myself to speak to Tom.

"Hallo, Tom!" I went over and gave him a perfunctory hug. "Sorry to keep you waiting."

Tom was pacing about and didn't look too happy. "What is it, Lottie? I've got things to do at the farm... I've got my field of mangel-wurzels being lifted to-day..."

I thought quickly and with relief remembered our new project in the village. Yes, I would ask his advice about that! "Um, it's about the war memorial they are proposing to erect on the village green, in honour of the war dead. Father is on the Memorial Committee and has now asked me to canvass opinions of local people, people of note who have lived here a number of years... he wants me to compile a detailed record of local men who have paid the ultimate sacrifice... Do you think that's a good idea?" I smiled brightly at him. Tom looked totally bewildered and stared at me in amazement. "You've brought me here to ask me that?" he said slowly.

"Couldn't it have waited?"

"It's a very important subject," I countered, feeling rather panicky inside, "Father wanted me to ask you, as the head of a respected local family." Flattery might help, I thought desperately. "The spirit of patriotism in the community is still there, but there is mounting disquiet about the heavy price to be paid, as I'm sure you realise." I had to lay it on thick to make it sound plausible, be a bit sanctimonious as befits a rector's daughter, I thought stoutly. "People want some recognition of the sacrifices made."

Tom picked up his cap and rose from the chair. "Yes, yes, of course I realise all that. Yes, naturally, I'm in favour of it, everyone is. Good idea, very commendable. Brave young men and all that, public recognition. Tell the rector I approve of the scheme. Now I'm afraid I have to go, Lottie, things to do. Is that all?" I could see he was completely mystified by my demands on his time and impatient to be off. His mangel-wurzels obviously meant more to him than any war-memorial.

But before Tom left I knew I had to broach the subject of his estranged brother with him again, as I still hadn't been able to see Luke to explain the happier situation with father and apologise, etc. I did want to see him in person to do this, not write a letter. I felt I owed him that as he had naturally seemed so upset about it all. So as casually as I could, when I was seeing Tom to the door, I said: "And Luke, is he living with George Thomson at Porlock now then?"

Tom nodded and grunted tersely. "As far as I know. Leaves me in the lurch. Don't know what's happening, I'm sure..."

I waved him goodbye, gritting my teeth in frustration and fuming inside. Because of this silly mix-up, I'm still engaged to Tom, even though I'm beginning to hate and despise him. And now, I thought wildly, how am I going to occupy my six young G.F.S. girls for two hours?

20th February 1915

The news of Tom's deception and secret lover has been nagging away at me, causing me sleepless nights and worrying days. It has been at the back of my mind that the proof I found in Tom's bedroom was not sufficient. I had to see for myself about this Miss Daisy Penhaligon living in Tiverton. I had to know it was true – but how was I going to do that? I knew no-one in Tiverton and father might be suspicious of me suddenly announcing I was going there. Then, all at once two things happened which presented me with the perfect opportunity. Tom said he was going to Tiverton to inspect an investment property that had come up (a likely story!) and Mrs Witherspoon happened to mention she was going there to see her daughter on Wednesday, the very day that Tom would be there. Would I like to accompany her, Mrs Witherspoon asked? There was an excellent market held there on a Wednesday, she said, and also I could meet her married daughter, Grace again. I had known her years ago in the village. She was expecting a baby in a few months' time and would love to see another young person, I know, said kindly Bertha Witherspoon. She's been confined to the house for a while. I would love to, I said, trying to contain my excitement at the amazingly convenient invitation.

I realised I would have to get away from Mrs Witherspoon at some point to find Daisy's cottage. So, in a moment of inspiration I invented Bessie, an old friend of my mother's that I keep in touch with and who lives there. I had heard she was ill, I lied through my teeth, and I would like to visit her and take her some flowers.

So tomorrow I am going (with father's blessing) in Mrs Witherspoon's horse and trap to see the delights of Tiverton town.

21st February 1915

Armed with a bunch of early daffodils from the Rectory garden, I arrived in Tiverton with Mrs Witherspoon. We were well rugged up, for there was a chill wind blowing. She dropped me off at the busy market, saying she wouldn't accompany me as she wanted to spend time with Grace. She showed me Grace's house near the village green and I said I would join them in about half an hour or so. I had made a note of Daisy's address, 5 Ivy Cottages and it was pointed out to me as fairly near by a stall-holder. I bought a pair of hand-knitted bootees to give to Grace for her layette, also some fudge for father who has a sweet tooth. Fortunately there were a lot of people about and so I wouldn't be too noticeable peering at a cottage. I put a shawl over my head in the style of the cottagers and clutching my flowers in my basket, I made my way down the little lane where a modest row of neat cottages stood, with postage-stamp gardens in the front. No.5 Ivy Cottages looked well-painted and tidily presented, but after a quick glance I hurried by to the corner of the street. And yes, it was indeed no surprise to me on reaching the end of the road to see Tom's car parked round the corner, proof indeed of his guilty presence. Even so, my heart turned over at the sight of it.

I waited a while under a tree watching the cottage at No.5, but then realised that by walking a little further on down the side street, I could see into the back gardens of the cottages. And yes, as I craned my neck I could actually see my fiancé Tom doing some digging in a vegetable patch in the garden. Oh! My heart missed a beat and a wave of anger swept through me. So this is how he spends his time 'looking at investment properties'!

The back door of No.5 then opened and a plump, well-built young woman came bustling up the path carrying what looked like a hot beverage in a mug. I recognised her at once from the photograph. Tom straightened up and took the mug from her, giving her a kiss on the cheek. Daisy smiled broadly and brushed Tom's jacket at the shoulders. It was a familiar gesture, made to someone who was obviously dear to her. She then turned and made some joking remark – I couldn't hear what exactly – and Tom then smacked her on her broad behind with a laugh. Oh! I shook my head. That was the last straw! I had seen enough. I decided it was time to join Mrs Witherspoon and Grace. Dumping the flowers in a nearby hedge, I pulled the shawl over my head and hurried back to the village green. Now I really did have proof of Tom's deception and infidelity. I was so shocked and angry, I thought about throwing my engagement ring in the hedge with the flowers, but decided I had to keep it on for appearance's sake, for now at least. I was fuming inside. To see my fiancé disporting himself with another woman in such a ribald fashion was more than I could bear. A humiliating scene, but one that was just another nail in the coffin of our engagement.

After a pleasant hour or so with Mrs Witherspoon and her daughter we returned to Tethercombe. I felt grimly satisfied that I had accomplished my objective. Now I just have to break it off with Tom, not an easy task, as I am finding. Being abandoned by Luke has really upset me. I feel utterly frustrated and depressed by the whole situation. I don't seem to have a friend in the whole world at the moment. And horrors! as I went to bed and peered at myself in the mirror creaming my face, I could see a nasty spot developing on my chin - aarghh! That's all I want!

25th February 1915

Porlock was a long ride across the moors. But I decided that to-day was the day for it. I had to make it up with Luke. When the morning dawned cold, but bright and clear with no rain or threat of snow, I donned my warmest riding clothes and saddled up Bessie. I knew most of the sheep farmers were lambing at the moment, so felt sure that Luke would be there, giving a hand.

As a small peace-offering for him, I had drawn a charcoal sketch of wild ponies on Exmoor, in their shaggy winter coats, sheltering beneath some stark, wind-blown trees. Maybe it would remind him of our ride on the moors together, a happier memory of a day now somewhat tarnished by gossip.

It took me nearly forty minutes to reach Dunkery Beacon and then to my dismay I saw the hills ahead on the Porlock ridge were shrouded in mist and low cloud and the rain began to fall. The gorse bushes were soon sparkling like yellow diamonds, as I galloped towards my love – for that is what he was, I knew now. I had to put things right between us. Despite the rain I was determined to carry on. I'd come this far.

The Thomson's farm was this side of Porlock on the edge of the moors and I reckoned I could make it within twenty minutes. My cape and skirt were rapidly becoming soaked through with the persistent drizzling rain, but I dug my heels into poor Bessie's side and pressed on. Soon the farmhouse came into sight and I could hear the sheep bleating as I approached. I remembered with a pang the incident in France Luke had related to me. I wondered how on earth he could bear to work on a sheep farm, hearing this sound all day. The wind had risen now and was blowing wildly through the trees near the house. It was very exposed up here on the ridge.

I cantered into the yard and in my hurry to dismount nearly slipped on the wet cobblestones in the courtyard. The sleety rain was still whipping in spiteful lashes against my face, stinging and cold. I looped the reins over a post and ran to the door, hammering on it, praying that Luke would be on the farm somewhere.

The stout figure of Mrs Thomson appeared in the doorway and she beamed when she saw me, but was obviously surprised to see a visitor on such a day. "Why, it's Miss Charlotte! What are you doing out this way in this weather? Come on in, my dear, out of the rain…"

I suddenly felt foolish as I followed her into the cosy farmhouse kitchen, the collie dog bounding up from the fireside to greet me, wagging his tail.

Yes, what was I doing there? I began to wonder.

"Sit down, sit down, m'dear. Why, you're soaked through, you poor lass!"

Mrs Thomson fetched a towel and shook her head, as I peeled off my sopping wet scarf and began drying my hair. This had a touch of déjà vu about it, I longed to tell her!

"Well, what can we do for you, Miss Charlotte? The men are working in the barns out the back there. There were six new lambs born overnight, and two of the ewes died, so we've had a real busy time feeding the orphans, had to put a couple in the oven they was so frozen…" Mrs Thomson tended to keep talking until you stopped her.

"It's Luke Trevithick I've come to see. Is he here?" I asked, my heart in my mouth.

She looked surprised, but then shook her head. "I'm afraid not, Miss Charlotte. He's up in London at the moment. Gone to see my Edward, George's brother. Something about a court case he wants to bring. Edward's a K.C. now, you know…" she added proudly.

My heart sank. Of course, I'd forgotten all about that! I knew he was planning to go to London to see Edward, but had no idea when.

"When will he be back, do you know?" I asked, trying to sound casual about it.

Mrs Thomson shrugged her shoulders. "Can't say, tomorrow or the next day. He didn't say. I think he was going to do some shopping while he was up there." She looked curious. "Is it urgent? Can I give him a message? I might be able to telephone Edward's chambers, if it's urgent, we're on the telephone now, you know, though I must admit the thing scares me half to death when it rings..."

Now I was starting to feel really embarrassed. "No, no, it's not that important. It's just that I heard Luke was living here at the moment and I needed to see him about something. It's not urgent, don't worry..."

Mrs Thomson went to the dresser and took some cups and saucers down. "Let me give you a cup of tea, dear, anyway before you go back home. Warm you up. It's such a nasty old day. Sit you down by the fire, my love, and get warm." She went to the range where a big kettle was steaming away and took down the tea-pot and tea-caddy from the shelf.

I suddenly remembered the little sketch wrapped up in my pocket and gave it to her to pass on to Luke. "Just tell him I came to see him and would like him to have this," I said, "he will know what it means."

Mrs Thomson nodded and smiled, as she gave me a cup of tea and piece of cake, chatting away about the weather and the farm. As I responded I stroked one of the orphan lambs curled up asleep in a basket on the big hearth. He looked so secure and peaceful, quite the opposite of how I felt at that moment. I sipped my tea, gratefully feeling the warmth from the cheery fire envelop me.

As I made my way out into the wet, windy courtyard once more I felt really depressed. What a fool I was! I'd come all this way, got soaking wet and for what? Luke wasn't here. So I was back to square one. Still out of favour with Luke.

* * *

"Now, what was his regiment again?" Doris Post sits at the Major's desk, pen poised, in the study of The Manor House,

Lottie alongside her a few days later. There is a large blotter on the desk, also a silver ink-well and a neat pile of folders. Nearby on the book-case is a smiling university photo of Ronnie taken on graduation day and other family photographs.

They are going through the grim task of compiling the latest local casualties from the war, 8 at the last count including outlying villages. Lottie has obtained a list of casualties from the Army base at Taunton and now they are linking them up with their local details, names of villages, ages, etc. And of course the date the men had died. It is a vital but painful task and Lottie is grateful for Mrs Post's assistance. When the Memorial Committee with the vicar as its Chairman had first discussed erecting a memorial in each village, no-one had any idea of the scale of the task.

But now with the war into its sixth month the casualties are mounting. Lottie certainly needs some extra help in compiling the records, on top of all her other duties. Accuracy is essential, so they are being very careful to make sure the spelling of the names is absolutely correct as well as the regiment, of course.

Lottie is entering all the details into a big ledger book in her best copperplate handwriting and this will be kept until the end of the war, when the names will be duly engraved onto the appropriate war memorials. She had thought of typing the list but had decided against. Handwriting somehow seems more personal and less official looking.

Lottie refers to her notes. 'The Royal Somerset Rifles' she replies to Mrs Post's question. And Mrs Post duly fills in a sheet in front of her.

"Let's have a little break now," says Doris, getting up and she rings the bell-pull by the big marble mantelpiece. Within a few minutes her parlour-maid, Ethel, smartly dressed in a black dress with white lace collar, starched apron and matching cap, enters the room and bobs. "Yes, ma'am, may I help you?"

"We'll have some tea in the front sitting room, please, Ethel and some of that delicious fruit cake Mrs Brown has made, thank you."

"Yes, m'm, thank you, m'm."

Mrs Post leads the way into the sitting room which overlooks the village green and is now flooded with late afternoon sunshine.

"My maid, Ethel, has got problems at home at the moment…"

Lottie looks over to her in concern as she sits down. "Oh?"

Mrs Post bites her lip. "Her brother Charlie has been invalided out – he's suffering from shell-shock. I went to see him the other day… Just terrible, poor young man. He shakes uncontrollably and then cries out at the slightest sound, claps his hands to his ears. It's just so upsetting for the family to see. They don't know what to do to help him."

"I'm so sorry to hear that," Lottie murmurs, "I saw a case of shell-shock myself the other day in Taunton – it's so distressing to see. Perhaps I should ask father to go and see him…?"

Doris shakes her head. "Thank you, but I don't think he's quite ready for that just yet. He's not good with strangers, though he is better with women." She sighs. "He used to be such a bright, cheerful young man as well, played cricket for the local team. He did spend a month at a convalescent home, that one on the Taunton Road and it seemed to help him. But then they said he couldn't stay any longer, they needed the bed, so sent him home. And now he's not doing so well. This terrible war! Anyway, we mustn't get morbid!" She goes to the mullioned window and looks out at the garden, her face worried and strained.

"Ah, the sun at last," Doris murmurs, "it's taken its time to-day."

Lottie joins her at the window and gazes at the sunlight filtering through the bare trees now bending in the wind, bordering the drive-way.

"It's always nice to see the sun in the winter, don't you think?" she says.

"M'm, it's telling us that spring will soon be here." Doris' warm brown eyes crinkle as she smiles. "Look, there are some daffodils out already…"

"…yes, and primroses too," puts in Lottie, pointing.

Doris says: "A real harbinger of spring. I adore the spring flowers…"

And Lottie suddenly feels a wave of sadness sweep over her. "Yes, mother loved them too. It was her favourite time of year." She feels emotional and full of memories.

"You still miss her, I know," Doris puts her arm around Lottie's shoulders.

Lottie nods, too full to speak.

"I miss her too," Doris says, "she was a dear friend to me – she was taken too soon, much too soon."

Lottie reaches for her handbag which she had placed by the armchair, as the door opens and Ethel appears with the tea-tray.

"I suddenly remembered, Doris, you said you would like a snapshot of mother if I could find one…"

"Why yes, if you have one to spare." The older woman begins to pour milk and tea into the dainty china cups.

Lottie delves into her handbag and brings out a photo and hands it to Mrs Post with a smile. "Here we are, you may keep that, it was taken the Christmas before she died. I've got another one of it."

As Lottie hands Doris the photo, another photo falls to the floor and Doris picks it up and glances at it before handing it back to Lottie. "Oh, there's another one here, I'll give this back to you."

Lottie is instantly embarrassed and a flush begins to creep over her face and neck, when she sees what it is. "Oh, thank you, I didn't mean…"

The photo is the one of Luke which she had taken from Three Chimneys farm a few months earlier. She always keeps them together in her bag.

Mrs Post casts a curious glance at Lottie, as she passes a cup of tea to her.

"That's Tom's brother, Luke, isn't it? Good looking young man."

Lottie nods, but then remarks awkwardly. "Well, um, I hope you like the photo of mother…"

Mrs Post wisely then prattles on about the photo of Lottie's dear mother and what a good likeness it is. And if any thoughts cross her mind as to why Lottie should be carrying a photo of her fiancé's brother in her handbag and not her fiancé, well, she is much too well-bred to utter them.

Chapter 12

MARCH

THE RECTORY
1st March 1915

Dearest Bella,

Thanks so much for your little note about the Sunshine Club children.

I am arranging with Matilda to meet them all at Taunton Station on the 18th March and will take them back to Tethercombe by motor coach, (provided free by the bus company) which in itself will be a thrill for them! I will look out for the famous Peter Plunkett wearing a red tie – but from your description of the pebblestone spectacles, buck teeth and balding head I'm sure I will recognise him! You are very withering in your comments about him, but he must be a thoroughly decent fellow to be involved in this charity work, so I reserve my judgement.

We are planning to take them to 'Three Chimneys' and show them around the farm, then give them a picnic (praying for a good day) in the fields, play a few games there, then take them all back to The Rectory for cocoa and buns before taking them back to the station again.

Anyway, it's a day out for the poor children. They have so little in their lives that these charities are a real blessing for them and I am pleased to help. However, please tell Mr Plunkett not to bring more than 10 children, as I don't feel we can cope with more than that. Also make sure they are all wearing shoes.

On the personal front, I have made my peace with father as you suggested and also written to Amy, but have been unable to contact Luke at this stage. He has been busy with the lambing at George Thomson's farm, also he went up to London recently, to see a barrister about bringing a court case against Tom to claim his rightful inheritance from his parents. It puts me in a difficult position, but I am trying to steer the correct course between them both. 'Diplomat' is my middle name, or at least I am trying!

Will close now and hope you are keeping well and saving for your bottom drawer. I am so thrilled for you! You couldn't be engaged to a nicer person. Ronnie Post is the tops!

Your loving sister,

Lottie

SECRET DIARY

3rd March 1915

Again noticed how shabby the furniture in the dining room and sitting room is becoming. It has been bothering me for a while and have decided I must do something about it. Father is hosting a special Memorial Committee meeting in May with a lot of important visitors attending, so it should be spick and span for that. Father would never notice in a month of Sundays! I suddenly remembered that before she died mother had actually gone into Dunster and chosen some material for this purpose from Hanburys, so it must be packed away somewhere. I owe it to her to get this work done.

I searched through the cupboards and found it, still packed in its brown paper parcel, along with the receipt. It was quite a big bolt of cloth, a lovely tweedy hard-wearing wool fabric of muted heather colours, quite a change from the dull, worn red velvet covering the chairs at the moment. I stretched it out. I was sure it would be enough to cover the sitting room furniture and dining chairs – there must be fifteen yards or more. I looked at the receipt – yes, 16 yards of wool fabric.

I decided to leave my typing to the afternoon and go at once to visit Mr Selby, the upholsterer in the village who we had used for many years. He was a dear, smiling little man and expert with his needle and sewing machine.

He greeted me at the door, the tape measure around his neck as usual and looking a bit harassed, as he was already dealing with another customer.

The small room was crowded with his two sewing machines and a cutting table, shelves full of materials of all colours and types, and boxes of matching reels of cotton, spare bobbins, also lots of big scissors hanging up. Once the customer had gone, however, he turned his attention to me and I told him what was required. It would be a sizeable job for him and hopefully would be useful to him, in these hard times. "I shall have to come and measure up, of course, Miss Carr," he said, looking doubtfully at his calendar. "I've got quite a bit of work on and I seem to have got behind. My assistant is off sick, you know..." He didn't seem his usual cheery self at all, but was dithering about, moving things from one chair to another and inspecting and measuring the material closely. "Ah yes, 54" wide, that's good.'

"As long as it's ready by the middle of May," I replied.

He looked relieved. "Oh yes, that would be all right, I'm sure." He gave a sigh and shook his head. "Sorry, Miss Carr, I'm not myself this week. Um, I had some bad news at the weekend."

"Oh, I'm sorry," I began, "not someone at the Front, is it?"

He nodded and sat down abruptly. "It's my nephew, Bertie. He was badly injured and they brought him back home, but then..." Tears began to well in his eyes. "I heard on Sunday he'd died of his injuries, in the Military Hospital at Taunton. He was only 28." He dabbed at his eyes with his handkerchief, sniffing. Mr Selby was a childless widower and I'd heard him speak with great pride of his nephew who was a popular butcher in Dulverton. I think in his mind he had taken the place of the son he had never had.

I put my hand on his shoulder. "I'm so sorry to hear that, Mr Selby. This war is such a dreadful thing for us all to cope with. Was he married?" He nodded. "Any children?" He nodded again. "Two little 'uns under five. His wife, Emily, is broken-hearted, doesn't know how she's going to manage."

I hugged him again. "Once she's over the shock, they will be a comfort to her – and to you. And don't forget, your nephew died serving King and Country. He was a brave young man." I found it so difficult to know what to say to people who had just received bad news. I decided to follow the old adage 'least said, soonest mended'. I pulled on my gloves and turned to leave. "Now, are you sure you are all right to do this work?"

Mr Selby made an effort to smile at me and pull himself together. "Yes, yes, Miss Carr – it will do me good – keep me occupied. Thank you for your custom. Now, shall we make a date for me to come up to the Rectory and measure up?"

And as I walked home my heart was full of grief for yet another victim of this awful, awful war, which just seems to go on and on. And yet another window will be decked out in black crepe and bombazine... It's becoming a familiar sight. Please God may it end soon.

10th March 1915

I have to record the special events of yesterday, so special I can't begin to describe!

I was (unbelievably) round at 'Three Chimneys' helping Tom with the accounts. Despite my changed feelings for him and even though incensed, I felt duty bound to answer his distress call when he asked me if I would go round and help him on Tuesday. Luke usually does it, so Tom is now having problems keeping the books in order. I'm not much good at figures, but I am methodical and can work my way through them slowly and carefully. So I agreed to help him just this once.

We had been working on the ledgers all the afternoon and progressed quite well. Late afternoon, we decided to stop for a tea break. About six o'clock Mrs Bryant had then departed for the day, as she had a family birthday party to attend.

We were sitting at the table and Tom was showing me some old studio portraits of their parents, when he suddenly cried out and clutched at his chest, complaining of breathlessness and tightness. "Can't breathe, Lottie, can't breathe!" he gasped.

I helped him to the armchair and fetched him a glass of water and Tom took one of his tablets prescribed by the doctor for his palpitations.

This seemed to help at first, but I then became very concerned as his breathing seemed very shallow and his complexion had now turned a nasty grey colour.

"Have you been exerting yourself unduly to-day, Tom?" I asked, suddenly suspicious he might have been over-doing it around the farm, against the doctor's advice.

He looked a little sheepish and admitted there had been a fire in one of the barns this morning. He had tried to help the farm labourers by moving a huge bale of hay which was just about to catch fire. I reprimanded him but didn't quite know what to do and felt very helpless. They still weren't on the telephone at the farmhouse. Luke had wanted to connect them up, but Tom (ever miserly) didn't think it was necessary. The nearest house was two miles down the road and above all I didn't like to leave him. Anyway, I hadn't even got my horse or bicycle with me, as Tom had picked me up earlier from The Rectory. I felt angry that I was in this ironic situation, in the light of recent events, but knew as a Christian I had to help him now he was ill.

I was just about to suggest making him a cup of tea, when Tom doubled up in pain and seemed to crumple up in the armchair, obviously in great discomfort.

Benny half asleep by the hearth suddenly pricked up his ears and ran to the door barking and a second later I heard the sound of hooves on the cobbles outside. "Thank God!" I ran out in the cold night air to see who it was. Luke, my saviour! I ran up to him, as he was dismounting and cried out: "Come quickly, Luke, Tom has collapsed... come and see..." I was nearly in tears now in my distress. I told Luke about Tom trying to put out the fire and lifting a heavy bale.

Luke tethered Rufus to a nearby post and put his arm round me, trying to calm me down. Then he led the way back into the big farmhouse kitchen and went over to look at his brother.

Tom was lying in the armchair, his eyes closed, his face an ashen grey.

Luke murmured some supportive words to him and propped his head up against the cushion and put his feet on a foot-stool. "We'll soon have you right, old chap…"

Then he turned to me, cursing that they weren't yet on the telephone. "I'll take Tom's motor and fetch Dr Witherspoon," he said tersely. And he was gone, backing the car out of the old barn and driving at breakneck speed down Turners Lane.

After what seemed an eternity, during which I made Tom a cup of tea, I saw the flash of the headlights and heard the two cars returning, swinging into the courtyard. And Dr Witherspoon entered the kitchen, nodding to me and going at once to see the patient, slumped in the armchair.

After a careful examination, the doctor suggested that he and Luke should help Tom upstairs to rest in bed. "I'll give him a strong sleeping draught so that he can sleep it off," the doctor said. This they did and I helped them settle Tom in bed, feeling guilty that I already knew this room quite well.

When we came downstairs again, the doctor turned to Luke and I. "Don't worry, it wasn't a heart attack, it's this irregular heartbeat of his, a severe attack of palpitations caused I believe by this extra exertion he had this morning. I'll arrange for him to have an examination at the hospital next week just to make certain." He smiled and patted my arm reassuringly. "Nothing to worry about, my dear."

"Thank God for that!" I sighed with relief.

"Thank God!" echoed Luke.

The doctor snapped his bag shut and moved towards the door. "Make sure he takes it easy for the next few days, Luke. And I'll let you know about the hospital appointment." Luke nodded.

I apologised for bringing him out during the evening and showed him to the door. We heard his motor-car drive away and Luke and I hugged each other with relief.

I suddenly felt completely exhausted and sank down into an armchair.

"Oh, Luke, I was so worried. I thought he was dying..." I said, and burst into tears, all the tension of the last few days suddenly overwhelming me. "I felt so helpless. I didn't want to leave him, but wanted to get help..." I sobbed.

Luke came over and comforted me, cradling me in his arms. "It's been very traumatic for you, Lottie. But he's all right now, nothing to worry about."

I shook my head. "Thank goodness you arrived when you did. But what were you coming here for...?"

Luke gave a quirky smile. "Rufus' saddle developed a bad crack, so I came back to get the spare one." He shrugged his shoulders. "It's providence, fate, call it what you like. Anyway, thank goodness you were here."

"Would you like a cup of tea?" I asked, but Luke shook his head and went to the sideboard, lifting the crystal whiskey decanter. "A drop o' the hard stuff for me, how about you, will you have some?"

I never usually touched spirits, but must admit I did feel in need of something stronger to pull myself together. I felt emotionally drained after seeing Tom so ill. "Well, perhaps just a tiny drop..."

As he gave me the glass, our fingers touched and to me the contact was electric. Luke linked his fingers with mine and our eyes met.

"Thank you for the sketch of the ponies, it's very good..."

"It was a bit of a peace-offering." I took a sip of the fiery liquid and coughed a little.

"I love it. That unexpected meeting on the moors was so special to me. Sorry I wasn't at the farmhouse when you called. I was in London."

Luke sat on the floor at my feet, still holding my hand, tracing round each finger up and down.

"What's happening about the court case?" I asked. "Is George's brother going to take it on?" As I spoke I was thinking a thousand things. I loved his dark eyes, especially his poor, scarred, drooping left eye, his firm lips, his deep low voice. I wanted to run my fingers

through his thick mop of hair, so close to me now. It curled round his ears in a most delightful way. I was thinking: I love you, Luke. It was suddenly crystal clear to me. What was I doing engaged to dullard, devious Tom? It was Luke I loved, darling Luke.

Luke's eyes sparkled suddenly. "Yes, he is! I'm so delighted. He said I stand a really good chance of claiming my rightful inheritance. The case will come to court towards the end of the year."

"That's marvellous news!" I cried, "I'm so glad for you!"

Luke shook his head. "You're a funny one, Lottie..."

I was a bit hurt. "Oh, thanks!"

Luke gestured helplessly. "First you support me at dinner, then you reject my advances in the hut. Then you tell lies about me, now you're pleased for me – I don't know where I stand with you."

But his eyes were amused as he searched my face.

"Luke," I began, "I came to the farm to tell you something. Tell you that I have now told father the truth, what really happened that day on the moors. I don't care about that silly gossip someone tried to invent. But I'm sorry if I hurt you, truly sorry."

Luke shrugged and smiled. "It doesn't matter now. But how are things between you and Tom?" he asked me gravely. "I have to know. It's important to me."

"To be honest, Luke, I'm beginning to realise I made a bad mistake when I became engaged to Tom. I think perhaps I was seeking security, not love after the death of my mother. There was never any spark there. And now I've discovered his deception and infidelity I don't even have respect for him anymore."

I nodded at his querying look. "Yes, I've seen the evidence – unbelievable! And he's got a child by her! I was so shocked." I shook my head. "I feel totally betrayed and quite understand why you told me."

Luke shook his head. "I was very torn. I wanted to tell you before but there was never a good moment somehow. I nearly told you when we were together in the hut on the moor, but held back. I had terrible rows with Tom about it when you became engaged. He only told me two years ago – he's kept it a secret all these years. Some skeleton in the cupboard!" He gripped my hand. "You deserve better, Lottie. I've thought that all along." Our eyes met in an unspoken acknowledgement of the deep bond between us both right now. Those magic feelings were stronger than ever, coursing through my body.

He suddenly leant forward and loosened the ribbon holding back my hair. "May I?" he said. My fair hair tumbled from its ribbon, the curls springing free and framing my face. "I love to see your beautiful hair about your shoulders, golden like the corn in summer." His poetic words made my heart sing. I smiled and squeezed his hand, colour tinting my cheeks.

"And Luke…" I was hesitant, but wanted him to know how it was.

"Yes, my little one?" His voice was tender and low, his dancing eyes scanning my face. He stroked my hand.

"I didn't want to admit how I felt about you, not even to myself at first. I tried to resist it out of loyalty to Tom. But now, well, it's too strong to ignore…"

Luke interrupted me, his fingers gripping mine tightly. "I'm glad about that, Lottie darling, because I'm madly in love with you and at this moment I'm quite desperate to kiss you…" An avalanche of kisses descended on me. He kissed my lips, my eyes, my ears and then my lips again, all the time undoing my buttons impatiently. We ended up on the floor in a tangle of limbs and I felt an overwhelming desire for him sweep through me.

And then I felt his hands on my breast and his body was hard against me. I heard him whisper those magical words: "I love you, Lottie! Now do you realise? I love you!"

11th March 1915

6.30 a.m. "The lark's on the wing, The snail's on the thorn, God's in His heaven, All's right with the world."

Robert Browning knew all about love and now, SO DO I!

M'm! I feel wonderful! My body is still throbbing, tingling and alive! I stretched my limbs luxuriantly in my bed and thought of Luke, over and over again.

As I grew up, I had been curious about the sexual act and in truth a little apprehensive about it. But Luke was so gentle with me at first and then, after I felt an initial stab of pain, he was increasingly passionate, leaving me aroused and breathless. I had gradually responded to his love-making and it had all seemed quite natural. He had dropped me off in Church Lane last night about eight o'clock and I had fled to my room to avoid father, pleading a headache.

"I am H.A.P.P.Y., I am H.A.P.P.Y., I think I am, I know I am, I am H.A.P.P.Y.!" I sang to myself the old gospel song, then padded to the looking glass to see if I appeared different. My reflection stared back at me, the colour high on my cheeks, my hair ruffled.

Yes, my eyes definitely look different – bigger, wider and more DECADENT somehow! I'm sure people will be able to tell I'm no longer a virgin. I shall have to wear high neck blouses and act very primly to fool everyone. But how can I possibly behave calmly at today's Prayer Meeting with all the village spinsters, including the Misses Tiptree, when my heart is pounding at the very thought of him?

I suddenly caught sight of my old dolls-house, stuck in a corner of my bedroom gathering dust. Kneeling down I stared in through the tiny mullioned windows and gazed at the neat little rooms with miniature figures and miniature furniture. As a child I had played with it endlessly, moving the little people about from living room to bedroom and inventing different scenarios for them, with guests coming to tea and the kitchen staff scurrying around with hot water and tea-pots. Playing house.

And yes, now, now I was a real woman, I could imagine myself running a real house, being part of my own real family, with lots of children chasing about and perhaps a dog and a cat. I turned away, my mind buzzing with future plans and my heart racing as I thought of him. 'Oh Luke, I love you, I love you!' I whispered to myself. Thank you, God, for sending me Luke, darling Luke! I can't wait till I see you again.'

THE RECTORY
20th March 1915

Dear Amy,

I thought I must write and say how much I enjoyed our meeting last week. It was really lovely to see you and hear about your post with Mrs Ponsonby. I thought your room was beautifully furnished and the view of Exmoor just delightful. It was very pleasant to walk into Porlock and have some refreshment at the little tea-room there. We must meet up again sometime. Perhaps you could come into Tethercombe on the bus one day and then come back to The Rectory for lunch.

Since I've seen you I've had an exhausting day with 10 children, yes 10! I rashly agreed to look after some London street urchins who are given occasional treats by The Sunshine Club, a charity Bella is involved with. So they all arrived one day last week and Matilda and I and Peter Plunkett from the charity took them by motor coach back to Tethercombe to see Tom's farm, have a picnic, etc. It went quite well, although the weather could have been kinder.

The children were dressed in such ragged clothes and looked so thin and un-kempt, but they all had fun and enjoyed themselves, thank goodness, which makes it all worthwhile. They had a picnic in one of the barns and saw the cows being milked. A lot of them didn't realise that milk came from cows even! They are completely ignorant about the countryside.

Afterwards we gave them cocoa and buns at the Rectory and Father saw them before they left. He gave them each a coloured text and said a blessing over them all, which I was pleased about. Poor little devils, they need a few blessings!

Well, I must close now and get ready to go to the Soup Kitchen. Matilda and I take it in turns now as we can seem to manage on our own. We are also now selling second-hand clothing at a stall there, which is proving very popular. When I had the street urchins here I managed to rummage among the clothing bins at the Hall and find them all an item of clothing each, which they seemed delighted with. One little girl was so pleased with her 'new' skirt that she went dancing all round the Hall in it, singing!

Hope to see you soon. How is Richard getting on recuperating in Exeter? And good wishes to Bertie too.

With love,

Your affectionate friend,

Lottie

* * *

"What shall we do with these things?" Mrs Post and Lottie are in the Village Hall a few days later, sorting through donated used clothing for the weekly stall. Mrs Post is holding up a red satin chemise and black frilly chiffon blouse. She laughs. "I don't think they're much use to our poor families, do you?"

Lottie giggles as she begins pricing a few items. "A warm pair of bed socks would be more the ticket or a woollen muffler…" She fingers the red satin chemise. M'm, it's my size, she thinks, and so pretty. Luke likes to see me in red. I might secrete that away later.

Mrs Post seizes hold of another box and begins to rummage through it. "What we're desperate for is more children's clothes. These poor families have so many children they always seem to be out-growing clothing."

Lottie piles up a few priced items beside her. "Perhaps we could advertise again in the Parish Newsletter. It might help. Or put a few posters up in Dunster or Taunton. Anyway, let's stop and have a cuppa', she suggests and she goes over to the big metal pot on the stove. 'You don't mind a tin mug, I hope, Doris?"

Mrs Post smiles. "Not at all, as long as the tea comes hot and sweet."

The two ladies sit down on the wooden bench at the side of the Hall, tired after the morning's activities. "So what's the news of Ronnie, have you heard anything recently?" Lottie asks.

Mrs Post shakes her head. "Very little news. The last we heard there was a big push coming up at Ypres, trying to regain some ground they'd lost earlier." She sighs. "It all seems so futile and such a loss of life. I pray to God it will end soon and our men will come home safely."

Lottie looks across at the older woman with genuine affection. She had been such a rock to Lottie since her mother died, always there with practical help or some sensible advice. And her support with the war records and the Sick and Poor visits had been invaluable. Lottie feels she couldn't do it on her own. It's such an emotive task, all the families seem so desperate, particularly now with most of the men away at the Front.

Suddenly the back door swings open and Tom comes in carrying some bulky bags under his arms. He touches his cap at Mrs Post and gives Lottie a brief peck on the cheek. "Morning, ladies, how are you getting on?"

Lottie forces a thin smile to her lips. "We've sorted and sorted until we can sort no more, haven't we, Doris? But we've got a lot of things to sell... What have you got there?" she asks looking curiously at the bags Tom has placed on the table.

"Some spare buns and rolls from the bakers. I was in there and he said he would drop them in for the Soup Kitchen tomorrow, so I saved him the trouble.'

"Oh, thanks, Tom that's good of you," Mrs Post smiles.

Lottie sips at her tea, keeping her eyes lowered. "Did you remember to pick up those other bags of clothes from the Misses Tiptree?" She speaks in a monotone, barely looking at Tom at all.

Tom looks rather flustered. "I don't remember you asked me to do that – when was that?"

"Yesterday," Lottie replies rather curtly, "I asked you yesterday, don't you remember? But please don't worry about it, someone else can do it if you're too busy."

Mrs Post glances anxiously at Lottie, sensing an atmosphere between the engaged couple. "I can ask Rodney to do it if it's a problem..."

Tom gives a nervous laugh. "No, no, don't bother the Major, I can do it, it's no trouble, it's on my way back to the farm." He gives Lottie a sharp look. "Well, I must be off back to Three Chimneys. Will I be seeing you later, Lottie dear?"

Lottie looks at him levelly. "Um, no, I can't come round tonight, Tom, but I'll see you in church on Sunday."

Tom gives a wave of his hand to Mrs Post and attempts to give Lottie a kiss on the cheek, but she turns her head away as he does so, ending up kissing her hair. "All right then, I'll be off now, bye!" Tom goes out the back door hurriedly again and Mrs Post looks hard at Lottie who is now studiously washing up her tin mug and some other dishes there.

"Everything all right between you two young people?"

Lottie shrugs. "Oh yes, fine. We can't be love birds all the time."

"And is Tom better now? I hear you had to call the doctor out last week."

Lottie nods, an enigmatic smile crossing her lips at the memory of the evening. "He's fine now, thanks. It was just a scare."

Mrs Post comes over to the sink, grabs a tea-towel and begins to dry up.

"Don't forget, my dear, engagements aren't set in stone. If there is anything wrong, now is the time to have it out in the open and discuss it. Don't leave it until you're married, that's too late. You can always break an engagement, remember that. That's what they're for really, to test the waters as it were." She put a hand on Lottie's shoulder. "I'm always here if you want to talk, you know."

Lottie gives Mrs Post a nervous smile, suddenly embarrassed at showing her true feelings in public. "Just a lovers' tiff," she laughs, "we're OK." And as they begin to tidy the Hall and lock up, Lottie thinks: I've given myself away now – Mrs Post must suspect all is not well with my engagement, but if she knew how close I am to Luke, she would be truly shocked.

As Lottie cycles through the village towards The Rectory, she nears the home of Charlie Bledisloe, brother to Mrs Post's maid, Ethel. She had called there once before recently on the spur of the moment, taking Mrs Bledisloe some eggs from Tom's farm. Doris' description of the poor young man had touched her heart and pricked her conscience. She had met

Charlie who was curled up in the foetal position on the sofa when she arrived. He had been very quiet and unresponsive at first. But after a short time he seemed to take to her, agreeing to walk in the garden with her, which his mother said later was a miracle. The spasms in his limbs became less frequent as she took his arm and they walked round the small cottage garden, admiring the spring flowers. Lottie was quiet with him, not talking too much and he seemed to become much calmer during her visit.

There was a piano in the small living room and after much coaxing Lottie had played a couple of tunes, Mendelssohn's 'Spring Song' and a Mozart minuet. She was not such a good pianist as Bella but could play adequately with music. Charlie's eyes had lit up at this impromptu recital and he had clapped his hands enthusiastically when she finished. "He loves music," said his mother, "it seems to soothe him."

While they had a cup of tea the conversation had switched to the Army and Lottie asked which regiment Charlie had been in. When he said 'West Country Fusiliers' Lottie had felt a *frisson* of excitement run through her. "Why, that's Luke's old regiment!" she cried, "you may know him – Capt. Luke Trevithick? He's my fiancé's brother, lives up at 'Three Chimneys' farm in Turners Lane. He was invalided out like you, but with a leg injury." The light had disappeared from Charlie's eyes momentarily at the mention of the word 'fiancé', but he still gazed at his unexpected visitor enraptured, as she sat there with her smiling demeanour, her blue eyes sparkling and her fair hair tumbling on her shoulders. It turned out that yes, Charlie did remember Luke and something resembling a smile crossed his face as he said so.

Although Lottie said nothing at the time, she began to think that perhaps Luke might agree to come and visit Charlie, to share a few jokes with him, remind him of the camaraderie of trench life. She remembered how good he had been with the disabled child before. Obviously such a visit would have to be treated with caution, remembering what traumatic memories Charlie had of his time at the Front. But it was an idea.

Lottie steps off her cycle and props it up against the cottage fence, glancing at her fob watch. She winces. Nearly lunch-time, she would have to make it brief. For Luke's possible visit was not the only idea she had had. She had another proposal to put to Charlie, after making some enquiries from her chum, Matilda Rowntree.

She knocks at the door and it's opened by Mrs Bledisloe, who smiles a welcome and waves her inside, wiping her hands on her apron. "How is Charlie to-day?" asks Lottie, for there is no sign of him in the small living room.

Charlie's mother shakes her head. "He's not so good today, he's very up and down. He doesn't sleep well, has nightmares, about the rats and the shelling. He's having a rest at the moment. But I'll be waking him up soon for his lunch," she adds, going into the kitchen to stir the tasty stew bubbling away on the stove, rich with nourishing vegetables. "I'm trying to build him up," she smiles, "he's got so thin and poorly."

"I won't stay long, Mrs Bledisloe, I'm sorry to call at this awkward time. In fact, it's probably better Charlie isn't here. I wanted to ask you something. I've got a proposal to make."

"Sit down, lass, what is it you wanted to say?"

Lottie sits on the edge of the settee, hoping Charlie's mother will agree to her idea. "You said Charlie had been in the convalescent home a few months ago – and he liked it there?"

"Oh yes, he was very happy there. It was quiet, lovely grounds to walk in, and yet he had companionship with the other chaps if he wanted it. And it was handy for us to visit. Yes, Amberley House was ideal for him. He was very sad when they said he couldn't stay any longer."

"Well, I've got a friend who used to be quite senior in the Red Cross in Exeter, Matilda Rowntree is her name. She helps me run the Soup Kitchen in the village now. I mentioned Charlie to her and she spoke to the powers-that-be in the Red Cross who run Amberley House. They remember Charlie as a fine intelligent young man, always polite and quiet. They don't judge people on their nervous illnesses. They see beyond that. They are used to dealing with that sort of thing." Lottie takes a deep breath. "They would be prepared to take Charlie back as a patient for a while and also give him some clerical work to do now and then, nothing too demanding, which I think would help his recovery."

Mrs Bledisloe's eyes light up and she clutches at Lottie's hand. "Why, that would be wonderful, Charlie would love it, I'm sure!"

"Well, that's what I wanted to ask you, *would* he love it? Are you sure? Could he cope with it? He would of course be paid a small wage for this work. I think it would build his self-confidence and take his mind off his personal problems."

Lottie glances at her watch and stands up. "Perhaps you could discuss it with him, and see how he feels about it. Let me know and if he likes the idea, well that's fine and I'll organise it. But if it doesn't appeal to him, well, it doesn't matter."

Mrs Bledisloe hugs Lottie to her in a spontaneous gesture. "Thank you, Miss Carr, from the bottom of my heart. You don't know what this means to us. Just you wait till his father hears about it." Her face is beaming, her eyes crinkling up as she smiled. Charlie's father is a cobbler with a tiny but busy shop attached to the forge.

"Well, I just hope he likes the idea," says Lottie, making her way towards the door. "I'll be off now. Give my love to Charlie." She reaches the door and then turns. "Oh and by the way, do you think he would like a visit from Luke Trevithick sometime? Just a short visit, see how they get on?"

"Perhaps he could visit him up at the Hall if he goes there," Charlie's mother says shortly. She opens the door, the spring sunshine flooding into the tiny hall.

Lottie nods sagely, one step at a time, she thinks. I shouldn't have mentioned that now, it's all too much for her to take in.

And she climbs on her bicycle, waving to a smiling mother in the doorway – a mother now seeing hope on the horizon for the first time in many months.

Chapter 13
APRIL 1915

SECRET DIARY

3rd April 1915

I still haven't spoken to Tom about our engagement. After the fiasco in February with the G.F.S. girls I was waiting for a suitable moment, which never seemed to come. I could feel the resentment building up inside me. But when Luke asked me again yesterday whether I had yet spoken to him about us, I realised I had to confront the matter. I knew that, if not, Luke would do it himself, and this I did not want. I have to tell him myself, face up to it and tell him in a civilised way. Obviously I must break our engagement, as now in the light of his betrayal I feel nothing but disgust for Tom and am deeply in love with Luke.

Luke and I have been very discreet in our meetings. Luke has access (through a soldier pal of his) to a cottage at Dunster and so we have been meeting there occasionally, going and leaving separately. It is in a very isolated position on the outskirts of the village and I know no-one in Dunster anyway, so I am sure we haven't been seen. But I feel so much in love, that I DON'T CARE if anyone does see us!!

Luke is the sun and the moon to me, I just adore him and live for each moment we meet. I feel ridiculously, impossibly HAPPY and have been flying through my duties, my typing, my Soup Kitchen, my Sick and Poor visits, my G.F.S. talks, as if I have wings, motivated and energised. I seem to have a new confidence inside me, as if I'm walking tall. The secret of Luke's love is enveloping me like a warm, comforting shawl. He is my first waking thought and my last. To my surprise I don't feel at all guilty. It seems perfectly natural for us to make love. We fit together perfectly, like two spoons. Luke takes care of the contraceptive devices, his rubber johnnies as he calls them, so I feel safe. When we meet in private we fall upon each other hungrily and a surge of love seems to take over my body. My breasts cry out for his touch and those magic feelings run through me like lightning.

However, I know my responsibilities and I have decided that I will tell Tom my decision after church on Easter Sunday. I did think about writing him a letter, but decided that was not the way to do it. And I need to set a definite date or I shan't do it.

6th April 1915

Heard from Mrs Bledisloe to-day and to my delight Charlie likes the idea I put to him and will be moving up to Amberley House soon. I rang Matilda and she is setting the wheels in motion for him to rejoin the patients there. I am so pleased about this and feel sure it will do him good and speed his recovery. Mrs Post was very chuffed about it when I told her and Ethel is over the moon and sent me a thank you letter, also her parents came round with a huge bunch of spring flowers from their garden for me in gratitude.

I am leaving mentioning all this to Luke and will wait a while until Charlie has settled in up at the Home before suggesting they meet up. I just feel it will be ideal for Charlie and do so hope he likes it there and does well. I mentioned it to father and he seemed very pleased with me for coming up with this scheme and organizing it all myself. As a little token of his esteem, to my surprise he presented me with a small box of sugared almonds, an unheard of luxury in Lent, and with the busy events of Holy Week approaching.

I had arranged to meet Luke at Dunster yesterday and rode over there as usual on Bessie. It's a long journey over the moors, but even further by road and more public, so I'm happy to ride. Once in the cottage (we both have keys) I made myself a cup of tea and waited for Luke. I kept peering out of the back window over the fields, but could see no sign of him. We had an agreement not to wait more than an hour, as it would mean he or I had been held up for some reason. So after an hour, although bitterly disappointed not to see him, I left and returned to Tethercombe.

As I passed Turners Lane on the spur of the moment I decided to call in on Tom, thinking it might be a good opportunity to prepare the way before the confrontation on Easter Sunday. But as I entered the courtyard I could see his motor-car was gone from the old barn.

Mrs Bryant appeared in the doorway, and Benny bounded up to me, barking excitedly, so I gave him a fondle and called out to her. "Tom gone out?" She nodded and came up, drying her hands on her apron. "The master's gone off to Taunton, Miss Carr. He's only been gone mebbe twenty minutes. Said to say if you came he'll be back after lunch."

"Thank you, Mrs Bryant. I'll be off then. Tell Tom I'll see him later."

"Did you want a cup of tea, Miss Carr? Mr Luke's here and I'm just making a fresh pot…"

My heart lifted. My darling Luke was here! But I wonder what happened?

I entered the sitting-room to see Luke's tall figure rummaging through papers in the drawers of the bureau. To see my darling so unexpectedly was a real treat for me. I felt a surge of sexual desire in my loins at the sight of him. He turned round in surprise when I called him.

"Darl… Lottie! How lovely to see you! Did you come to see Tom?"

We had to be careful when Mrs Bryant was about, but I moved over to him and lightly touched his arm, gazing up at him. We could hear Mrs Bryant now in the kitchen and Luke put his arms around me and gave me a deep kiss. "Darling, what happened?" I asked.

"Lottie, I'm sorry, so sorry. I called in here first thing this morning to get some papers to give to Edward Thomson – unfortunately Tom was still here and we got into a big row. He's got wind of the court case, vowing to bring a counter-action. It got a bit nasty, I'm afraid. He's gone to Taunton to see his solicitor now. So in the end it got so late I couldn't come over to Dunster. Sorry, my sweet." He kissed my nose and then, obviously distracted, continued looking through the drawer. "Forgive me, sweetheart, but I'm still searching for this wretched paper. It's a copy of the Codicil I'm looking for. That was added at a later date and specified I was to receive my share on turning 25. The solicitor has got the original, but there's a copy here somewhere…"

Mrs Bryant entered the room with a tray of tea-things and then left, closing the door.

I shook my head as I poured the tea. "I wish to God it was all out in the open, our relationship. It would make it a lot easier."

Luke glanced at me rather sharply. "Well, you know what the answer is, Lottie."

"You haven't said anything to Tom, have you, Luke? Or even hinted at it?"

He shook his head. "Not a word. I am discretion itself."

I gave a deep sigh. "It's been worrying me. I feel so resentful now. But I've now decided, I'm going to tell him after church on Easter Sunday when we go for a walk. I'm feeling quite nervous already."

Luke straightened up and put his arms around me, smiling and hugging me to his broad chest. "Darling, that's ripping news! Soon the whole world will know that we are in love!" And he brought his lips down on mine in a passionate kiss. "M-m, love you, love you..." His eyes were dancing before me. "Tell you what, Lottie. When it's all out in the open, I'll take you up to London and we'll go to a Music Hall, perhaps the Coliseum, that's the best one. It's such great fun. I went recently when I was up there. And there's a new musical on, "The Belle of New York", everyone's talking about it. And we could look at some art galleries as well." He hugged me anew and I laughed back at him enjoying his enthusiasm.

But Luke hadn't finished. He seized me and began to whirl me around the room, dancing. "Hey, I've got a great idea! Let's climb Dunkery together and shout it to the whole world that we're in love, once we reach the top!" We kissed again and I could feel those magic feelings running through me. I felt exhilarated and on top of Dunkery already.

We were standing in front of the window which gave onto the courtyard. And as we embraced I suddenly saw a movement there, out of the corner of my eye. I fully turned to the window and there was Tom standing in the courtyard, hands on hips, looking through the window at us. My stomach turned. All my limbs stiffened and I stood frozen for a moment entwined with Luke, looking back at him. How long he'd been there I don't know, but the look on his face was thunderous, as he turned on his heel and entered the house.

Luke and I broke away from each other and I stood immobile, my head bowed, feeling completely aghast. I hadn't wanted it to happen like this. My heart began to hammer in my chest. I couldn't understand why he was back so soon. I hadn't even heard the car. Luke cursed aloud and we stood together to face his brother, as he entered the room.

Tom stood in the doorway, arms folded, legs apart, an angry red flush creeping round his neck. "So this is what goes on when I'm out. And how long has this been going on?" he demanded.

Luke was very cool. "We didn't expect you back so soon, Tom, what happened?" he asked, facing him, arms also folded across his chest.

Tom explained stiffly his car had broken down and he'd had to walk back. But then he said in a sneering tone. "Now, Luke, what's your explanation? So, you couldn't keep your dirty paws off her, you had to seduce her, did you, like all the others. It didn't cross your mind to leave this one alone, as she is my fiancée..."

Luke took my hand and tucked it under his arm possessively. "Lottie was intending to tell you very soon, Tom. I'm afraid she has had a change of heart. She wants to break your engagement. Lottie knows all about Daisy and William at Tiverton and feels completely betrayed. We're very much in love and intend to get married. I'm sorry to cause you any distress, but that's the way it is."

Tom looked stunned for a moment, then started to bluster, denying any wrong-doing, but then he turned to me. "Is this true, Lottie? I want to hear it from you."

I nodded, suddenly feeling defiant and angry, thinking of his appalling deception, his paramour in Devon. I faced Tom's hostile gaze and lifted my chin. "Things seem to have changed between us, Tom. You are not the man I thought you were, the man I became engaged to. When I heard about your infidelity I was totally devastated." I shook my head. "So I'm afraid I have to break our engagement." And I slipped my ring, that symbol of trust and commitment, off my finger and placed it on the table.

I was going to say more, but he seemed so upset I thought I should hold my tongue. I was rather put out that Luke had spoken before me. I had wanted to tell Tom myself, I had rehearsed in my mind what I was going to say. But I had left it too late.

Tom spluttered in an apoplectic fashion at me and then turned on Luke, blaming him for leading me astray, an innocent girl, and warning him he would now receive nothing, nothing at all from his due inheritance. He seemed breathless and I was concerned he would collapse, remembering his heart condition.

But then he turned suddenly and went up the stairs, sighing and holding his head and beginning to weep loudly when he reached the landing.

I could see Mrs Bryant peering anxiously round the kitchen door. I was really upset and began to cry myself. Luke pulled me close and I nestled against his rough, hairy hacking jacket. "Darling," he said, stroking my hair, "don't get upset, we knew we had to face him some time. At least it's all out in the open now, we have no secrets anymore. We can love each other openly. There's no deceit anymore and we can begin to plan our marriage. It doesn't matter about the money. We have each other. That's all that matters."

I knew what he was saying was true, I knew it made sense. But I hadn't wanted it to happen like this. I hated rows and confrontations, they caused so much trouble. I had wanted to tell Tom in a civilised fashion, but had procrastinated and so it was my own silly fault.

9th April 1915

Must record something which happened today. I was in the village doing some shopping when I saw a knot of people gathered round a car. An incident had just occurred, it seemed. Then I saw it was Tom's car, with Luke driving it! I hurried over to see what had happened. To my horror as I approached I saw that Charlie Bledisloe was in front of the car, lying on the ground. But Luke was by then bending over him solicitously and helping him up.

"What happened?" I asked a passer-by, "did the car hit him?"

"Oh no," he said, "the lad stepped out in front of the car as it was driving off, he just seemed to lose his balance, and fell down. The driver braked hard and stopped immediately."

I went over to join Luke and make sure Charlie was all right. Someone brought out a stool and a glass of water for him from a shop. Luke was crouching beside him. "Are you all right, old chap?" Charlie nodded and to my amazement didn't seem too badly affected. He looked up as I stood beside him and nodded at me, breathing heavily, still in shock.

Luke smiled. "You know Miss Carr, I'm sure?" Our eyes made contact. We had agreed to be discreet in public.

Although his hands were trembling, I could see Charlie was only shaken up, so I smiled back and introduced them. "Luke, this is Charlie Bledisloe – Charlie, Luke Trevithick. I was hoping you two would meet, but not like this!"

Luke gave a grin and punched Charlie lightly in the chest. "Hey, you were in my regiment, weren't you? The West Country Fusiliers." Charlie nodded. "We're the lucky ones, eh, Charlie? Still got all our limbs. Do you remember Private Harry Benbow?" Charlie nodded vigorously. "Lost a leg at Ypres, did you hear? Taken it uncommon bad. He's up at Amberley House now – I met him in the Military at Taunton when I was there."

"Charlie's going back to Amberley House soon, aren't you?" I said, smiling.

Charlie gave an unexpected grin. "G-good up there…"

Luke stood up and stretched his limbs. "Well, when you're there, can you do me a favour, look out for Harry Benbow, he's a decent sort – his people live over Winsford way. He needs a few friends to come to terms with his injury, buck himself up…"

"I w-will, I w-will," Charlie stuttered, nodding.

Luke looked at his watch. "Excuse me, but I have to go now, have an appointment in Dulverton. Glad you're all right, old chap, no harm done, eh?" He stuck out his arm and shook Charlie's hand. "You be more careful next time crossing the road, promise me. You gave me quite a scare, I can tell you, pal. Can I give you a lift home?"

I spoke for him. "I'll walk you back, Charlie, it's only round the corner..."

"I'll see you up at Amberley sometime, Charlie," said Luke, climbing into the car. "I go up there from time to time. Bye for now." And with a wave of his hand, Luke drove away.

I looked after the car as it went down the street. How I loved this man, my darling Luke. He had just the right manner with Charlie, compassionate and caring yet jocular, speaking to him like a mate would to a pal in the army. And I didn't know he already visited Amberley.

I went to walk Charlie home, but he stuttered out: "The b-bread, the b-bread, I've g- got to g-get the b-bread..." I was going to pop in the bakers and get it for him myself, but thought it wiser to let him do it himself, it was good for his confidence to carry out these tasks.

Well, well, I thought as I walked Charlie back home nearby, I wanted them to meet and now they have. But I never thought it would be like that.

15th April 1915

Easter has passed in a blur of church services and flowers and I have spent it at home quietly with father. I was even drawn into conducting Sunday School in the vestry on Easter Day, as Miss Clements was indisposed, and must admit my heart wasn't in it. I usually love teaching the children from the illustrated Children's Bible, but not on this occasion. I felt distracted and my emotions were so mixed up I didn't even make any plans to see Luke, although he had other ideas.

He arrived unexpectedly on Easter Monday carrying what seemed to be a large hat box and some flowers for me. We walked in the garden together, so as to be private from father, who was busily occupied drafting a cross letter to the Church Times in his study. I was curious about the hat box. "What have you got there?" I laughed, as he presented it to me.

"It's a present for you. An Easter bonnet! I bought it in London when I was up there recently. Hope you like it."

I opened the box and took out the hat, wrapped in pink tissue paper. It was a pretty cream straw with two pale pink roses at the back and a pink brocade ribbon all around the crown. Delightful! "Why, thank you, Luke! I love it, it's so pretty!" I gave him a brief kiss.

Luke seemed pleased at my delight. "Try it on, go on," he urged.

We were out of sight of the house now behind the hedge bordering the vegetable garden and so I popped it on, wishing I had a mirror. "How's that?" I paraded before him, smiling.

Luke held my hands and gazed at me. "My perfect English rose. It really suits you. I bought it impulsively, when I was killing time before the train went. I spotted this little milliner's shop. Glad you like it."

He hugged me as we stood there in the kitchen garden and I wished, how I wished, I could trumpet our love to the whole world.

Now we are both estranged from Tom we should, I suppose, be announcing our engagement and going to choose a ring, but I don't feel ready for this yet somehow. I felt great relief to have broken my engagement to Tom, but now (to my surprise) I had begun to feel cautious. Self-doubts were beginning to creep in. Was I being too hasty? I loved Luke, adored him, but I had made one mistake, I had to be certain I was doing the right thing this time. I still felt rather piqued that Luke had stolen my thunder, as it were. I tried to explain all this to him and hoped he wasn't offended by my cautious attitude. But I wasn't sure he understood how I felt. Anyway, we reluctantly agreed not to see each other for a couple of weeks, until our emotions have settled down somewhat.

But when I saw him disappearing down the driveway on Rufus I didn't know how I was going to bear it. And, once I had tried the pretty hat on again and had a quick look in my bedroom mirror, I hid the hat box away at the back of my wardrobe. Hopefully soon I will be able to wear it with pride, with Luke alongside me.

So, for the most part lately, I have been the dutiful daughter supporting her father during Easter, this season of renewal and re-

birth, which I usually love so much. I have told father my news that I am no longer engaged to Tom, but so far haven't said anything about Luke. And I certainly didn't tell him about Tom's infidelity. Poor father couldn't cope with that! I don't want more recriminations and explanations. He took it very well, I thought. In fact he seemed especially kind to me, as if he was glad to welcome me back in the fold, now he was no longer sharing me with a stranger. Maintaining the status quo is very important to father.

27th April 1915

Popped in to see Charlie at the Home today, went for a walk in the grounds with him. We picked a few bluebells in the wooded area there. He seems much improved – his limbs still tremble at times but his spirits are much higher. He likes it there and is doing some clerical work once or twice a week, copying patient notes from doctors' notebooks into a big record book. I even ended up having an impromptu game of ping-pong with some of the lads there. Despite my opponent only having one arm, he still beat me! They were all so cheerful despite their injuries, quite remarkable.

One of the lads had brought a copy of the 'Wipers Times' back from the Front and they were all laughing as they read it. This Ypres news-sheet roughly produced in the rest camps was full of dark humour and helped keep up the spirits of the soldiers, fostering much joking and camaraderie. The boys would go to these camps behind the lines for a few days for a much-needed shower and rest, medical attention, or some social life in the local <u>estaminets</u>, before returning to the hell of the trenches again.

Silly me, I had fondly imagined that the soldiers were just fighting all the time! I spoke to the Nursing Sister and she said Charlie is one of their most trusted patients – and very good at interpreting doctors' dreadful scrawl! Think I will continue to visit regularly, also try to see other patients there, maybe Harry Benbow. Perhaps Doris Post would come with me occasionally?

I did ask after Private Benbow and the sister said he was still in a depressed state, but that Charlie had been taking him round the grounds in the wheelchair occasionally and having quiet halting chats with him. So in a way they were both helping each other. It makes you well up when you see these brave young men, blinded or maimed by the war, being led about so trustingly by the nurses. I wear my favourite perfume and put on my prettiest dress when I go, as I feel it might cheer them up to see (or smell!) a female after all the deprivations of life at the Front. The nurses and VADs there do such a wonderful job. Most of the lads are amazingly positive and enjoy the camaraderie, laughing and joking with their chums and the nurses. But a few are (understandably) very bitter, particularly those who have lost limbs. One man I spoke to reacted badly when I happened to mention my fiancé. "Pretty girl like you, no doubt he's blessed with two legs, eh?" he said and then rattled off angrily in his wheelchair, minus both his legs. I felt so embarrassed.

28th April 1915, 11.30 p.m., London

Am writing this hastily late at night after today's traumatic events. Fortunately father was out when the mysterious phone call came earlier to-day. He had gone to a Parish Council meeting at Dunster and I was having a cup of tea in the sitting room about two o'clock, when Mrs May came in to say Aunt Hilda was on the telephone. That in itself was odd, as she rarely telephones us, so I was instantly curious. But when I heard her voice, I realised something must have happened. She sounded very unlike herself, quite shrill and almost panicky. But as usual she came straight to the point.

"Can you come up here right away, Charlotte? It's a bit of an emergency. I am just about to go on holiday to Scotland, the taxi is on its way and Bella is acting very strangely." Aunt Hilda always had an authoritarian manner. But this was definitely an order, not a request.

When I enquired in what way my sister was 'strange', all she would say was that Bella had received a phone call and then immediately gone to her room and closed the door. Aunt Hilda had tried knocking and calling her, but found she had locked the door and there was no response, just muffled sobs.

Aunt Hilda apologised for leaving Bella in the lurch, as it were, but she had arranged to meet friends at Kings Cross to catch the overnight train to Edinburgh at 4 p.m. She had tickets and so had to leave immediately. "So," she said, "can I rely on you, Charlotte, to come up straight away and look after Bella? She must have had bad news or something. I don't like to leave her on her own in this state. My housekeeper is here of course, but she needs you, she needs the support of her sister." Naturally, I agreed.

What alternative did I have? I immediately packed a small bag, changed my clothes, tidied myself up and left a note for father. I also asked him to let Matilda know as I was due at the Soup Kitchen the next day. I knew where the key was hidden, so I raided father's cash box in his study to provide myself with some money. Fortunately there was quite a tidy sum there, as he had just been to the bank.

I consulted the Bradshaw, found a fast train about four o'clock, then summoned Potter to bring the pony and trap round to take me post haste to the railway station at Taunton. Mrs May seemed very concerned at my sudden departure, but happier when I said I had left a note for father. However, she seemed even more vexed that I wouldn't be there to eat the nice piece of fish she was cooking for dinner! "Fresh trout," she said, "caught only this morning in the River Exe by Sam Potter, what a pity!"

It was only when I was on the fast train speeding towards London that I realised I hadn't let Luke know my plans, or asked father to inform him. And of course father didn't even know that Luke was now my best boy, anyway.

I arrived at Aunt Hilda's elegant Georgian house in Chelsea at 8.30 p.m. I was tired and hungry, having only eaten a chocolate bar and a bun at the Station before I'd hailed a taxi-cab. The cab journey then had to be diverted round the back streets, as there had just been a serious traffic accident with two fatalities. Several ambulances were racing through the streets clanging their bells, overtaking omnibuses and horse-drawn carriages in a most alarming manner. But the driver seemed to take it all in his stride in typical Cockney fashion.

"We'll get you there, miss, never fear!" he laughed confidently.

The house-keeper showed me into the sitting-room, but as there was no sign of Bella I asked to be shown her bedroom, explaining I was her sister.

I listened intently at the door, but could hear no sound. A tray of untouched food was by the door. I tried the door, still locked. I gave a timid knock. No reply. I knocked again, louder. "Bella, it's me, Lottie. Please let me in."

I heard a movement inside and then the door was unlocked and Bella stood there. I hardly recognised her. Her beautiful green eyes were swollen, red-rimmed and blurred with tears, her dress was creased and her titian hair was ruffled and unkempt. But at least she seemed glad to see me and hugged me tight. "Lottie! Come in..." She closed and locked the door behind us.

The room was dimly lit, just one bedside lamp illuminating a corner of the room. But I could just see the posters up on the walls proclaiming "Votes for Women" and "Fortune Favours the Brave". I put my arm around her shoulders. "Bella, what is it? Aunt Hilda telephoned me to say you were upset. She's had to go to Scotland, I'm afraid. She sends her apologies. Whatever is the matter?"

To see my super-confident, effervescent sister reduced to tears! I felt as if my whole world was collapsing around me. I hadn't seen her crying like that since – since mother died all those years ago. It was then I thought of Ronnie. It must be Ronnie. My stomach lurched in fear.

I sat beside her on the bed, waiting for her response. Hardly daring to say his name I then ventured: "Is it, is it Ronnie?"

She nodded, and began weeping again. "I still can't believe it. I had a call from Major Post late morning to say he'd passed away yesterday. They had a wire from the War Office this morning."

I clung to her and we sobbed together. "Oh, Bella, Bella! No, no, not dear Ronnie! I don't believe it. Was he killed in action, what happened?"

Bella lay back on the pillow and stared up at the ceiling, blinking her eyes hard. "Oh, no, it was nothing noble like that – he died of dysentery in the field hospital at Ypres – ironic, isn't it, he was such a dedicated soldier and he died of dysentery..."

She sniffed hard and made an effort to control herself. "You know, it's funny, I've been expecting it all along, but not now. I didn't expect it now – oh, God! And we were so happy together..."

Her voice was bitter as she punched the pillow. "This damned war! How I hate it..."

I held her hand. I didn't know how to console her. Suddenly all my own trifling worries faded into insignificance. "You mustn't upset yourself, Bella. Will you be coming back home? Will there be a memorial service for him?"

Bella nodded miserably and blew her nose. "Yes, I think so, the Posts seem to want one. You will be there, won't you, Lottie? I need your support..."

My sister looked up at me, her eyes suddenly distraught and desperate. I began to answer, wanting to reassure her. "Yes, of course, Bella, I'll be..."

But she interrupted me, her eyes fixed on my face, suddenly alert.

"...you see, Lottie, that's not my only problem. I was going to tell you very soon, I saw the doctor this week – I'm pregnant with Ronnie's child..."

I drew in my breath sharply in disbelief. "Bella!" Yet another shock! We clung together again. She began to cry quietly once more and I hugged her shaking shoulders. I think she was incredibly relieved to have told someone her secret at last. She shook her head and sighed. 'I feel terrible, I've got such a headache, all this crying...'

All I could think was 'How on earth will we ever tell father?' But then I pulled myself together.

"Let me fetch you a glass of water and you can take some aspirin, and I'm sure you must need something to eat," I said and went over to the dressing-table where there was a carafe and glass. But as I was pouring the water I couldn't help noticing a typed letter lying open amidst the hair brushes, jars of cream and perfume bottles. It was stamped 'TOP SECRET' in big capital letters and headed: 'War Office, London' and clearly addressed to Miss A. Carr. A few key words jumped out at me:

"…valuable contribution … enemy territory … commend your bravery … successful outcome … next assignment…"

I froze with shock. So, on top of everything else my sister was a spy! My suspicions had been well-founded. When I thought of the terrible danger she must have been in, my heart turned somersaults. That was the last straw!

I went back to the bedside with Bella's glass of water, my hands shaking and mind whirling with a thousand emotions and problems, so many problems to be overcome.

29th April 1915

Bella has decided to keep the news of her pregnancy secret until the grief over Ronnie's death has subsided somewhat. I think this is wise, as people can be very prejudiced against unmarried mothers. There is a real stigma attached to them in today's so-called 'modern' society.

I feel so deeply for Bella in her grief over Ronnie's death and want to give her as much support as I can. I am so shocked by the news myself – I can hardly believe we will never see his laughing face again. I had been genuinely fond of Ronnie and we are going to miss him so much in our social circle. He would have made such a lovely brother-in-law, not to mention father. I still remember him at the Fete dressed up as the clown, capering about the Rectory lawn amusing the children and running the Skittles game. Cracking jokes at my engagement party and dancing the tango with Bella. And addressing the Scouts meeting, looking so smart in his uniform. And of course only a few months ago, looking so ecstatically happy when they turned up unexpectedly with the flowers to announce their engagement. There are so many memories.

The Memorial Service is now scheduled for early May. It will be such an emotional ordeal for us all to get through. As for the news of Bella's secret espionage work, hopefully now with her pregnancy that will fade into the background. I sincerely hope so – I don't want any more shocks.

30th April 1915

I have tried to make contact with Luke but without success. I rang George Thomson's farm at Porlock and spoke to Mrs Thomson. But to my surprise she said that Luke is no longer living there. "Independent young man, he is," Mrs Thomson laughed down the phone. "So we offered him an old shepherd's cottage on the moors. It's sound and dry, if rather basic, but he seems happy enough there. And he's paying us a peppercorn rent for it. It's over near Tor Point somewhere, I believe. We miss him in the house and he was welcome to stay, even though we've got my niece staying at the moment. But he was adamant he wanted to be off on his own."

I felt badly that I hadn't contacted Luke to let him know my movements. Then I heard he had come round to see me the day after I left. When father told him I was in London Luke was most surprised and didn't seem too happy, according to father. I felt rather uncomfortable at this news. But I do hope that father explained why I was in London. I feel sure, though, Luke must have heard about Ronnie's death by now on the local grapevine and put two and two together.

* * *

The 10.33 steams out of Paddington Station heading for Taunton, crowded with passengers and quite a few servicemen in uniform. Lottie and Bella settle back in their seats, relieved to be on their way back home, but desperately sad that their reason for going back is the Memorial Service. Bella had volunteered to drive, but Lottie had insisted they travel by train. In Bella's present physical and emotional state Lottie felt it was just too long a journey by road.

Lottie glances at Bella as the train leaves the smoky metropolis and heads west into the lush green of the countryside. She seems perfectly composed thank goodness and is bearing her grief with the utmost fortitude and courage. Her usually vivid features are now pale and drawn, her beautiful green eyes downcast, as she flicks absently through a magazine. Bella is wearing a black coat over a sombre grey dress, relieved by a white silk scarf at the neck and a stylish black straw hat sits on her auburn hair, a small veil covering her eyes.

She squeezes Lottie's gloved hand in her lap. "Thanks for coming, Lottie. You've been marvellous. You're the only one I wanted to see.' Lottie nods, gripping her hand. 'You're doing well, Bella, we'll get through this together."

She had tried to boost Bella's confidence the previous evening. "The baby will be a comfort to you and to Ronnie's parents. It will be a living reminder of your love for Ronnie. And don't worry about how you will manage. We will all look after him once he's born..."

But her words voiced an optimism she didn't really feel. Lottie knew Bella would face terrible social problems as an unmarried mother, of prejudice, bigotry and ostracism. A lot of people were very strait-laced and could be very hurtful at times in such situations. But Lottie also knows Bella is a very strong character and that ultimately with the support of family and friends she will overcome these problems, once she has recovered from the shock of Ronnie's death.

Lottie can't begin to think how they will ever break the news to their father. Being of strict morals and the older generation, she knows he will be shocked beyond belief. But he will just have to accept the news like everyone else, give his support to Bella and perhaps look forward to becoming a grand-father instead of moralising, she thinks defiantly.

As the fields flash by and the train carries Lottie nearer and nearer to Luke, she begins to feel guilty. Guilty that she had left him so suddenly recently without any word and guilty that she had perhaps neglected him before that, when she had ended her engagement to Tom. Does he still love me, she wonders? What reception awaits me when we meet? Lottie knows she loves Luke desperately and is aching to see him.

The train stops at Bristol and several soldiers and sailors alight and yet more board the train with heavy kit bags on their backs. Then it's onto the final leg of the journey and the train begins to slow down again, eventually steaming into Taunton Station about two o'clock.

And as the two sisters gather up their baggage and spot

their father's bespectacled anxious figure waiting on the platform, Lottie's heart skips a beat. She is back in Somerset and only a few miles from Luke.

Chapter 14

MAY 1915

THE RECTORY
6th May 1915

Dearest Amy,

I am sorry I haven't been in touch lately, but events have overtaken me and my usual routine has had to be abandoned. I won't go into all the details, but I am no longer engaged to Tom Trevithick.

I do remain friends with his brother, Luke, but he has now left home and is somewhat estranged from Tom. I will tell you all about it at a later date. I can't explain in a letter.

You may have heard that my sister Bella's fiancé, Ronnie Post, has died at the Front. Bella is distraught at this news of course, but holding up remarkably well in the circumstances. I have been staying with her in London for the past two weeks to give her my support. We have just returned to The Rectory for the Memorial Service in his memory to be held in our church this coming Friday, 8th May, but naturally I don't expect you to attend, as I don't think you knew him, did you? He was the finest young man possible and I am very upset about his death myself.

I will get in touch with you again, once the Memorial Service is over and Bella and I will try and resume our lives in some degree of normality again. For poor Bella it is the most terrible tragedy, but she is a very strong character and she has her busy job at the Language School to occupy her.

Forgive me for writing this short letter, but do hope all is well with you and that the news is good of Bertie and hope that Richard is making good progress.

Your true chum,

Lottie

SECRET DIARY

8th May 1915

Before I record my own personal events of 8th May, I must make a comment about the disastrous loss of life which occurred on 7th May off the Irish coast. The Cunard liner 'Lusitania' travelling from America to Liverpool was sunk by a German torpedo with over 1,200 lives lost, men, women and children. There has been such shock and horror about it, also riots all over the country protesting about the barbarity of such an appalling act of warfare against innocent civilians. Let us pray to God that this ghastly war will soon be ended without further loss of life. Father is going to mention it in his sermon on Sunday and will offer up prayers for the bereaved, as there is such strong public feeling about it.

And now to record my own happenings, which of course pale into insignificance in comparison with the 'Lusitania' disaster, although I'm sure Bella doesn't take this view with her recent terrible loss.

Father conducted Ronnie's Memorial Service today with his usual dignity and compassion and the eulogy spoken by one of his fellow officers was so sincere and moving, I was choked with grief and emotion. Captain Hugh Cardington spoke of Ronnie's generosity of spirit, what an inspiration he was to his men and his dedication to King and Country. But mainly, he said, he would be remembered for being a fine human being. He commanded respect and yet he had the common touch. He will be sadly missed in the barracks, the officer said, as well as here in Tethercombe, his home community.

I had of course written a letter of condolence to the Posts, as I was particularly close to Doris. I wanted to speak to them privately about the death of their beloved son, but this was not the right time. I would speak later on, perhaps at luncheon to-day.

My heart ached for Bella and I clutched her hand as she bowed her head, and the choir sang 'The Lord's My Shepherd'. Her face was drawn with grief, her bearing erect in her sombre but stylish black hat and coat. Bella, Aunt Hilda and I were sitting with the Posts and their family to give them our support. Ronnie's belongings had now been returned. So it was particularly poignant to see his own cap and badges, his belt, ceremonial sword and medals displayed on a plinth surrounded by lilies in front of the pulpit.

Aunt Hilda had returned early from her holiday in Scotland and come down from London. She had met Ronnie on a couple of occasions and was deeply distressed by his death. As father led the choir up the aisle and the packed congregation began to file out of the church, I scanned the pews for Luke's tall figure. But there was no sign of him. I was dismayed. I couldn't understand it. I was sure he would be there. He and Ronnie had been at school together. In fact Luke had apparently told Major Post quite definitely he would be there when he had expressed his condolences to Ronnie's parents at the weekend. I searched the figures leaving the church yet again, but Luke just wasn't there. I was bitterly disappointed.

I saw Tom slipping quietly out of the church door and thought of following him to ask him Luke's whereabouts. But stopped myself just in time. Of course, I'd forgotten. The two brothers were still at loggerheads because of the court case.

Overhead the church tenor bell was tolling its solemn tone, that sad, grieving sound that seemed to haunt me forever. As I heard it I suddenly realised with a jolt I had completely forgotten the 25th April, the third anniversary of mother's death, in all the drama of recent weeks. Please forgive me, mother, I prayed.

I somehow got through luncheon at home with Father, Bella, Aunt Hilda and the Posts, making sympathetic noises and polite conversation. I managed to say a few private words to the Posts about dear Ronnie, although words seem so trite and inadequate at this sensitive time. I longed to tell them about Bella's baby, as I felt this would give them a glimmer of hope in the darkness. But it was not my news to divulge and besides their grief was too new and raw. They were both utterly devastated to have lost their precious only son. Doris was her usual well-mannered self, but desperately quiet. The Major looked desolate, completely broken-hearted, his eyes stricken with grief.

He was now speaking fervently about a plaque of polished stone which he was intending to erect in the church in Ronnie's memory. He was thinking of including a quotation from Rupert Brooke's poem 'The

Soldier' on the stone. It was very poignant and appropriate, I thought, particularly as the poet had recently died at Skyros, a few days before Ronnie:

> *"If I should die, think only this of me;*
> *That there's some corner of a foreign field*
> *That is for ever England..."*

But despite all the sadness, my mind kept wandering, I'm ashamed to say. I could only think of Luke and wonder where he was. And when after the meal Bella said she would like to rest for a while and the Posts departed, I seized on the opportunity.

I changed into my riding clothes, went to the stable and saddled up Bessie. I made for the shepherd's cottage Mrs Thomson had said Luke was renting near Tor Point. After the two weeks in London, and the stifling emotion in the church and at lunch, I was glad to be 'en plein air'. I had to see Luke. I suddenly realised I hadn't seen him for nearly three weeks. I looked around the open moor and breathed in the fresh air. M'm, it felt good. It was a mystery to me why Luke hadn't been at the Memorial Service. I had to find out what had happened. I was suddenly in a fever to see him, and spurred Bessie on to gallop even faster.

I was approaching Tor Point and could see the shepherd's cottage now coming into view. My heart lifted when I spotted Rufus grazing in a paddock at the back of the house. Luke must be there. But did he already have a visitor? I could see another horse tethered to the post outside the front door. It was an unfamiliar horse, a big dappled grey mare.

I began to feel slightly uneasy as I dismounted and looped the reins over the post. Knocking somewhat timidly on the door, I waited in the porch and my heart began to bang against my ribs uncomfortably.

The door swung open and there stood a stunning young woman, dressed in a long gown of blue cotton. I had never seen her before in my life. She had dark curly hair and startling blue eyes which now swept over my figure in an appraising manner. "Yes?" was all she said imperiously. I tried to speak, to ask for Luke, but the words wouldn't come. For my eyes were suddenly drawn to a figure lying stretched out on a bed in a room off the tiny living room. It was Luke. His head was turned away from me, but all at once I was horribly aware I should never have come.

Colour flooded my face and I took a step backwards. I was mortified, convinced I had interrupted a liaison between them both. "Excuse me, I'll, I'll come back later," I muttered barely audibly and quickly remounted Bessie and galloped away over the moors.

My heart was thumping wildly and tears began to stream down my face. So this was why Luke hadn't attended the Memorial Service! I didn't know who this young woman was, but he was obviously smitten with her and in the throes of 'la grande passion' – and I had walked in on them! I felt deeply hurt and totally rejected.

I should never have come! How I wished I could go, get as far away from Tethercombe as possible, go back to London even. But I blamed myself. It was my fault for not keeping Luke fully informed of my actions. What a fool I was! I loved Luke, truly loved him and now he had found someone else!

My eyes were blurred with tears, my thoughts in a turmoil, but as I rode back to the Rectory a plan began to form in my mind. Yes, I will go back to London with Bella and Aunt Hilda tomorrow. I could help her with the charity work for the Sunshine Club and any other charities Aunt Hilda is involved with. Anything to avoid the humiliation of staying in Tethercombe and seeing Luke with another woman in the village. Anything is preferable to that.

Once back at The Rectory I had calmed myself down. And over dinner I made my suggestion as tactfully as I could. Much to my surprise they both accepted the news quite easily.

In fact Bella immediately assumed I was suggesting it to support her in her hour of need and thanked me profusely, making me feel guilty that it was for purely selfish reasons I was considering it.

But father was naturally rather put out and aggrieved. "Who will look after me?" he said rather piteously, staring accusingly at me.

"Nonsense," said Bella briskly, "Mrs May takes care of your every need as you well know…"

"...and I'm sure my friend Matilda Rowntree would always do a bit of typing and office work for you," I put in, "I'll give her a ring tonight and arrange it all."

"So," I smiled round at everyone, "it's all settled then. That's good." Now I had come to a decision I felt a lot happier, pushing Luke to the back of my mind, or at least, trying to.

15th May 1915

Have been working for a charity with the grand name of the Queen Mary Relief Clothing Guild for the past week. It is mainly housed in an old mansion in Pimlico, but there are other 'depots' all over London. We are sorting through donated used clothing for disabled and unemployed ex-servicemen – this is then packed in boxes and sent to the central depot based at St. James Palace for distribution. My chief companion in this work is Joe Tremlett, a cheerful young man (a doctor's son from Hertfordshire) rejected by the War Office due to colour blindness.

After several mornings doing this rather monotonous work I was seized upon on arriving at the office by Poppy Travers, a socialite turned manager. "This is desperate, darling. Can you type by any chance?" When I nodded she said the secretary had called in unwell. "I've got all these reports to be typed up. Terribly boring, I'm afraid, mainly lists and corresponding figures, so make sure you get them right. Would you mind? You are an angel! I might even be able to wangle a couple of theatre tickets if you can do it all by five o'clock. You are a love, that's wonderful! Oh, of course, you're Bella Carr's sister, aren't you, so you're bound to be a poppet!" So how could I refuse? Everywhere I go I am introduced as Bella Carr's sister, so feel I have a fearsome reputation to keep up!

At 5.30 having finished all the typing and with a headache and a crick in my neck, I was presented with two theatre tickets and a bowl of soup and a ham roll. I tried to find Bella to see if she wanted to accompany me, but was told she was busy doing emergency work as a volunteer ambulance driver – my dear sister is quite amazing! But I know she is desperate to keep busy to assuage her grief.

Joe then suddenly appeared in the office and agreed to go with me. We spent a pleasant evening together at the Music Hall show. He is an amusing chap and had me in fits of laughter with his comments about various passing folk. We went on the open-top bus to Drury Lane and sat up the front on the top deck. It was such fun! He pointed out all the famous landmarks to me as we passed them.

I have warmed to Joe from the start. He came to my rescue on the first day when I was dumped unceremoniously in the tiny office by Peter Plunkett at the Pimlico depot. Surrounded by piles of clothing and boxes, with myriad bewildering lists to be checked off, the phone ringing constantly, I was getting rather flustered when Joe walked in and calmly took over. He explained the system patiently to me, checking stuff in, sorting and packing and then checking clothing packs out. It is quite simple when you get used to it and I soon had it organised after a fashion with Joe's help.

"We should have a lot more volunteers here but they've been 'loaned out' to another depot at Hampstead who were short-staffed," he explained. "Queen Mary is making a visit there next Tuesday and they're trying to get up to date with everything." He gave a grin. "The ladies are looking out their best hats."

I was impressed. "Is the Queen likely to come here on a visit, do you think?"

Joe nodded. "It's quite possible. She is very involved with all these charities that carry her name and likes to see at first-hand how they are doing."

How wonderful! I have great admiration for Her Majesty the Queen – she is involved with so many different charities and always has a smile and a word of encouragement for the hard-stretched volunteers. A lot of them are middle-aged and older women who find the work very tiring, but they give their time willingly and cheerfully.

When I got home to-day to Auntie's lovely house in Chelsea, I suddenly realised how tired I was and slumped into an armchair, exhausted. Since coming back to London a week ago I have been working non-stop, either at the Sunshine Club or for the Relief Clothing Guild – the only time off has been that theatre trip with Joe.

Haven't even had time to do my weekly manicure or see much of Bella.

Had a phone call from father this evening, which made me guilty I hadn't phoned him. I had promised him I would ring him regularly to keep in touch.

"Sorry I haven't rung you, father. Bella and I have been so busy with the charity work up here – it's frantic, you would never believe it. How are you getting on, is everything all right with you?" I asked.

Father's familiar rather reproving voice came floating over the line. "Yes, I'm all right, Lottie dear, but I did hope to hear from you before now. You did promise, you know. You and Bella are keeping well, I trust?"

Father always does have a way of making me feel guilty. "Yes, thank you father," I answered, "we're both fine" (better not tell him about Bella's morning sickness). "But has Matilda Rowntree been to see you as I arranged?"

"Yes, yes," father said, "she has, Lottie dear. She's very efficient I must say, but I find her, um – a little over-bearing, I must admit. Do you think you will be coming home soon, dear?"

I gave an inward groan. "Um, I'm not sure, father. A couple more weeks perhaps, then maybe I'll be back with you."

Father was obviously disappointed. "Oh, I did hope, but then, I realise you have your, um, you sound very busy up there with your charity work. Oh, and the house is upside down –" He sounded quite distraught. "I wish you were here, Lottie – that upholsterer chappie, Mr Selby, keeps coming and taking furniture to be upholstered, but it's nearly all been done now, looks quite good, I suppose, I don't know really. I've got that important meeting next week here with the councillors about the Memorial, so it needs to be finished by then." Father seemed rather peeved and flustered, but he continued.

Oh, and by the way, that young man, Luke Trevithick came round. He seemed surprised to hear you were in London again. I said you were up there supporting Bella. He's been ill with this influenza that's going around. That's why he wasn't at the Memorial Service, apparently. He was very cut up about Ronnie's death, naturally. He's back at the Thomson farm now, they're looking after him."

Must admit my heart skipped a beat at that news. But I felt confused and mixed up. And I rang off quickly, saying dinner was ready.

And now as I'm preparing for bed, Luke's face keeps appearing before me, his handsome, familiar face. Have I been too hasty in leaving Tethercombe? Was I too quick to judge Luke? Who was the young woman in the hut?

I don't know, I just feel too tired to work it all out. All I know is that tomorrow Joe and I have got to pack up and despatch 150 boxes, as well as answer numerous telephone calls – and look cheerful about it.

I will be counting boxes in my sleep tonight…

Chapter 15

JUNE 1915

Ennismore Gardens
Chelsea
1st June 1915

Dearest Amy,

Just a quick few lines to keep in touch and hope that you are well.

Bella and I have been really busy for the last few weeks. It is so hectic up here. We took the Sunshine Club children on an outing to Margate for a day, that went well recently. Then we have been involved in a lot of Queen Mary's charities, mainly the Relief Clothing Guild, sorting and packing used clothing, so pretty dull stuff, but all the volunteers are so friendly and nice that the time seems to fly by.

There was a Zeppelin airship raid over London last night which was frightening, the first we have had I believe. I actually heard it approaching, it makes a strange humming noise – it sent shivers down my spine, I can tell you. I was just going to bed but Bella and I went out and saw this ominous dark shape in the sky and then explosions and smoke a few miles away, in Hackney and Stratford. Seven people were killed and 35 injured, you may have read about it in the newspaper, a shocking new development in the war, after the previous bombings at Great Yarmouth and Kent.

We had great excitement last week as we had a personal visit from Her Majesty at our depot which was such an honour. The Queen was so gracious and dignified and so interested in everything we were doing.

We have also done some work for the Needlework Guild doing patchwork quilts, etc., mending shirts, etc. and even been packing up food parcels for the needy and serving in soup kitchens (which I do know about!).

The poverty, unemployment and homelessness in London

caused by the war is on a scale not dreamed of in our quiet village. People are living 10 to a room or are out sleeping rough in doorways, it's appalling. You see these poor disabled men out on the streets selling matches and buttons, it's so sad.

One of the patchwork quilts completed by a group of ladies was so beautiful with materials of vibrant jewel colours that Bella and I decided to buy it for Aunt Hilda. We gave quite a large donation for it. She has been such a brick to us that we felt we wanted to express our appreciation, in recognition of her kindness in looking after us both since Ronnie's death. She was delighted with it.

Bella is coming down to Tethercombe this weekend to see the Posts. She wants to keep in touch with them, they are just so heart-broken about Ronnie. She is bearing up quite well. Trying to keep busy seems to be the answer.

I may be back with father soon, as he seems to be missing me (can't think why!). Matilda Rowntree has filled in for me, but she is busy with the Soup Kitchen and other activities and it is not fair to expect her to look after father for too long.

So hope to see you soon. Will get in touch once I'm back.

Hope all is well with you. Bye for now,

Your loving Lottie

SECRET DIARY

5th June 1915

At last I can write my Diary! Have been so busy it was impossible before this. Bella has now spent the weekend with the Posts and broken the news to them of her pregnancy. I did personally think it was too soon after R's death, but she wanted to tell them before her figure starts showing too much. Although they were initially very shocked, they seemed very pleased as well in a quiet sort of way, she said. I think it will give them a ray of light at the end of the dark tunnel they are in at the moment and, should the baby be a boy, it would be such a joyous thing for everyone. I know dear Bella is hoping and fervently praying for a boy. I have told her she must be careful not to overdo it with her charity work and also she must start going for regular checks at the hospital to make sure everything is all right with the baby. The due date is 15th November. She hasn't had the courage to tell father yet, but has sworn the Posts to secrecy and says she will tell him next month when she will be nearly 5 months and it will be beginning to show. Must confess I am quite excited about becoming an auntie – I might even start knitting a little matinee jacket or something (poor baby, I'm not a good knitter!).

While Bella was in Tethercombe she told me she bumped into Luke who was with his chum, George Thomson and his cousin Mabel in the village. When I asked her (casually) to describe her appearance, it sounded just like the mysterious girl I had seen in Luke's shepherd's hut. Dark curly hair, blue eyes, rather abrupt manner. She is a widow, apparently and has a young son and is staying with the Thomsons to get over her husband's death at the Battle of Mons several months ago. Bella said Luke kept asking after me and asked for our address up here so that he can write, so that is promising. But until I know how it is between him and this Mabel, I am doubtful about our relationship. I still love Luke, of course, and think about him all the time, but seeing him with that girl and now hearing she is still in Tethercombe has made me question my feelings. Oh, woe is me!

Saturday, 8th June 1915

Had a letter from Luke today! Also some beautiful flowers were delivered from him, so I feel ecstatic. They are gracing my dressing-table as I write.

The flowers are red long-stemmed roses and beautifully packaged and the card just said 'To my darling Lottie, missing you – all my love, Luke'.

Then the morning post was delivered bringing a letter from my darling and in it he explains a lot of things, so I feel my silly doubts were completely unjustified.

Apparently he began to feel ill with this influenza the day before Ronnie's Memorial Service and sent a message via the shepherd that he couldn't come to dinner with the Thomsons as usual that evening. George's cousin, Mabel, who is a VAD nurse and was staying with them offered to go the next day with some remedies, take his temperature, etc. It was while she was there that I happened to barge in and jump to all the wrong conclusions. Silly me, what a fool I was, but I wasn't to know, was I? She was such an attractive young woman that I was suspicious of her, but according to Luke she is, in fact, rather curt and a real 'bossy-boots'! Hearing about his illness I felt terrible I hadn't sent a note or something, but have been so busy.

Luke ended the letter saying he was desperate to see me and asking when was I coming back to Tethercombe? 'If you're not coming back soon' he wrote, 'please write to me and tell me you love me. I don't know where I stand with you, Lottie. I love you desperately and want to marry you. So please put me out of my misery and return to me, darling. Your loving Luke.'

* * *

So here I am back in Tethercombe! Father is so pleased to see me it is quite touching. He never stops beaming at me. 'Shall we go and pick some strawberries from the garden together?' he suddenly says, after lunch, while I was admiring the newly upholstered furniture.

"Of course, father!" I smile and put my arm through his. Potter seems quite surprised to see us as we make our way over the lawn to the kitchen garden, but gives us a wave as he trims the lawn edge. "Nice to see you back, Miss Charlotte," he calls.

Father puts his arm around my shoulder. "I've missed you so much, Lottie. It *is* lovely to have you back." His spectacles begin to mist up. "I've been quite lonely without you."

And yes, it is lovely to *be* back, back home where I belong. The winding country lanes, the wide open moorland, my own quiet room overlooking the churchyard. After London with its hectic pace of life and frightening air-raids, Tethercombe is a little haven of peace and tranquillity. The roses on the front terrace are so beautiful this year – yes, almost as lovely as the bouquet of roses that Luke sent me last week. But they were very special and his letter even more so. It made me realize he does still love me and, more importantly, that I still love him.

Now I'm back and know that Luke is just a couple of miles

away I am suddenly impatient to see him. I have missed him so much and am only just beginning to realize it. I sent him a brief note thanking him for the flowers last week and told him I was coming home this week, so hopefully I will see him soon.

We pick quite a few strawberries and are taking a rest on the garden bench when Mrs May calls from the kitchen door.

"Miss Charlotte! You have a visitor!" Her face is beaming and behind her and then striding across the lawn is the tall figure of my darling Luke. I realize with dismay I am still in my travelling clothes, but as I see him rapidly approaching it doesn't seem to matter anymore.

Father mumbles a greeting and disappears into the house. And suddenly Luke is there, right in front of me and his arms are enfolding me to him.

My heart is doing somersaults and I can hardly breathe.

"Lottie, Lottie! At last you are here!"

"Oh Luke, Luke!"

We gaze at each other, our eyes locked and then Luke holds me at arm's length. "Let me look at you, my darling girl." He embraces me again and his lips seek mine. "Lottie, we never should have parted, I thought I would lose you." He shakes his head. "When I heard you had been to the Music Hall with a young man, I didn't get a wink's sleep."

"...that was just Joe from the office," I smile. "And this Mabel, you're sure she means nothing to you?"

Luke's eyes flash scornfully. "Of course not! She's just George's cousin! You're the only one for me, Lottie, you know that!"

And as I feel his arms around me, I do know that. We kiss deeply and I run my fingers through his thick, wavy hair. Those magic feelings are coursing through my body once again.

"Promise me you will never go away again," Luke says sternly.

"Never again," I promise. "Unless you are with me, of course."

"Just try and stop me." He wags his finger. "You're only

allowed to go up to London with me beside you from now on, understand?"

I nod obediently and salute. "Yes, sir."

"We'll go up next week and buy the most beautiful engagement ring money can buy. That reminds me, I must speak to your father! Then we'll have tea at The Ritz…"

"…or Fullers in Regent Street, it's cheaper…" I put in, then add, "and feed the ducks in St. James Park…"

"…then go on to the theatre to see 'The Belle of New York', then have supper at The Savoy, and then…" His eyes sparkle.

"And then, sir?"

Luke squeezes my hand as we walk back to the house. "We'll find a Pullman sleeping car – it doesn't really matter where it's going."

THE END